EVANESCE

Shining Warm Wishes!
Sarah

SARAH LASHBROOK

tellwell

Tellwell Talent
www.tellwell.ca

ISBN
978-0-2288-6274-1 (Paperback)
978-0-2288-6275-8 (eBook)

This book is dedicated to:

Marie, who never wakes me from my dreams - even when my dreams make me nearly impossible to live with. You are my life.

Terry, for the gentle and loving push to complete this project, with the smartest of reminders that at any point I can always scream pineapple, pineapple, pineapple. I am grateful to have your friendship.

To the little girls out there that do, or have, even in the slightest way, identified with Mia. I see you. It's not your fault. You were a good kid worthy of so much love. This is for you.

Warning: descriptions of child physical abuse, verbal abuse, and sexual abuse, ahead. Please practice your best self care and seek help if you feel that this story brings up emotions that are hard to handle.

Call your local mental health provider, local authority, visit a nearby hospital, or call a friend.

In Canada, you can call the Mental Health Helpline at 1-866-531-2600

If you are under 18: Kids Help Phone 1-800-668-6868 or Text 686868 to have a confidential conversation with a real person.

Be safe friends.

ev·a·nesce

evəˈnes/

verb literary

verb: **evanesce**; 3rd person present: **evanesces**; past tense: **evanesced**; past participle: **evanesced**; gerund or present participle: **evanescing**

pass out of sight, memory, or existence.

Prologue

1987

9:42 a.m.

The room was cold and so was the coffee.

Mia wasn't sure if almost eleven year olds were allowed to drink coffee but she didn't care. Not today anyway. Not anymore. Momma was going away.

She had been waiting a long time for the lady in the red pantsuit to come back. This was the second time Mia was meeting her. Both times she wore the same clothes. She had forgotten her name, but it didn't matter much to Mia. She wasn't going to know her for long and they were never going to be friends. Mia noticed the pot of black coffee that sat on the counter with mugs, cream, and sugar placed beside it. She helped herself to some. Being new to drinking coffee, she didn't know 'how she liked it'. Momma used that term all the time. Every guest that came through their doors and sat down, Momma would make them a hot beverage and ask, 'how do you like it?' They would respond with a different ratio of cream or sugar, depending on the sweetness they preferred. One guest surprised them all one day by asking for honey. Bee poop! Mia couldn't even imagine drinking bee poop let alone being confident enough to ask someone else to put it in your coffee for you. But Mia knew better than to question her parent's guests.

Mia put in a small amount of sugar and a lot of milk. She remembered Daddy said once that he liked his coffee as white as Jesus. She liked a lot of things her Daddy liked so she did the same. She just wasn't sure exactly how white Jesus was, so she guessed.

It was cold from the first sip.

But drinking it passed the time waiting for the red pantsuit lady. She had walked Mia into the room more than fifteen minutes ago, told Mia to sit down and relax. She said she would be right back. Mia had a different idea than red pantsuit of what *right back* meant.

9:57 a.m.

The walls were made of shiny grey bricks similar to the ones in Mia's school basement. The desk, also grey, the chairs all wooden and small. What a boring look, Mia thought. The only thing that made the décor better was the smell of citrus in the air. It livened things up a little.

The entire right side of the room held file cabinets. Mia wondered how many files were tucked away inside. Four hundred and sixty-two was her guess, but she was bad at math.

The left side of the room was where she found the coffee bar that she snuck her cold coffee from. There were bookshelves on either side of it. The books were boring looking too. They seemed to fit in. They all had the same words in their titles: crisis, help, behaviour, and shelter. They didn't sound at all appealing to Mia.

The only noise in the room was a *tick, tick, ticking,* of a wall clock. A constant reminder to Mia that time was going by and red pantsuit still hadn't returned. Mia wouldn't be surprised if she never returned. People did that a lot. They went away and never came back, especially if Mia told them things about her life. Red pantsuit knew about Mia's life. If she hadn't run away already, Mia soon, would tell her to go.

Mia reached across the desk and grabbed a pen from a holder. She looked around for a piece of paper but found none. She decided she didn't care. She took the lid off of the pen and gently rubbed the ball tip over the skin on her hand. She drew a figure 8. Satisfied, she placed the lid back on and put the pen away.

10:06 a.m.

Mia straightened out her pink dress. Aunt Colleen suggested that she wear it that day. Said people would see her beautiful childlike personality better in a girly dress. Aunt Colleen also told Mia to be brave and speak only the truth. Mia could do that. She didn't like lying. Lying always got her in trouble with Momma and with Jesus.

She took another sip of coffee, swung her feet back and forth under the chair, and looked around some more. The room needed a window. The dead Aloe Vera plant on the counter needed a window too, and maybe some coffee. It was dying. Mia got up from where she sat and walked over to the plant. She poured her leftover coffee into the dry soil. Maybe that would perk it up she thought. It always perked Daddy up. She returned her empty mug to the mat that she took it from. Turning it upside down like the other clean mugs so no one would know it was used. She returned to her chair and continued to wait. She looked up and counted the dots on the ceiling but even that got boring once she hit a count of two hundred dots. Mia wanted out of the room.

10:11 a.m.

The door to the room opened. Mia looked back behind her. Red pantsuit was back.

"Sorry about that. I just needed to get some information from a colleague first. Are you doing okay in here?"

Mia nodded. She stared at red pantsuit's long curly brown hair. She wished her own curly hair were as pretty. Red pantsuit didn't seem to have any knots in her curls like Mia did. Mia also liked how her bangs were teased high above her forehead. If Mia was braver, she would have told her how much she liked her hair, but she couldn't. Compliments made friends, and Mia didn't want any friends. Not today.

"Good. I know we have met before, but just in case you forgot, my name is Katherine."

Mia gave Katherine the smile she seemed to be looking for.

"Did you enjoy your coffee?"

Mia nodded yes even though she didn't really enjoy it.

Katherine sat down. Mia looked at her more closely. She did a quick assessment in her head. Clean and smells like perfume, Momma's age, probably likes soap operas, wears pants, good smile, and likes red.

"Do you know why we are here today Mia?"

"To talk about Momma?"

"That's right. To talk about your Momma," Katherine paused for a moment. She flipped open a file. "Specifically, what you and your Momma do together."

Mia wasn't sure what she wanted to know.

"You mean when Momma is mad?"

"Yes. And when she is happy. When you are together. What things do you and Momma do when it is just you and Momma? Alone. In your special time. Do you feel comfortable telling me these things?"

Mia thought about it for a moment. Katherine was trying to trick her. Momma said people would if they were asking about special time. Momma said no one would understand if she told them, so she had to hide the truth. Mia still remembered how. Momma said that Mia just needed to find a story other than the real one and give it a lot of detail. If she did, people would forget why they were asking her. They would get caught up in the story instead. But Mia wasn't sure if she wanted to find a story today. Especially not if they were already spying on her.

"That depends," she said.

"Depends on what, Mia?"

Mia looked around the room. She eyed every corner she could. She saw no camera's or recorders but that didn't mean that they didn't have any. Momma told her to always be aware of her surroundings. To be smart. Especially in a hospital or police station. Cameras were everywhere. Mia figured a court house office would be the same. She replied in the smartest way she could.

"Depends on how you knew I had a coffee?"

Chapter One

1986

One Year Earlier

Mia sat at her desk with a pen and notepad.

<u>Nina</u>
Lives alone
No kids
Likes to listen to loud musik and dances around her living room
Has 2 dogs, cheeto and?
Seems fun - likes to laugh

Mia paused and rubbed her fingers over the dents in the desk. There were many. Her desk belonged to her mother, her grandmother, and her great grandmother before that. It was hers now. And she couldn't wait to pass it on to one of her own daughters one day.

When her touch got to the desk drawer, she poked her baby finger into a small hole. The handle no longer attached, she envisioned what it might have looked like. Gold with a twisted knot as decoration, she decided. Maybe even a white flower in the middle, a white porcelain flower with blue edges.

Mia sat back and admired her desk. In many ways, it reminded her of her grandmother. She had scars as well. Scratches and dents just like the wood. Mia looked at the names etched into the desk: Kathleen, Mary, Lee-Ann, even a George with a heart around it.

Mia thought about scratching her name into the wood on more than one occasion but hadn't yet. Her desire to be remembered was not yet greater than her fear of tarnishing the desk with such ugly letters as M I A.

"Mia, are you in your Sunday dress yet?"

Mia jumped back from her reverie. She looked over at her good Sunday dress lying on the floor in the corner. Momma would kill her if she saw what she had done with it.

"Almost!"

She got up and grabbed the dress, nearly tripping over her own two feet. She paused to listen for Momma's footsteps. Heard nothing. Relieved that she had time, Mia took off her pajamas and put on her Sunday dress. Once buttoned up, she grabbed her dirty pajamas from the floor and ran them down the hall to the hamper. She stopped and looked at herself in the full-length mirror on Momma and Daddy's door. The dress was beautiful. It was long and flowing, pastel pink, with perfectly lined frills from the waist down. It was a shame that she had to ruin it by being the one to wear it.

"Mia, it's almost church time. I don't want to have to come up and get you."

Mia didn't want that either. She knew she had some time though. Momma was still talking in her Southern voice. Momma talked funny when she was feeling good. The voice started when Momma was a teenager, after she watched a movie called *Gone With The Wind*. An actress named Vivien Leigh played Ms. Scarlett who Momma loved. The way Vivien walked and talked made Momma feel one with her. Momma said that ever since that day she started to talk and walk like her. When Momma got mad though, she often forgot that she wanted to be Southern.

"Coming, Momma."

Mia ran back to her room and closed her notepad. She opened the desk drawer and hid the book under the rubber mat that lined the bottom of the wood. She smoothed the lining back out and placed a few things on top of it. Satisfied that the notepad was hidden well, she closed the desk drawer and left her room.

Momma was waiting for her at the bottom of the stairs.

"I swear child, that hair is straight from the devil himself. So many curls going this way and that. We should just shave your head. Save us all a lot of stress, not to mention teach ol' Lucifer a thing or two. Don't mess with the Pratts!" Momma licked her fingers and ran them through Mia's curls. The curls didn't respond to the spit. Instead they rebelled and went frizzy and rogue.

"Well, I guess God is going to have to deal with disappointment today. Your hair will have to do. Your daddy is waiting in the car and we still have to clip your nails."

Mia smoothed her curls as best as she could then followed Momma to the kitchen. It was Sunday, and every second Sunday Momma clipped her fingernails.

She walked over to the sink and placed her fingers over the edge. Momma stood beside her and clipped the nails one finger at a time. Short. Quick. Painful. Mia leaned into her mother a little for comfort. It was the one time that Mia could feel and smell her mother beside her, against her, and didn't have to fear. Momma's body warmth mixed in with the strong smell of her perfume: red roses mixed with maple syrup, was almost like a hug. And Mia liked hugs. It always felt so wonderful.

Momma blew on Mia's fingers when she was done. Rubbing them to make sure they were smooth. Once satisfied, she told Mia to go get her shoes and coat on while she rinsed the clippings out of the sink. Mia did as she was told. Jesus and her Daddy were waiting.

"The book of Mark reminds us of what the Lord wants from us. What He needs from his lambs. Mark 16, verse 15 and 16 tell us: And he said unto them, go ye into all of the world, and preach the gospel to every creature. He that believeth and is baptized shall be saved; but he that believeth not shall be damned."

Mia looked up at her daddy on the pulpit. He was a magnificent man. Not very tall, but commanded a room as though he was. His dark hair curled around his head like a tilt-a-whirl. When it got too long, Daddy would always have it cut short. It gave him headaches if he let it grow. Right now, it was near cutting length. The whole crowd, every Sunday, looked up at him as if it was the Lord himself talking on that stage. He could say anything and they would nod and shout Amen after. He had power. He had class. He was loved. Mia admired that. People listened to her Daddy. They actually listened. He was their leader.

Daddy, also known as the amazing Reverend Richard Pratt, was a good man. He healed people, listened to their woes, and cried when others around him were hurting. Mia always saw the softer side of him on Sundays. She liked it. It was quite a contrast to her Momma. Momma never showed any real emotion other than anger. Which was okay for Mia. She knew what Momma was like. It was as Momma said, her childhood had made her mean. But Daddy was different. He said Jesus saved him long ago from heartache and pain. Made him a changed man. Mia never knew her daddy before Jesus fixed him. But she knew him now. He was good. He was her light. *Her* happy. He never once put his hands on her in a way that would make Jesus angry. He made Mia feel safe. She thanked Jesus every night for her Daddy.

When church was over Mia always had a few free moments to play with some of the other children. She was 9, and although most of the kids were younger than her, she still had fun. She looked forward to it every Sunday. Daddy would have to say goodbye to the parishioners and add those who needed it to the prayer list, and Momma would always catch up with the other mothers and make plans to meet for teas and lunches later that week. These tasks always left 20 minutes open for Mia to run around and have fun.

Jason was her favourite despite being only 5. He would follow Mia around the way the churchgoers followed her daddy. Jason called her Mena, which always made her laugh. He had golden blond hair and sky blue eyes. His lips were a soft pink colour, and trembled every time he was about to say something Momma would consider to be against Jesus's good will. The neatest thing about

Jason, Mia thought, was his birthmark. On his left arm he had a dark red mark that was shaped like a spiders web. Jason didn't like it but Mia did. She always tried to encourage him to believe it was a sign that he was part superhero. Sometimes that made Jason smile. Other times, he just shrugged her suggestion off.

Mia, face pressed against the wall, finished her count to ten, before she yelled, "Ready or not, here I come!" and turned to look around the basement for those who were hiding from her. Jason came out right away and stood beside her. He didn't understand the game. Mia patted him on the head and told him he did a good job. Jason smiled with admiration.

"Wanna know where the others are?" Jason asked innocently.

"No," Mia replied. "That would be cheating."

Jason nodded with disappointment. Mia started to look around. She searched behind the puppet stand, under the serving tables, and behind the doors. It wasn't until she went into a Sunday school classroom that she found the first kid.

Jason pulled at Mia's shirt. "I know where they are, Mena."

Mia smiled. "No, Jason. That would be cheating. Cheating is wrong, especially in God's house."

Jason nodded again, more disappointment showing on his face.

Mia kept looking in the other Sunday school rooms. Four rooms, and no other kids were found.

Mia came back to the main room and looked around. She was puzzled. Jason again pulled on Mia's shirt. She ignored it. He tugged harder.

"No! Jason, that's cheating I said."

But instead of nodding this time, Jason just pointed towards the stairs. Mia looked over. Her Momma was standing on the last step, shaking her finger to the breaking point.

"Mia Lee-Ann Elizabeth Pratt! Running around in your Sunday dress. Quit your being ugly. You know better than that young lady."

Mia stood frozen. Jason sidestepped behind Mia until he was out of sight.

"Sorry Momma."

"Sorry you did it, or sorry you got caught?"

Mia knew there was no answer that was proper, so she didn't give one.

"Upstairs now. It's time to leave."

Mia nodded. She waited until Momma was out of sight. She turned and gave Jason a hug.

"Thanks for all of your help. I need you to take over for me and go find them all, okay? It isn't cheating if you need to take over for the seeker. It isn't your fault."

Jason smiled and headed off to do his new duty.

Momma was talking to Frank when Mia found her. Frank was Daddy's best friend, and the local washer and dryer repairman. He was a short bald man who looked much older than he was. Daddy said it was probably because his soul was so old that his shell looked wrinkly. Mia wasn't convinced. Momma was making arrangements for him to come over the next night to fix their dryer. It had been acting up for Momma lately. She said he should stay for dinner too. Frank lived alone in a trailer. He didn't have a wife at home to cook for him like Daddy did. Momma said it was because he liked his girlfriends' young, and no young woman these days stuck around for a big heart. They only wanted money. And Frank didn't have money.

A home-cooked dinner sounded great to him. He said Momma's cooking was his favourite. Momma laughed at that, the way she laughed at Daddy whenever he asked her to go to bed early. With that laugh, Momma would sway her hips back and forth, back and forth, until she remembered how much she hated her flat butt. Then she would touch it, twist her body forward again, and laugh harder to hide her shame. Mia knew that Momma did this often, but she had never watched it happen in front of Frank before.

Momma excused herself on account that she had to get her *spawn* to the car before she misbehaved anymore. Mia suspected that she was the spawn her Momma was talking about but she wasn't quite certain. Momma walked away in a hurry, with one hand covering her face and the other hand dragging Mia. Daddy was in the car waiting already.

They weren't in the car more than 5 minutes when Momma reached back and threw a set of yard clothes at Mia. The pants button hit her right in the eye.

"Momma!" Mia cried. She looked up at her Momma with just one eye open.

Momma turned and looked out of the front window. After a few moments, Momma found some words.

"I told you not to play in your Sunday dress. If you can't respect that then you don't deserve to have them. Take if off right now and put on your play clothes. I will return that dress tomorrow."

Mia looked at her daddy for help, but he just started driving. He stayed silent for most of the ride home, until they got to their own street. Then, without turning his head, he reached over and held Momma's hand.

"It'll be okay. She's just not there yet."

Momma nodded then looked back at Mia and smiled. Momma was always right.

Chapter Two

Mrs. Gentry looked at her watch. Satisfied with the time allotted, she yelled to the class to put their pencils down. Mia didn't mind. She couldn't figure out the last math question anyway. She'd rather get it wrong with no answer, than with a stupid mistake. Momma always told her that mistakes are what she was good at. But Mia wanted to change that. She wanted to be smart. She wanted to be good at something else. She figured, if she left this question blank, then Mrs. Gentry would just think she was slow and had run out of time. Not stupid because she didn't know what 8 times 7 was.

Mrs. Gentry seemed to like Mia. She told Mia many times that she wondered what was going on in her little mind. Mia never got around to telling her but she didn't think that mattered. It was like the two of them spoke to each other without an ounce of language. She was the best teacher Mia ever had.

"Don't forget we have our weekly spelling test tomorrow. The words of the week are in the back of your agenda. Read them over. Write them out. Memorize them. Do anything but write them on your hands. This is the last mini test before the big one. Study hard, kids."

Mia looked at the back of her agenda book to make sure the words were there. Eyeing them, she smiled. Easy words. Tomorrow would be a breeze. Mia was so focused on the words she hardly heard the bell ring. It wasn't until her classmates charged their way to the lockers, that she realized it was home time. She didn't often like home time. School was a much kinder place to be even if no one loved her there. One day someone would. That she was sure of.

"Oh, one more thing kids," Mrs. Gentry called out over the chaos of getting coats and shoes on. "There is a letter at the door you all need to grab. Bring it home and show your parents. There is a writing contest, entries due next week. The winner gets free admission into this summer's creative writing program. For all of you aspiring writers, this might be just the thing you are interested in. The writing theme this year is *what makes you special*."

Mia was excited about this news. She always wanted to be a writer, a real writer like Stine or Martin. She looked over at the pouch attached to the classroom door. It was filled with pink papers. She ran over right away and grabbed one. She was going to start writing tonight.

Abby was waiting for Mia by the big tree in the left corner of the schoolyard. She always waited there for her. Today, Abby's short brown bob, coupled with the tights and jumpsuit she was wearing, made her look several years younger than she actually was. Abby was 8, but today she looked 6.

Abby and Mia got along great. They lived together, kind of. Mia's house was a semi, a house made into two houses. Abby's family lived on the other side of Mia's. It was nice to have a friend so close. Mia was never allowed to actually go over and visit, but they always walked home together, and in the basement, they had a hole in the wall that they could talk through. Face to face. They called it their spy wall.

Mia had discovered the spy wall accidently one morning when hiding underneath the stairs, away from Momma's shaking fist. After a while, she heard Momma's steps coming so she moved some boxes around to fit behind them. To be extra hidden. When Mia moved the one box she saw a light come through the wall. The hole was at least 6 inches wide and tall. The next day after school, Mia told Abby about it. Abby ran home right away and found the hole on her side of the house. The two girls had used it to communicate ever since. Sometimes, Abby was kind enough to pass Band-Aids through the hole, when they were needed for school. Most days, if the cuts were too bad, Momma would keep Mia home. But sometimes, Momma forgot to check Mia over. Mia hated going to school with cuts. Her

hurt a fly. She always smiled and said, 'bonjour' to Mia when they passed in the hall. Mia wanted to know her better. Mia thought Jessie would be good at hugging but she had to make sure she was kind first.

"A boyfriend? But she's old. She's like 40."

"I know. Eww." Abby wrinkled up her nose as she said 'Eww'. Mia did as well.

"Okay, let me write this all down."

Mia pulled out her pen, and for the next 20 minutes, documented every new juicy detail that Abby was spilling. After that, they played a cassette tape that Abby had brought. It was by someone named Cher. By quarter to 5, Abby was gone.

Mia rushed downstairs to start preparing dinner. Tonight was the night that Frank was coming over to fix their dryer. If Mia didn't have dinner started, Momma would throw a fit.

Dinner was easy. Spaghetti. They often had spaghetti when company was coming. Mia had just finished browning the meat when Momma walked through the door late, around 5:15. Tired and beaten down, Momma walked slowly into the kitchen, inspected the food Mia was preparing, tasted it, then nodded and went on to the living room. She sat down on the couch and turned the television on.

"Did you get the garlic bread out?" Momma called from her place of rest.

"Uh huh."

"What did I tell you about proper language?"

"Sorry Momma, I mean yes. Yes, I did get it out."

It must have been the right answer because Momma didn't say another word until Daddy and Frank walked in together 30 minutes later. They were laughing and talking like two grown men do. Momma must have dozed off because she startled pretty bad when the men walked into the living room. Momma jumped off the couch, ran her fingers through her hair, and straightened her dress real nice, before saying hello.

Mia had the table set and ready for everyone to eat. Daddy suggested that they all eat first, including Frank, before he went down to check on their machine. Frank took off his tool belt and sat at the table. Mia served everyone then sat down to a plate of her own spaghetti.

"Frank is going to be a counselor at Bible camp again this summer, Mia."

"The first aid lead, actually," Frank corrected Daddy. "I'm running the medical emergency cabin. I'll be there for all of the families and their kids. You included sweetheart." Frank winked at Mia when he said sweetheart. She smiled back. He was a nice man, that Frank. And her Daddy liked him, which made him even more special. Frank was always patting her on the knee telling her how beautiful she was. She liked that. He made her feel nice.

Mia was excited to know that Frank was going to be at Bible camp. Every summer, Daddy booked the family a cabin and they would spend two weeks on Manitoulin Island praising Jesus and living in the woods. This year, Jason's family was going too.

"Frank says you can stay with him this Friday, when your Momma and I are at the potluck. Isn't that nice of him? He offered it up himself."

Mia nodded. She hated being home alone at dark.

Dinner took them nearly a half hour to eat because everyone was talking so much. It could have taken longer but when Mia went to reach for a second helping of spaghetti, her Daddy kindly reminded her that gluttony was a sin. And that she shouldn't eat more than what she first took. She was grateful for the reminder but wished she had given herself more spaghetti in the first place. Momma had two helpings. So did Frank. But they were adults, and from what Mia saw, adults were excluded from God's list of sins. At least the good Christian ones that her parents knew were. Next time, she would be more aware of her stomach and how empty it was.

Frank thanked Momma for the delicious meal before he went downstairs with Daddy to have a look at the dryer. Mia almost corrected Frank on who he should thank for cooking it but thought better. Momma needed to feel good today, and Frank's compliment did that.

Mia started cleaning off the table. She was almost done when the mistake happened. She went to grab the good serving plate off the table with two hands and her one finger caught on the tablecloth, sending everything flying to the floor. Including Momma's good serving plate. It smashed into a thousand little pieces. Mia knew Momma was upset. That good feeling Frank just gave her left running from fear. She could see anger in Momma's face.

Daddy called from the basement to ask if everything was all right. Momma said yes. Mia wanted to yell to her Daddy or Frank for help, but she didn't. Instead she focused her pleas on Momma.

"I'm sorry Momma. It was an accident. I'm sorry."

Mia knew to keep her eyes directly focused on Momma. No turning away. It hurt more if she didn't see it coming.

"I am so sorry," Mia said again.

Momma didn't want to hear any of it. She grabbed Mia under the arm and pulled her out of the living room and up the stairs to the bedroom wing. Momma stopped at her room for a minute to grab the key. Mia hated the key. The key meant darkness, and hunger, and monsters. Momma pulled Mia into her room and slammed the door behind them. Mia didn't need to be told what to do. She knew. She went straight to the closet and sat down on the floor. She heard the lock snap. Mia was trapped, in the dark, for the night, or until Momma decided to unlock the door and let her out.

Chapter Three

Mia sat at her desk and read the writing assignment topic out loud to herself. She sat and thought about it. Thought about when she was told she was special. One time, she read in a Readers Digest magazine that the best stories were the ones where the author wrote about things that were familiar. *Write what you Know*, the article was titled. Mia would do just that.

She knew when she was most often told she was special.

What makes me special by Mia Pratt

What makes me special is that I like to be happy. Always.

Happiness is the key to life, Aunt Colleen says.

If you ask Momma even my stupid is special.

She says it all the time. Mia, you're a special kind of stupid.

Daddy says I give special kisses when I have peanut butter on my face.

Momma says I give special kisses too. She asks for them during our special time in her room.

I think I should be at this writing camp because I can work hard

and write alot of good stuff. I want to be a writer forever. I can do it.

Writing is special to me.

Mia Pratt

Mia looked at her paper. She was proud of what she wrote. She thought Momma and Daddy would be too. She couldn't wait to show them.

Daddy was going to be late coming home today. He had a doctor's appointment for the problem he'd been having with his legs. They just didn't want to work like they once did. Daddy had troubles getting up and down the stairs. Some nights, he slept on the couch in the living room just to avoid the walk to his room.

Momma didn't like it when Daddy slept down there but he did it anyway. Mia liked that about him.

Momma said she was going to be late as well. She was meeting her friend for tea. Mia was on her own to feed herself. She liked these nights. Mia could eat until she was full.

Mia read over her writing assignment one more time before she headed downstairs to get some food. As she ate her third peanut butter and jelly sandwich, she pictured what writing camp would be like. She bet there would be a lot of kids there just like her. With stories they wanted to write. Mia had a lot of those. Stories. The nights Momma made her sleep in the closet, she would stay up and create grand stories of princesses and castles, with kings and queens. It helped her pass the time. Mia didn't like darkness. It scared her. But her stories made it better. Stories made everything better. Except the ones that she made up where her parents were killed and she moved in with new families. Those ones made her stomach hurt the next day.

Mia finished her food and cleaned up the table and the dishes. It was almost 6 o'clock. Soon she would have to go over to Frank's. Momma said if they weren't home by 6:30, she needed to walk herself over to his trailer so he could babysit her. Momma and Daddy had the potluck to go to that night that and they would be out late. Mia knew she could stay home alone, but was really thankful for Frank offering to babysit her. She wouldn't have to be scared late at night. Her house made a lot of noise.

Mia ran upstairs and took one last look at her assignment. She noticed she spelled the word a lot wrong. It was two words not one. She erased what she had and fixed it up. Convinced that she had the winning paper, Mia rolled it up, put an elastic band around it, and brought it into her parent's room. She left it on her Daddy's pillow. He could read it when he got home and tell her if it was good. She could hand it in on Monday when she went back to school. Daddy was going to be so proud. Mia just beamed at the thought.

Chapter Four

Before leaving, Mia pulled out her book for a refresh.

<u>Frank</u>
Lives alone in a traylor
Daddys best friend
Hasn't had hair since he was 25
No girlfriend
Fixes washers and dryers. Can't fix ovens
Bad at skipping
Goes to church every Sunday, Bible study too
Smells like gasoline all the time
Makes funny jokes
Likes to eat.
Can pull a quarter out from kids ears with magic

Frank's trailer smelt like fish. It was Friday, and Friday was the day to eat fish Frank said. Mia wondered silently if he kept them alive in a tank somewhere inside the trailer, it smelt that strong.

Mia sat on a chair, or a table, she wasn't quite sure which. It looked like both. It was really just a piece of wood that hung from the wall with a small cushion placed on top. The cushion had many holes with stuffing sticking out. It looked like it was just thrown on top of the wood. Like it didn't belong there. Nothing in the room looked comfortable.

The space was small. Mia could see to the other side of the trailer from where she sat. She saw the sink to the right that had at least a week's worth of dishes piled up. Most of the dishes had dried food still clinging to the porcelain. To the left she saw the door to the outside, and a mini fridge built into a cupboard, that she could only assume was full of fish.

The trailer became really skinny after that, with just a walkway leading to the bathroom and a room in the back. Even though there was a curtain up, it wasn't quite closed and Mia could see a bed in the back. She could see Frank's bedroom.

As she continued to size up the trailer, she watched Frank pace. He scratched his baldhead as he looked around for something for Mia to do. He said things like 'Umm,' and "Ah,' before telling Mia that his living space wasn't very kid-friendly. Mia didn't mind. It didn't take much to entertain her. She once killed three hours with a paperclip, string, and a straw.

Frank finally settled on television as a way to pass some time that evening. He twisted the knob on the television until he found a movie. Frank reached under the middle couch cushion and pulled out a rolled-up TV Guide magazine and flipped to that days' date. He ran his chubby pointer finger down the paper until he found the current time slot. He slowly read aloud that the movie was about a young boy who was trying to get on a kids' soccer team, even though he couldn't kick a soccer ball to save his life. Mia said that she was interested in watching it, so Frank left it on.

The movie was pretty funny. Mia laughed. Frank watched half the movie with her. He sat beside her and rubbed her leg. But after a bit, he went to his bedroom. He stayed there for the rest of the movie.

When the movie was over, Frank said it was bedtime. Mia wasn't tired. She told Frank this and he offered to get her some books to read while she tried to nod off. Frank only had encyclopedias so Mia read those. He had a whole shelf of them. She started out with the first one on the letter A.

She read about Africa first. She didn't know that Africa was the world's second largest continent. Next, she read about the Amazon, and Anacondas before she got to Anatomy. She found that the most interesting. There were so many systems in the human body, the skeletal system, the muscular system, and the cardiovascular system to name a few. There were about 700 named muscles in the body as well. Mia knew about 6. She had a lot of learning to do yet.

Frank came in and checked on her a few times. She always told him she was fine. But this time, when he came in, she asked him about Anatomy. She wanted to know if Frank knew about how many muscles were in the human body. Frank was surprised at the amount too.

He sat down beside Mia for a while and read the book with her. They read about the immune system, and the urinary tract. Mia didn't like that one. She hated the smell of pee, and even more, talking about it.

When they moved onto the male and female reproductive system, Frank got uncomfortable. He suggested that maybe Mia save that section for when she could talk about it with Momma and Father. Mia corrected Frank. Jesus is my father, she said. Daddy is my dad.

Frank smiled and said he understood. He said the sentence again using the word Daddy instead. Frank learned quickly. Mia liked that.

Frank said goodnight and went to bed. Mia stayed up reading a bit longer. It was about 15 minutes later that Frank called to her from his bedroom.

"Are you still reading, Mia?"

"Yes."

"Are you not tired?"

"No," Mia lied. Truth be told, she was exhausted, but too interested in what she was reading to put it down.

There was silence for a few moments before Frank called back, "Wanna come learn something else about the reproductive system? Something that isn't in that book?"

Mia was intrigued. What could he know that the encyclopedia didn't? Her gut told her that maybe she should put the book down and go to bed but she knew that it wasn't polite to say no to an adult.

Daddy always said that you learned more from listening than from talking.

Mia got up from her homemade bed on the couch, with the encyclopedia in hand, and walked into Frank's bedroom. Frank was pleased that Mia wanted to come learn.

"In the bathroom there is a pair of scissors and a razor. Grab them and a wet towel. I'll show you what happens when you shave a man's private areas. It's how babies are born. Just don't tell your parents. They would probably want to tell you themselves. We wouldn't want to disappoint them or get them in trouble."

Mia was excited to learn how babies were born. Momma never told her. Momma said that that's the kind of stuff she should learn in school from the people Daddy paid taxes to. Mia was very thankful to Frank. He was smart. She never knew you needed to shave a man to make a baby.

Chapter Five

Mia woke up in bed at her own house. She wasn't sure how she got there. Probably Daddy. The last thing she remembered was leaving Frank's room to head back to her pillow and blanket on the couch. Frank had given her some medicine to help her sleep because she couldn't find her tiredness. Her brain wanted to think more than sleep.

She thought back to Frank's baby making lesson the night before. A penis is really ugly, she thought. Mia couldn't believe that something so ugly came from Jesus. She thought everything God made was beautiful. Not everything she now knew.

Mia still wasn't quite sure how babies were made though. Frank was so happy with himself for teaching Mia that she didn't feel it was proper to put her stupid on him and ask more questions. She understood that the white stuff made a baby, but how could a baby be made when the white stuff just went into a cloth? Did you hide that cloth somewhere special until it created a baby? That couldn't be right. She did know that babies came from the inside of a woman's belly. How did it go from the cloth to the Momma's belly? Did she wipe herself with it?

Maybe, Mia thought, this was the other way to have a baby? Not the awful way Momma said Mia was born: in section c at the hospital. Momma said Mia couldn't come out of her down under parts as a normal child would, that would have been too kind of Mia. Momma said she had to let that mean old doctor rip into her with a knife and pull Mia out of her birthing sack. Ruined Momma's figure that day, she said. Mia always felt bad for that. She often saw Momma looking in the long mirror, checking out her stomach and her backside, pulling her shirt up, and pants down to see the scar. Momma was sad whenever she looked. Probably because she was beautiful before Mia was born, and all ugly after. Momma's words, not Mia's. Most days, Mia thought Momma was pretty. She would have to ask her momma why she was born by section c and if it had anything to do with how Momma handled the cloth.

Mia felt pretty confident that she wasn't going to end up with a baby in her belly. She didn't touch the cloth. Frank did touch her privates though. Frank's touch hurt. Frank's fingers were rough and his nails were sharp. Frank needed to let Momma clip his nails too.

Mia stayed in her bed staring at the ceiling for several minutes before she remembered her paper. She had left it on Daddy's pillow. Did he read it yet? He must be so proud of her this morning.

Mia leapt out of bed, got dressed, and ran down the hall to see if Daddy had read it. As she passed her parents room, she could see that her Daddy was still sleeping. Daddy never slept in. He must be real tired she thought. That was okay. Momma was up. Maybe she'd read it. Mia could wait to hear from her Daddy about what he thought. She would get Momma's thoughts first.

Mia could smell bacon as soon as she got to the bottom of the stairs. When Mia rounded the corner into the kitchen she could see Momma dancing at the stove. She was whistling a church song as she flipped the bacon from one side to the next.

"Morning Mia," Momma sang to the tune of her song.

"Morning Momma."

Mia grabbed a cup, went to the fridge, and poured herself some orange juice. She leaned back against the wall to sip on her drink. She watched Momma continue to dance and sing.

"You're happy this morning," Mia said.

Momma just smiled.

Mia watched Momma's pajama dress flow back and forth across her legs. Even her pajama dress seemed happy. Mia loved mornings like this.

"Do you want some eggs?"

"Yes please."

"How many?"

Mia debated this for several moments. If she said one and was still hungry, she wouldn't get more. She knew she wanted at least two. What if after two she was still hungry? But Mia knew that if she asked for three eggs Momma would say she was being a pig and maybe Momma would then tell her that she couldn't have any. She went with the safe option.

"Two please."

Momma looked back at Mia and smiled.

"Daddy's going to be up soon, Mia. I'm letting him sleep a little. He hasn't been feeling so well lately. Doctor says it's on account of him having diabetes. Pretty bad too. He will be going on insulin Monday. I think it's from all the fatty food you been cooking this family. You gave your Daddy diabetes. I will start cooking from now on."

Mia didn't know what to say. Was Momma right? Had she been killing her Daddy with the food she had been making? Poor Daddy. Daddy said long ago that fear was a wasted emotion. It only made things more complicated. Of course, sometimes she still got scared, like in the dark, or when Momma had that look of the devil, but mostly, she stayed calm. If she acted afraid, Momma would just get madder. Or pain would hurt more. And mostly, Mia wouldn't be able to think properly. And Mia always had to think about what she was going to say or do when Momma was mad. No, she didn't feel afraid for Daddy, she felt sad for him. She felt sad that she had hurt him. Mia hated hurting people. Especially Daddy.

"Is he dying, Momma?"

"Don't be so dramatic child," Momma said with a snarl. "He's sick, that's all. But we can both help him be better by not allowing you to cook for him as much. You haven't killed him yet. I don't plan on letting you either."

Mia nodded. She felt horrible. Daddy was always so good to her. And she had hurt him. She would have to fix this. Momma seemed to say that she could fix it. Mia wasn't going to cook Daddy another thing.

Momma finished the eggs and the bacon. She put it all out on the table before heading upstairs to wake Daddy. They both came down 5 minutes later ready to eat.

Daddy had Mia's paper in his hands when he sat at the table.

"What's this?"

"My writing assignment for school. It's a contest. The winner gets to go to a summer writing camp."

"Writing camp?" Momma said confused. "We can't afford to send you to a writing camp. We already paid for the whole family to head to the Bible retreat this summer. We have no more money."

"It's free. If I win."

Daddy started to unroll the paper when Momma reached over and grabbed it from him.

"Now, I made a special breakfast here for Daddy. Don't you go bothering him with silly things like storytelling and writing camps! If you want to enter that contest, go ahead. But don't you bother your Daddy with nonsense like this."

Mia wanted to cry but didn't. Momma hated tears. She said no one loves anyone who cries. Momma was right. Every time Mia cried, people walked away. But sometimes it was hard not to cry. Like right now. Her storytelling wasn't nonsense. Daddy would like it. She knew it. But Momma said different, and that made her upset.

"But…" Mia started to argue but her Daddy cut her off.

"Your Momma is right, Mia. She made a lovely breakfast and we should concentrate on that. Besides, it's probably the winner anyway. I will read it when it is in the paper. I can see the headline now." Daddy put his hands up high and waved them through the air. "Fourth grader writes the most stunning piece of literature ever to grace the earth."

Mia smiled at her daddy's enthusiasm. His arms swung out wide as he said the word earth. She knew it. Daddy knew it. Her paper was brilliant. Daddy didn't even need to read it. Daddy liked Mia's storytelling.

Momma rolled up the paper and put the elastic back on. She handed it back to Mia.

"Go put this in your school pack so you don't lose it."

Mia grabbed it from her mother and did as she was told.

Breakfast was great. Momma even cleaned up afterward. Mia didn't know what to do with herself so she went up to her room and worked on her spy book. Abby had found out more information about Nina and told it to Mia through the hole in the wall earlier that morning. Mia had to make sure that the notebook was updated. After doing that, Mia took a shower and got dressed. They were headed to Aunt Colleen's that night for supper and she wanted to look her best. Aunt Colleen was Daddy's older sister. She was in her fifties by now, but looked like she was twenty-five. She always wore jeans and rock t-shirts. Daddy had tried to get her to know Jesus more than once but she never wanted to make his acquaintance. Aunt Colleen told Daddy that she and Jesus weren't a match. And they were never going to be. Daddy just chuckled and told her that one day they would be, and that he and Jesus could wait until she was ready.

They arrived at Aunt Colleen's house around 5. She was cooking her usual steak and baked potatoes with green and yellow beans. Mia loved Aunt Colleen's cooking. Aunt Colleen was mellow, as mellow as they came. Once, when Mia was there, she dropped a glass on the floor while being reckless. Aunt Colleen just said, "That's okay Mia, I had too many glasses anyway." And that was that. Mia cried, and Aunt Colleen said there was no room for tears. That Mia had actually done her a favour by making one less glass for Aunt Colleen to wash. No anger. No sadness. Just calmness. And Aunt Colleen didn't leave after Mia cried. She stayed. Momma didn't share that calmness. She was so mad at Mia for dropping that glass, that when Mia got home, Momma told her exactly how disappointed she was. Mia spent two hours in the closet because of embarrassing Momma with her clumsiness.

Aunt Colleen's house was large. It was big and white, with a matching fence going all the way around to the back. In the back yard there was a pool. No one Mia knew, except Aunt Colleen, owned a pool. She liked to go there in the summertime to swim. Daddy would never let Mia go there by herself though. Even if Aunt Colleen said she would pick her up and drop her off. Daddy said Mia couldn't go until Aunt Colleen accepted Jesus into her heart.

The house used to belong to Mia's Grandparents. The year Mia was born, her Grandparent's car was hit by a train. Grandpa went to heaven instantly. Grandma lived but had a lot of injuries. Aunt Colleen quit her job and moved in with Grandma to help her with bathing and feeding. Aunt Colleen had a lot of money saved from her divorce settlement so she could make it work. She said she was only planning to stay until Grandma got stronger, but Grandma never did. Aunt Colleen ended up moving in permanently and still lives there today, even though Grandma passed a few years ago. Momma sometimes told Daddy that he should be living there instead of Aunt Colleen, since the house was paid for and everything, but Daddy only ever shrugged his shoulders in response. Daddy told Mia once that if he was meant to own a big house, the Lord would have provided one for him. He didn't, so Daddy was staying put.

Aunt Colleen met Mia at the door with a big hug. She grabbed Mia's arm and pulled her inside.

"How is school going Mia?" Aunt Colleen asked as she helped her out of her coat.

Mia told her that it was going well. She also told Aunt Colleen about the writing contest and the summer camp. Aunt Colleen asked her what kind of stories she would write if she got into the camp. Mia hadn't thought about it she said. But she sure would tonight.

They all sat in the living room and chatted for a while. Momma seemed unhappy sitting in Aunt Colleen's dirty old recliner. She had so many nice pieces of furniture, yet Momma always sat in that same chair, then complained about it the entire ride home. Mia suggested once that maybe Momma should sit in another seat next time instead, but Momma thought that was a dumb idea. Well, she never said that exactly, but the look Momma gave Mia did.

Finally, after a half hour, Aunt Colleen put dinner on the table.

"You're growing up fast, Mia." Aunt Colleen seemed proud. "You have a boyfriend yet?

Momma answered this question for Mia. "No. She can't date until she is fourteen."

Mia nodded.

"Fourteen? Well you have some time I guess. Are there any boys you like?"

"No. Not really. Boys don't really talk to me. Except for Jason, from church, but he's only 5."

"A little young now, but when you're 25 and he's 21, it isn't going to matter." Aunt Colleen winked when she finished her sentence.

Momma didn't like this conversation. She told Aunt Colleen as much. Aunt Colleen was never really bothered by Momma's crankiness. She just waved her hand at Momma and said, "She's nine, almost ten. This stuff is going to come up sooner than you know, Lee-Ann. Better get used to hearing it on the sooner. Before you know it, she's going to have her period. She's going to be asking to go out on dates, and wondering where babies come from. These years go faster than you think. Better to hear them coming than to be surprised when it's too late."

Momma just kept eating her beans, the yellow ones first, then the green. Aunt Colleen seemed to notice Momma's discomfort, and talked more.

"Girls these days are maturing faster than we did as kids. Mind you, they aren't getting married as young, but sex and drugs are coming up earlier and earlier."

"Don't talk like that in front of her," Momma chimed in. "She's just a baby."

"I'm not a baby!" Mia said, finally entering into the conversation.

Aunt Colleen touched Mia on the arm in support.

"You are only nine," Momma said.

"Almost ten."

"A baby," Momma responded, looking happy that Mia made her point for her.

"Fourteen is just around the corner, Lee-Ann."

"That corner is several blocks aw…"

"I already know where babies come from," Mia jumped in.

"Really?" Momma laughed. "I know what I told you, and that ain't the truth. I told you to wait until your teachers show you with proper diagrams. And that ain't happening until grade seven. You are only in grade four."

"I still know."

Aunt Colleen laughed. "See Lee-Ann, they learn these things in schoolyards now."

"Is that where you learned what you think you know about babies, Mia? Some schoolyard chatter taught you everything? I'll have you know those kids don't know either. Why none of those kids are old enough to have had any babies. They are guessing. You need to be smarter than that."

"Not from the schoolyard Momma, Frank taught me."

"Told you," Momma corrected. "I wouldn't believe anything Frank tells you either, child. He has never had a kid."

"Not told me. Taught me. Showed me how they are made. I know about the white stuff. I seen his. I even touched it."

Well you would think that Frank was right there in the room with his ugly penis sticking out, the way all three adults looked at Mia. Daddy almost choked on his steak. Momma started screaming at the top of her lungs until Daddy went over and comforted her. Aunt Colleen stopped laughing instantly and looked at Mia with tears in her eyes. She stared for what Mia felt was a lifetime. Aunt Colleen looked over at Momma melting down, and Daddy trying to help. Aunt Colleen shook her head and focused back on Mia. She stood, picked Mia up, and carried her straight to the bathroom holding her tighter than she had ever been held in her entire life.

Mia could still hear Momma screaming in the kitchen. Mia was really confused.

Aunt Colleen shut and locked the bathroom door and made Mia tell her the entire story. It took a while because Mia couldn't remember all of the details even though it was just the night before that it happened. But by the time Mia was done telling the little bits she remembered, Aunt Colleen was so upset.

"I'm sorry I made you cry."

"Oh sweetie," Aunt Colleen said. "This isn't your fault. And you didn't make me cry. Frank did."

Mia was more confused now.

Daddy came knocking at the door.

"Open up the door," Daddy said.

"One minute, Richard," Aunt Colleen responded.

Daddy knocked harder.

"I said open it up, Colleen. We need to go," Daddy said. "Lee-Ann is quite upset. We need to take her home so she can get some medicine and some rest. This is hard on her."

Aunt Colleen ripped the door opened. For a moment, Mia thought she was going to punch Daddy right square in the face, but she didn't. She just stood there and scowled at him like he was an alien.

"Hard on Lee-Ann? Richard!"

"Mia, it's time to go."

Mia got up and walked to her Daddy.

"Richard, you need to call the police."

"She's my child, Colleen. And he's my best friend. And we aren't even really sure what happened. I will deal with this if it is needed, don't worry, but I need to think about it first."

"What is there to think about, Richard?"

"I am a man of God, Colleen. He will give me the answers."

Mia walked with Daddy down the hall and to the entrance. Aunt Colleen followed behind him. He handed Mia her coat and shoes. Mia started to get dressed. She noticed Momma was already in the car.

"Seriously, Richard? You don't need to wait until God tells you. I can tell you what you need to do right now."

"Stay out of this Colleen."

Aunt Colleen knew what she was up against. Nobody got between Daddy and Jesus. She knew how stubborn he could be on the subject. Aunt Colleen crouched down and got really near to Mia's face.

"You need anything, you call me okay?"

Mia nodded.

"I love you sweetheart."

"Don't love me. Love is for dreams, Aunty. That's what Momma says. And we're not dreaming."

Aunt Colleen shrugged and moved her face to Mia's ear this time. "Momma doesn't know as much as Aunt Colleen," she whispered. "Love is what makes dreamers, love is for everyone."

Mia left with her Daddy. Both Daddy and Momma said nothing all the way home. Mia was confused as to why Daddy and Momma were so upset with her when Aunt Colleen wasn't. Mia wondered if Frank was upset with her too.

Chapter Six

Mia walked up to Mrs. Gentry with a rush of excitement. Monday had finally come and she could hand in her writing assignment for camp. Yesterday was the longest day of waiting she had ever experienced. She stared at her rolled up paper for hours wondering how she could make it better. But she couldn't. It was just perfect.

Daddy had come to her room after church and again refused to read it. He sure was confident that it was the winner. He wanted to wait to read it like everyone else. Mia could understand that.

Daddy also talked to her about Frank. He said he was waiting until God, or his son Jesus told him what to do. He said that Frank was trying to do something right for Mia, but instead did something that was wrong. He was misguided. Daddy wanted to see how God thought he should proceed. He wanted to make sure that Frank got the proper help.

Mia couldn't understand why Frank needed help. Nor why Daddy felt that it was so bad that God had to get involved but she didn't question Daddy. He always knew what was right. Daddy told her yesterday, "Mia", he said, "you don't always have to understand what is going on. But you do have to believe that this is what God's plan is for you, for everyone. Things happen for a reason, Mia. You will understand when it is time for you to."

Mia had nodded at Daddy and he smiled back. He said she was his good little girl.

But today was another day. *The* day. Mrs. Gentry wouldn't refuse to read her paper. Finally, someone was going to see it.

"Here is my writing assignment." Mia did a small dance as she handed over her paper to Mrs. Gentry.

"I look forward to reading it, Mia," Mrs. Gentry said as she grabbed the paper from Mia's hand. "I wish you luck."

Mia appreciated that extra bit of luck Mrs. Gentry was giving her. She wanted to win this contest in a really bad way.

Mia took a seat at her desk and pulled out her workbook and pencil case. The math problems for that morning were already on the board, and she knew she needed all the time she could get to complete them. Math was not her best subject.

She looked around the room. Most of the kids were hard at work except for Crystal who never did any school work at all. Mia often felt bad for Crystal. She always had messy hair and dirty clothes. Mia wondered what her parents must have been like. Did they not let Crystal shower or wash her own clothes? Maybe their washer and dryer didn't work and they hadn't yet met Frank? Mia was sure grateful her parents washed her clothes and helped her with her hair. She was lucky.

Crystal stuck out her tongue when she caught Mia staring. Mia put her head down in shame and continued on with her math questions. She was deep in concentration trying to figure out what 11 times 12 was when she felt a hand on her shoulder. Mia jumped back hitting her knee on her desk as she did.

Mia unintentionally screamed out. She didn't like surprise touches. Every kid in the class looked over at her. They all started to laugh. She had disrupted the class. Mia knew what that meant. It meant the back of the room desk was hers the rest of the day. But instead of getting mad, Mrs. Gentry just bent down and looked deeply into her eyes.

"Mia, honey. Can we take a walk?"

Mrs. Gentry never asked her to take a walk before, Mia thought.

"I'm not done my math yet."

"That's okay," she said. "You can finish it later."

Mia couldn't believe her ears. You can finish it later was not a sentence that Mrs. Gentry said to any student. Mia put her workbook and pencils back in her desk and stood up. Mrs. Gentry informed the classroom that she would just be outside, and she expected everyone to stay quiet and continue their work.

Mrs. Gentry led Mia out of the classroom. She saw that her teacher had her writing assignment in hand. Mia became hopeful that Mrs. Gentry was going to tell her she should start packing now for writing camp. What would she pack? she wondered.

The two left the classroom. Mrs. Gentry closed the door behind them then pointed to two chairs stationed nearby in the hall. Mia sat down first, then Mrs. Gentry next. Mia couldn't keep the smile off her face.

"Did you read my paper? Do you think it will win?"

Mrs. Gentry smiled. But it wasn't the smile one would use when they are about to talk about a masterpiece. It was more like the sort of smile she had seen before with Jason, when he was trying not to cry.

"It's not good?" Mia asked feeling worried about her story's worth for the first time.

"No, it's wonderful."

Mia smiled again.

"I wrote it right away. I just knew what I wanted to say."

Mrs. Gentry put her hand on Mia's head.

"How did you come up with what you wrote?"

"I just wrote about what makes me special," Mia offered in response. "It's all the truth. That is what makes me special."

Mrs. Gentry nodded before she pulled Mia into a hug. Mia never saw Mrs. Gentry hug anyone. Mia felt uncomfortable. She pulled away.

"Sorry," Mrs. Gentry said.

"That's okay," said Mia.

Mrs. Gentry cleared her throat too many times for a normal person. Mia was worried she was getting sick.

"Are you okay, Missus?"

Mrs. Gentry nodded.

"Mia, some of these things you wrote about are not things that…are maybe just a little…are things that concern me. I think

I need to call someone in to talk to you about them. Would you be okay with that?"

Mia wondered what would need to be talked about.

"Why Missus?

"Well," Mrs. Gentry added. "Like I said, some things you wrote concern me. I want to make sure that everything is okay."

Mia felt her insides deflate.

"What did I do wrong? Why don't you think I'm special?

"Mia, I…"

"Why?"

That's when Mrs. Gentry lost her ability to speak. Mia hated when people had no words to speak. It scared her more than anything. But Mrs. Gentry just sat there staring at Mia. Mia couldn't believe it. If Mrs. Gentry didn't think she was special, no one else would. And the writing camp wouldn't for sure. If she didn't get in for free, Momma would never pay to let her go. Mia was upset. She looked at Mrs. Gentry hoping she was wrong but Mrs. Gentry didn't change her face. Mia was going to cry. She couldn't cry right there. Not in front of her speechless teacher. Mia knew that her words wouldn't be enough right now. And that made her mad on top of her sad. Mia had no choice. She reached over and grabbed the paper right out of Mrs. Gentry's hands and ran. Mia ran like she had never run before. She ran down the hall, down the stairs, and straight out the front door. She was leaving school early that day. She was breaking the rules. She was throwing away the last little piece of her that she thought she had to offer. Mia was throwing away her kindness.

Chapter Seven

Mia rushed into the house. She didn't even take off her shoes, she just ran straight to her bedroom. She was wrong for leaving school and she knew it. She needed to be punished. Mia knew what Momma would do; Momma would put her straight into the closet without dinner. But Mia had to cook dinner tonight because it was a work night. Momma would be too tired. Momma said Daddy would have to try to survive Mia's cooking a little longer, because Momma couldn't make it every night. Jesus would have to work a little harder for Daddy this week.

Mia should at least be punished until dinner, she thought. She would punish herself until it was time to start cooking. Mia opened up the closet door. It was harder to get the nerve to get into it when Momma wasn't behind her screaming. When Momma was screaming at her, the closet almost seemed like a great trade for Momma's anger. But Momma wasn't there. There wasn't anybody threatening to beat her into next week. It was just Mia, and Mia alone that had to get inside that closet. And Mia didn't want to. But she was bad. She disrespected an adult. This had to happen.

Mia opened the closet door and looked inside. With the light from the room shining in, it didn't look as scary as it normally did. But she had to shut the door once she got inside, and that didn't sit well with her at all.

Mia knew there was no time to waste. If she was going to properly punish herself, she had to do it now. Momma would be home in two hours. She needed to do her punishment then get down to the kitchen so food was on when Momma came in the door.

Mia took one last look to study the closet then she closed her eyes and slowly walked inside, closing the door behind her. Once it was shut, she sank to the floor and wept.

Darkness had a funny way of making Mia realize how she needed to fix things. She realized today that she needed to just explain to Mrs. Gentry that maybe she didn't write things properly. That maybe if she told Mrs. Gentry about what made her special she would see it better. Maybe her sentences weren't what they needed to be yet. But she was working on it. She wrote everyday so she could be better. She just needed to be better. That was all.

Mia thought about how she could be better for many more minutes before she decided she had a plan. Once she was confident that her plan would work, she got up and opened the closet door. Her eyes took a moment to adjust to the light, several moments in fact. She was only feet away from her bedroom door when she smelt the strong and familiar scent of roses and maple syrup. Mia stopped. She turned her head slowly. Momma was sitting on her bed, shaking her leg vigorously, reading Mia's writing assignment. Momma had her mad face on. Mia's heart jumped. She debated running back to the closet but knew that she would have to pass Momma again to do so. And Mia was not willing to pass Momma. Not right now.

Mia's heart was running for her.

Why was everyone upset with her assignment?

"You little bitch!" Momma said under her breath.

Mia didn't like the b word. It meant pain.

"Momma?"

"How could you write this?"

Mia didn't know what to say.

"This leaves me very concerned."

"Mrs. Gentry said that too! What did…"

Mia didn't get to finish her sentence before Momma stood up and screamed.

"You showed this to your teacher?"

Mia hesitated but nodded.

"I handed it in. But don't worry. It won't go far. Mrs. Gentry doesn't think I'm special. She said so. Said she was concerned over what I wrote and that I needed to talk to someone about it."

Momma screamed again. She ripped up the assignment as quick as she could. Ripping and ripping until no piece was bigger than a quarter.

"Momma stop! That's my writing!"

Momma didn't stop. She kept tearing pieces smaller and smaller, grunting and screaming each time she separated one word from the other.

"Momma!" Mia knew she shouldn't argue with her Momma's decisions but she couldn't help it. Mia wanted writing camp so bad, and Momma was taking her chances away. How could she explain to Mrs. Gentry now? Mia could only stand there and watch.

When Momma was done ripping the papers as much as she could, she dropped the last piece on the floor and charged at Mia.

"Do you know what you've done?"

Mia didn't. But Momma did. She grabbed Mia by the hands and pressed them against the wall. Mia was held there, unable to move from the plaster.

"Momma please! That hurts! Let go of my hands."

Momma didn't care. Momma held Mia there tight. She spat right in Mia's face. Mia wanted to wipe Momma's spit out of her eyes but she couldn't. Momma had her hands too tight. Mia couldn't see.

Momma drilled her knee straight into Mia's stomach. Mia's breath was so scared it left her body. Mia struggled to pull her breath back in but her stomach hurt more than it ever had. It wouldn't let Mia breathe.

Momma hit Mia with her knee three more times before she stopped, and that was only because Mia threw up her entire lunch onto Momma's shoes.

Momma let Mia go. Mia dropped to the floor, landing in her own vomit. Mia only had time to wipe her eyes clean before

Momma pulled off her shoes and threw them at Mia, both hitting her on the head as they landed.

"You stupid, stupid girl. You don't know what you just did. You better not tell your Daddy and hurt him like you just hurt me. You will need at least one of us to try to love you over the next few weeks. And that ain't going to be me. You better pray that he has the strength to see your goodness somewhere under all this horrible."

Momma pulled Mia out of the way of the door so she could leave the room. Mia stayed on the ground for a few minutes. She held her stomach with her vomit soaked hands. Putting pressure on it was the only way to make it feel a bit better. She needed to get her breath back before she could attempt sitting up. She moved her Momma's shoes out of the puke, and wiped them off on her own clothes. That gave Mia the energy to sit up. She leaned back against the doorframe. Her breath was making an appearance in her lungs again. She was thankful.

Momma was sure mad about her writing assignment. Mia still didn't know why everyone was so upset about it. Mia just knew she did something really awful.

"Mia, hurry up and get your ass down here. Dinner won't cook itself you know."

Mia tried to stand but her stomach hurt too much. She bent over and held it tight again, giving herself one last moment of relief before she had to suck it up and move, pain or not. She couldn't disappoint Momma more by not making dinner. Mia had to do her responsibilities no matter how hurt she was.

"Coming Momma," Mia found a little breath to respond back.

"Move it a little faster, Mia. And make sure you wipe all the puke off of you before you come down. No one wants that in their dinner. And bring my shoes. You need to start them in the laundry sometime before Jesus comes back for us."

Mia grabbed Momma's shoes and stood up. She looked over and noticed the torn pieces of her paper on the floor. Mia finally allowed her tears to fall.

She thought it was the winning assignment. But no one else did. That made her sad. And mad. Mad at Daddy for telling her it was. Mad at herself for thinking she was special. Mad at Jesus for making her want to be a writer. Mostly, she was mad at herself for being so damn ordinary.

Chapter Eight

Mia pulled the pork chops out of the pan. The smell of them made her stomach turn even more. She didn't want to eat. She thought she would vomit again if she did. Mia just wanted to go to bed but she couldn't.

She set everyone's plates up in the kitchen this time. Mia knew that Daddy wasn't going to be happy with his new diet. She didn't want to taunt him with having bowls of food on the table in front of him.

She gave Momma extra food. Momma ate more when she was upset anyway. And Mia had upset her something awful today. Mia was already killing Daddy she didn't want to kill Momma as well.

She put enough on her own plate to make it look like she was eating a healthy amount, but not more than she could force down. She filled Daddy's plate up with vegetables, cheese, and pickles. All things she didn't cook.

Once they were ready she brought in both Momma's and Daddy's plates first then returned to the kitchen for her own.

Daddy's face was contorted when she went back to the table.

"What is this, Mia?"

"Dinner!"

"Are these appetizers before my meal?"

"No," Mia said. "That *is* your meal."

Daddy was as confused about his meal as Mia was about why he didn't want it.

"Mia, go get your Daddy a proper meal."

"But Momma, you said…"

"Enough Mia, we don't need your input. Just go get Daddy what he is asking for."

Mia didn't want to. She didn't want to kill her Daddy. She hesitated.

"I didn't cook anymore pork chops," Mia admitted. "I gave you Daddy's, and I took one. There are no more."

Momma looked at Mia with great disappointment.

"What is going on in your head today, child? Do the proper thing. Give Daddy your meal and go upstairs to think about what you did to him."

Mia looked down at her food. She was a little relieved. She handed Daddy her meal, and he returned the favour by giving her his plate. Mia took it and went up to her room.

Mia didn't leave her room until the next morning when Momma came in and told her to get dressed in 5 minutes. Mia did as she was told and was downstairs in record time.

"Where are we going?"

"The police. It's time to tell them about what Frank did," Momma answered without even looking at Mia.

"Why would they care?" Mia asked. "I thought we were only telling Jesus?"

Momma ignored Mia's questions. She just continued to get ready and silently encouraged Mia to do the same.

The police station was quiet. The only sound was an officer or two typing on their computers. Mia sat in a cold black chair that was in a line-up of many against the wall in the registration area. She watched Momma talk through a glass partition to the only cop around who was willing to listen. He nodded his head several times before he opened a door to the back and held his hand out for Momma and Mia to follow. Mia got up and walked to where she was asked to go.

The officer led them into a dark room where they waited. Once alone, Momma told Mia to stick to talking only about Frank and what happened the night she went over to his house. She also told Mia that Daddy didn't need to know about this from her. That Momma was going to tell him. Lastly, Momma made sure to tell

Mia not to talk about her camp writing assignment anymore, or what Mia thought made her special. Momma told her she wasn't special and no one would understand why she thought she was. Mia listened to everything that Momma had to say and made a mental note of it all so she wouldn't screw it up. She played it over and over in her mind until a new officer came in. She was a woman. Mia felt more comfortable.

"Hi, my name is Officer Tawes. You can call me Karen. You're Mia?" She asked looking at Mia. Mia nodded.

"Hi Karen, I'm Lee-Ann, Mia's mother. Thank you for your time." Momma started petting Mia on the head. "My poor child has been riddled with fear and sadness ever since this happened. We really need to do something to help this poor dear."

Momma was talking weird. Mia wasn't riddled with fear or sadness from Frank. Yet, Officer Tawes nodded and comforted Momma as best as she could. She told Momma not to worry, that she would take good care of her baby. Momma nodded and got up to leave the room as Officer Tawes asked her to.

"Momma? Don't go." Mia liked the petting Momma was doing. She didn't want Momma to go. She wanted Momma to comfort her. She also worried she would say the wrong thing and Momma wouldn't be there to catch it and stop Mia from saying too much.

"Can you give us a minute, Karen?' Momma asked Officer Tawes. The officer agreed and left the room.

Mia's stomach hurt. She wrapped her arms around her covered belly bruises.

"Listen Mia, Momma needs a coffee. I don't want to listen to what you need to say. Momma has enough stress without hearing what you let Frank do. Just say what I told you to say, listen to the officer, and I will see you when I'm done my coffee. And for heaven's sake, don't cry. You aren't pretty when you cry. Or maybe you should cry. It might look better. I don't know. You decide."

Momma tapped Mia on the shoulder. Mia so wanted Momma to stay.

Momma opened the door and left, and Officer Tawes came back in to replace her.

"Okay, Mia. Let's have a chat."

Mia told Officer Tawes everything that happened that night. She didn't think it was bad enough to be telling the cops so she added a few minor details to make it sound worthy of tattling.

The officer nodded a lot and when they were done, she told Mia that she did a great job. Mia was relieved. Officer Tawes asked Mia to wait outside so she could talk to her Momma for a few minutes. Mia opened the door and told Momma to go in. Momma was inside the room for just ten minutes before she came out crying. Mia did it again. She made her Momma cry.

Mia didn't go to school that day. Momma said it was best if she stayed in her room and thought about what she had done. How she had hurt people. She hurt Momma, she hurt Frank, and she hurt Daddy. She may have hurt Mrs. Gentry's job too. Momma also explained how Daddy was supposed to go on insulin but chose not to. Daddy said Jesus was going to heal him. Momma wondered out loud if he was making that decision because he couldn't handle one more stress in his life after everything Mia was putting him through. Mia now wondered that too.

She stayed up in her room and waited. She knew once Daddy came home she would have more sadness to fix. He didn't want her to tell the police what happened with Frank. Daddy knew that Frank just made a mistake. Mia knew that too although she didn't know what the mistake was exactly. She was a little confused. She wondered if Jesus was going to explain things to her too.

Chapter Nine

Mia could hear Daddy yelling from all the way in her room. He was upset with Momma. Mia got Momma in trouble. Mia was screwing things up all over the place.

Momma and Daddy were fighting so loud that they didn't hear Mia walk past them to the front door. As she was getting her shoes on she heard Daddy say to Momma that she had betrayed him. Momma said she had to because of Mia's damn writing assignment. When Daddy asked what that had to do with anything, Momma was too embarrassed about Mia's bad writing to tell him. She just told Daddy that he would have to trust her.

Mia left the house as quietly as she could. The door barely made a sound as it closed. She looked over at Abby's house. The family car was parked in the driveway. Abby had to be home.

Mia walked up their front steps. Most of the wood had been chipped away, so she stepped carefully and slowly on the way up. She knocked on the door. Abby's mom answered. Mia asked her if Abby was available to come out and play. Her mom said yes, but Mia would have to wait a moment for Abby to finish cleaning off the supper table. Abby's mom asked Mia if she would like to come in. Mia said no.

"Are you sure? Come in out of the sun."

"I can't. But thank you kindly," Mia responded. "I will wait right here."

Abby's mom nodded then closed the door. Mia wanted to go in to see what Abby's house looked like but knew if she did, she would be in more trouble than she already was. Momma said Mia wasn't allowed in friend's homes. Momma was worried that if Mia did go in, she would start comparing her life to theirs. And that wasn't very Christian like. To compare your life to that of others. Especially sinners. Mia needed to appreciate what the Lord had provided her with.

Abby came out a few minutes later. They decided to go and do a little spying. They had a new person that Mia wanted to spy on.

"Who?" Abby asked excited.

"Her name is Karen Tawes. She's a police officer."

"You want to spy on a police officer?"

Mia nodded. She knew how dangerous it was but she needed to do it. Mia used the spy game as a way of getting to know people that may get close to her. Mia hated surprises. And she hated not knowing someone. She needed more information. She wanted to see if she could trust Officer Tawes.

"Where do we start?" Abby asked.

"The corner store. We find a telephone booth and look in the phone book for her address."

Abby liked that idea. The two girls jumped on their bikes and headed down the street.

Thirty minutes, and two wrong addresses later, the girls were comfortably sitting in a bush watching Officer Tawes through her kitchen window as she made herself a late dinner.

Abby noted everything she could on a piece of paper.

<u>Karen Tawes</u>
Wears jogging pants
Eats green apples while cooking
Has a cat likes to dance with him making super
Lives with a boy hes cute
Watches tv
Has a big house

Mia always liked being the one who documented things because Abby's writing was messy. But she knew how much Abby liked doing it too, so she let her every once in a while. Mia felt today was a good day to let her write it. Maybe Jesus would see her kindness and it would make Him feel better about all the mistakes Mia had made recently.

The sun was starting to set when they decided to leave their post. Abby handed Mia the notes before going back into her house.

"Here, put these into the master book."

Mia nodded and grabbed the paper. She waved good-bye to Abby and watched her walk into her home before Mia even attempted to open her front door. If she got busted, she didn't want Abby caught in the crossfire. Mia couldn't add Abby to the list of people hurt by her.

Once Abby was inside, Mia opened the front door slightly. She heard no noise. She opened it up fully. Still quiet. Mia inched her way to the front hall closet and hung up her jacket and put her shoes away.

Mia slowly peeked around the corner. The television was off and the house was still. No one was around.

She walked as quietly as she could to the stairs. She heard voices coming from the top floor. Where were they?

Mia took the steps one at a time. Taking care each step she took. Getting closer and closer to her parent's voices, she noticed the sound was coming from their bedroom. Momma and Daddy were in there with the door closed. Mia moved a little faster. She snuck by their room on her tippy toes. Daddy's words were still upset. So were Momma's. Momma asked Daddy to pass her a magazine then shouted that he didn't have to throw it at her. Daddy replied by telling her to get it herself next time then.

Mia made it to her room. She barely got inside before Momma's door opened.

"Mia?"

Mia's heart sank.

"Yes, Momma?"

"I'm thirsty, go downstairs and get me some water will ya?"

Mia looked at her Momma confused.

"Don't look at me like that. Water. Comes from the tap. Go get me some."

Mia nodded and quickly headed back to the stairs. She wasn't caught. Momma didn't even know she had gone out. Mia felt a slight thrill that she knew she shouldn't have. Mia had broken a rule and it felt oddly good.

Mia grabbed a cup from the kitchen cupboard and turned the tap on. She placed her finger under the running water until she felt it was cold enough for Momma's liking. She filled the cup up. Mia turned off the tap and turned around. Momma was standing behind her.

"Momma!" Mia startled. "You scared me. I was just going to bring this up to you."

Momma grabbed the cup from Mia and placed it on the counter. She put her pointer finger up to her lips and said "shhhh!"

Mia felt concerned.

"What's wrong Momma?"

Momma just smiled. "Let's go sit and talk on the couch. Have some special time."

"I'm tired Momma," Mia hoped Momma would care.

Momma grabbed her by the hand and pulled her to the couch.

Mia sat down.

Mia's eyes started to water. Her sore stomach couldn't handle anymore of Momma. Mia wasn't sure her heart could either. She tried to wipe her tears away before Momma saw them but she couldn't do it fast enough.

"Do I need to get the packing tape?"

Mia shook her head. She hated the packing tape. Momma used it on Mia's mouth when Mia had tears. Momma knew the tape stopped the whining. If Mia were to cry with tape on her mouth, her nose would get plugged. And if Mia's nose was plugged, then she couldn't breathe. Crying meant suffocation. Mia would rather go off in thought in her head then deal with the tape and no breath.

"No Momma, I'll stop crying. I promise."

Momma nodded.

She started telling Mia all about her stress. She talked to Mia about how she couldn't find anyone to care. How she just wanted to die. Momma told Mia about how she would kill herself one day. Mia didn't want to hear what Momma was saying. When Momma was done with her words, she grabbed Mia's hand and put it on her belly.

Momma may not have caught Mia sneaking in but Jesus obviously did. She was being punished as she should. And with that thought, Mia allowed her mind to wander off somewhere more pleasant than the couch.

Chapter Ten

"Mia, you're back! I was worried about you." Mrs. Gentry looked at Mia with happiness. "I am so happy to see you."

Mia liked the thought that maybe Mrs. Gentry was happy to see her. Especially after Mia ran out on her two days ago. She was also relieved to see that her teacher still had her job after all of Mia's nonsense.

"Can we go outside and talk again?"

Mia didn't want to go back out but she felt she had no choice.

Mia headed to the hall, Mrs. Gentry followed. She grabbed Mia's hand as soon as they sat down. Mia pulled her hand away. The only time people grabbed Mia's hands was to hold her down or tie her up and she didn't particularly want to be held or tied at school. The kids would make fun of her.

"I talked to your Momma yesterday. She told me what happened to you."

Mia wasn't sure what Mrs. Gentry was talking about.

"She told me that you had something very awful happen to you, but you went to the police station yesterday and told them all about it."

Mia realized she was talking about Frank. Mia nodded.

"She also told me that she saw your paper and that you were quite confused over who did what to you. That you had bad dreams about what had happened, and you blamed others for a while."

Mia was confused.

"She said that you got confused about Momma checking you out after he hurt you. I thought your Momma hurt you. That was my mistake. I'm sorry if I frightened you."

What was Mrs. Gentry talking about? Why did Momma say that?

Mia wanted to ask Mrs. Gentry what she was talking about but Mrs. Gentry just kept talking.

"Your Momma helped me see what you were writing about. I'm so sorry. I did call someone in to protect you but realize now that isn't needed. They will still come in tomorrow and talk to you but it's only a talk. I will tell them about my mistake. Is that okay?'

"Yes," Mia said.

A part of Mia wanted to tell Mrs. Gentry that she was wrong. That Momma was wrong too, but Mia was only 9. And 9-year olds didn't call adults liars. Especially when those adults were your Momma and your teacher. Mia didn't want to make Mrs. Gentry feel bad about her mistake. Mia wished Mrs. Gentry were smarter. But she wouldn't tell her that either.

The rest of the week passed quickly. Mia talked to the protective services people like Mrs. Gentry said she needed to. They were kind. Mia asked them what was going to happen with her paper she wrote, and if she could still apply to writing camp. They didn't seem to know anything about the contest. Mia had a feeling that her chances of making it to writing camp were gone.

Aunt Colleen called Mia twice that week to check up on her. They had a good conversation the second time. Aunt Colleen explained how she wanted to come and get Mia and spend some time with her but Daddy said they were really busy that week. Mia told Aunt Colleen that they weren't that busy, but then instantly felt bad for maybe making Daddy sound incorrect. Aunt Colleen said it was okay though, that she already figured Daddy wasn't being truthful and she wouldn't tell him that Mia thought the same. Aunt Colleen promised Mia that she would see her very soon because she had a hug to give her.

Church day came on Sunday as it always did, and Momma had to tell Mia to hurry up and get ready again. Today was the Sunday Mia needed to get her fingernails clipped down smaller; this required a few extra minutes.

Momma said it was important that her nails were clipped short. Then she couldn't hurt Momma with her nails if she decided to be one of those girls who got rough with their Mommas. Mia wasn't one of those girls but she understood Momma's fear. Nails hurt. Momma got Mia with her nails often. It's too bad that kids couldn't help Momma's clip their nails. Mia would be the first to sign Momma up for that if they could.

This church day was different than most church days. Mia felt like everyone was staring at her. They all gave her looks of disappointment. Even Jason didn't come near Mia. Every time she tried to talk to him, his Momma would shoo him away.

Momma on the other hand had looks of love. All the women in Momma's tea group came over and offered Momma hugs. Mia heard a few of them tell Momma that they were sorry she had to go through molestation charges. They wished Momma strength from Jesus. Momma was kind. She thanked them for their concern. She said she would need them to pray for her, and maybe spend some extra time with her having tea that week.

Frank wasn't at church. Mia wondered if he went to jail like Momma said he might. But right before they left, Mia overheard Daddy say to a parishioner that Frank was just home with the flu bug. He needed their understanding and faith.

Mia walked down the hall as soon as the last prayer was completed. She looked up at some of the artwork from the Sunday school kids. They were paintings of the three Crosses of Calvary. One kid put Jesus on the middle cross, using the imprint of the side of his hand to do so. Mia thought it was quite brilliant.

She was contemplating some of the other pictures on the wallboard when she felt a large hand touch the top of her head. Mia tried to twist around to see who it was but he was holding on so tight that she couldn't move. He started speaking in a loud alien language, shaking as he did. Mia knew enough about Daddy's teachings to know he was speaking in tongues. The language the Lord had given him. Mia tried harder to twist around and see who was praying for her so intently but all she managed to do was bump herself straight forward into the wall instead. That's when it happened. The man screamed loudly, "I revoke you Satan, I revoke you right now. Get out of this small child!"

Mia didn't like what was happening.

"Stop!" Mia cried.

But he didn't. Mia started to cry a little.

"Please, just stop."

The man didn't hear her over his continued shouting. Or he didn't want to hear her. Mia couldn't decide.

Satan? Did she really have Satan inside of her? Or was Satan trying to get inside of her and he was stopping it? She couldn't have Satan inside of her then she really would be unlovable.

Mia stopped trying to see who the man was. Instead, she stood still and waited for him to be done. She knew that sometimes no fight was the best fight. Before long, she felt his hand lift up from the top of her head as he shouted Amen. Many Amens were returned to him. Mia turned around and noticed that it wasn't just this man praying for her, but many other parishioners as well. They all gave the old man satisfied smiles and walked away. Mia just stood and watched them leave, stunned at what had happened.

Nobody played with Mia after service. She sat alone at the bottom of the stairs waiting for Momma and Daddy to finish up what they were doing. Sometimes, Mia thought, the Lord's house was an awful lonely place for a building that had so many worshippers inside.

The next day, Momma was already out for her first tea date of the week. She kept Mia home from school so she could attend tea with her. Mia didn't like that. She wanted to be at school and not at tea. Momma said Mia was needed with her though.

Mia sat and listened to Momma as she told the ladies all about what Frank did. The ladies oooo'd and ahhh'd with every detail.

Mia didn't want to listen to what Momma was saying. She didn't like that the church ladies knew how dumb she was. Mia liked when they thought she was cute. Momma accepted hugs from all of the ladies before paying the bill. Mia guessed Momma hadn't quite got all the hurt out of her system yet because she told the waitress at the counter about Frank as well, when she asked Momma why Mia wasn't in school that day. "My daughter was molested," was Momma's reply. Momma said it while pretending to cover Mia's ears but she heard it loud and clear. "Now she can't seem to not be near me." The waitress nodded to Momma like she understood exactly what Momma meant.

Momma brought Mia from one tea to another, three teas in one day. All of which included the same conversations. Mia just wanted to go home. It was nearly 4 pm before Mia got her wish. Momma pulled the station wagon up to the front door and Mia ran out of the car like it was on fire, only to stop dead in her tracks once she reached the steps. At the top of the stairs was a box wrapped in the most beautiful wrapping paper, with a big red bow on top. The card attached said, To Mia, Someone to start loving. Love Aunt Colleen.

Mia picked it up and ripped it open before Momma even got to the stairs. It was a box, a beautiful box with the most gorgeous doll inside. The doll had long brown curly hair just like Mia's. The box said she was a big sister dream doll, and a paper exposed inside told Mia that her name was Lucy. Mia was so happy. It was her first doll. She always wanted a doll. Aunt Colleen knew her. That made Mia feel a bit of the special she seemed to have lost in the past few weeks.

"Who gave you that?" Momma asked.

"Aunt Colleen. Oh, please Momma, can I keep her?" Mia pleaded as she pressed Lucy against her chest.

"Well, I can't exactly say no, now can I? That Colleen never asks before she gives. So inconsiderate that one."

"I can keep it?"

"For now," Momma agreed.

Mia picked up the mess of wrapping paper she made and headed into the house behind Momma. The phone started ringing as they entered the unlit hallway. Momma stumbled as she rushed to go answer it.

Mia took off her outside clothes then headed to the kitchen to throw the torn wrapping paper out. She looked at Aunt Colleen's card once more and decided to keep it. She walked through the living room and past Momma. She heard Momma on the phone say thanks to Officer Tawes for her help and that we would be sure to be in court July 20th. That we would just be getting back from the Bible retreat the week prior to that. Momma had told her that our lawyer hadn't called yet but that she looked forward to hearing from her. Mia didn't stick around for the rest of the conversation. She headed upstairs with Lucy, hoping a doll snuggle would stop the words 'court' and 'lawyer' from sounding so scary.

Chapter Eleven

The next few weeks went by quite quick for Mia. Momma and Daddy barely spoke to each other. Daddy was still mad that Momma took the Frank situation out of God's hands. Daddy was mad that he now had to explain to his congregation why he went to the police about the matter. Mia heard Daddy say to Momma that he was hoping that he would have God's blessing when and if he did. The parishioners would understand his reasoning if he could tell them that it was Jesus who told him to do it. But Momma took that chance away. He vowed that he might never ever forgive her for what she had done. Momma reminded him once that Jesus teaches forgiveness and Daddy nearly popped an eyeball out. Mia knew that if Daddy couldn't forgive Momma, he probably wouldn't ever forgive Mia either.

Momma tried many times to get playful with Daddy but he just pushed her away. Momma didn't like that at all. Mia didn't either. Every time Daddy pushed Momma away, Momma would slap Mia in the face. She said it was to remind Mia of the pain she had caused Momma.

Daddy still refused his insulin from the doctor even though his legs were not getting better. His feet were starting to hurt now too. Daddy was getting more and more tired as the days went on. A few times, he even came home and went straight to bed. No supper or anything. Mia didn't mind those days. It was a day she didn't have to worry about killing her Daddy with her food. But she still sometimes felt worried for him. Daddy would go to bed at 5:30 in the evening and not come back down until early the next morning. Daddy said he just needed to change his diet. He said it like it was a new idea. Mia wanted to tell him Momma figured that out long ago, but she didn't want to be a show-off.

It was now the last week of school and Mia was feelings. She was excited for summer vacation but sh about going to court and facing Frank. She didn't w Daddy sad over his friend.

Mia was also going to miss Mrs. Gentry. Mia wouldn't see her all summer. When she returned to school in the fall, Mia would be in grade 5. Mrs. Gentry didn't teach grade 5. Mia would have a new teacher. Mia always felt sick when she had to meet her new teacher, another new person to have to learn about.

The bell rang and Mia packed up her stuff. Mrs. Gentry started the day handing the kids back a lot of their projects that they had been working on throughout the year. Mia had most of hers sitting under her desk. She had to gather them and somehow fit them into her backpack.

"Class, before everyone leaves for the day, I want us all to give a big clapping congratulations to Mia, who was the only one in Grade 4 at our school to make it into this summer's writing camp."

Mrs. Gentry looked over at Mia and smiled. Mia couldn't believe her ears. She made it into the writing camp? How was that possible? Momma ripped up her writing assignment right in front of her. Mia didn't want to say anything about that in front of her classmates. She instead sat at her desk and listened to the cheers that were erupting in the room. It only lasted a few moments before kids went about getting themselves ready for home, and soon, leaving out the class door. Mia had slowed her getting ready process down so that she could be the last to leave. She needed to ask Mrs. Gentry how she made it in with no paper at all.

Mrs. Gentry sensed that Mia was waiting to talk to her, so when the last student left, Mrs. Gentry made her way over to Mia to help pack.

"Wondering how you made it in without an official entry?"

Mia thought Mrs. Gentry was amazing. How she could see what Mia wanted to say, before she said it blew her mind. Mia wanted to tell her that but instead she just nodded.

"Well, you see, every year we are allowed to have one student go at our discretion. That means, we get to choose one kid between grades 4-8, to attend the camp, that may not have gotten in, or applied. Since you took your writing assignment and we never saw it again, I knew you wouldn't get in."

Mia listened intently, nodding at every point Mrs. Gentry made.

"Since you didn't *officially* enter, but I knew what you wrote and how wonderful it was, I thought I would put your name forward to Mr. Fig, the Principal and suggest that you be the one student we ask to get in. I know how bad you wanted to go. He agreed that you were the one, so did the people at the camp. You're a special person, Mia."

Mia smiled. Mrs. Gentry liked her paper after all. *And* she said she was special. Mia had a grin so wide she thought she might swallow her own ears.

"The only problem was that it is a paid spot. Money had to be given to the camp to have you there."

Mia's smile faded. Momma and Daddy would never pay for her to go to writing camp.

"Don't frown yet," Mrs. Gentry smiled. "I said was and had not is and has. Remember our lesson on tenses?"

Mia nodded, curious about what Mrs. Gentry was about to say.

"Last week we had a volunteer come in and say they wanted to work at the writing camp this year, as a fulltime volunteer. They will stay there all day and all night. She asked about you and if you made it. When we told her you did but only as a school request and that money would be needed, she offered to pay for you too."

Mia's eyes lit up. "Really? Someone paid the fee for me?"

Mrs. Gentry nodded.

"Who?"

"They asked to remain anonymous. I can't tell you their name. But someone out there also thinks you're special, Mia. You have a mystery angel looking after you."

Mia loved the thought of having her own angel, a mysterious one at that.

"Now I have an envelope for you. Bring it home and make sure your parents sign it before the school year is done. The camp is held at Bakers Camp Ground this year. It's two weeks starting the third week of July."

Mia nodded and grabbed the envelope. She zipped up her backpack and did something she rarely ever did. She hugged Mrs. Gentry without being prompted. Mia was headed to writing camp.

Mia kept the envelope in her pocket while she made dinner. She was going to show Momma and Daddy together at dinnertime. They were sure to be proud of her today. Mia decided that she was going to make coated chicken and mashed potatoes for dinner. The smell alone was sure to make her family happy. Daddy especially. Mia didn't like that Daddy was eating the food that she was cooking, but he told her that he realized not eating would kill him faster. Mia decided that if she were going to kill Daddy, she would rather kill him slowly than fast.

She had been making dinner since she was 7. That was two years of her cooking Daddy had consumed already. She wasn't sure how long diabetes or bad cooking took to kill someone, but she figured she still had some time left with him. The way Jesus spoke to Daddy all the time, Mia was sure Jesus would probably tell Daddy before He came to take him to heaven. And Daddy hadn't said anything about that yet.

Momma and Daddy returned from work on time. They came home hungry. Mia wanted to give them the envelope along with their food but was too excited to wait. Instead she handed it to Daddy as soon as his shoes were off.

"What's this?"

"Read it. It's from Mrs. Gentry."

"Did you run your mouth at school again?" Momma asked.

"No, Momma!" Mia answered.

Daddy opened the envelope. Mia stared at him with glee. She studied his face as he read it. His expression didn't change. He didn't smile. Maybe he needed to read it a second time? Maybe he didn't quite understand what it said?

But Daddy didn't read it a second time. Instead he passed it to Momma. Momma read it. Her expression changed. She looked angry, then upset.

"Mia, how could you get into this program? You didn't keep your assignment?"

"I know Momma. One kid is allowed in without an assignment every year. I didn't know. Mrs. Gentry said I was the kid chosen this year. She said I was special."

Momma snorted.

"Special. What they mean by that is charity. You were chosen because they felt sorry for you dear. No Pratt takes a pity invite. We're better than that."

Mia looked at her Daddy. Surely he felt different.

"Daddy?"

Daddy just looked at her softly.

"I'm sorry dear. Your mother is right."

"But Momma," Mia whined. "It isn't a pity invite. Mrs. Gentry told them about my paper and said it was good. I got in cause of my writing. And I had a mystery person donate and pay for my fees. It wasn't free. It just is because someone else donated money."

Momma did not like that answer. Her shades of red came out again.

"More talking about that paper and what you wrote. Well I'll be. I'm at a loss for words child. Just simply at a loss. I won't reward that nonsense paper with giving you two weeks at camp having fun."

Mia felt tears welling up. She tried desperately to stop them but she couldn't. They flowed down like a waterfall.

"Stop your crying Mia. It won't help you. Your Daddy and I said no. And besides, if God wanted you to go, he would have made it so you got in for free. Then it would have been His will for you to be there. Jesus doesn't want this Mia, and neither do we."

Mia wiped away the tears she felt on her cheek but her eyes just kept crying.

"I really want to go," Mia pleaded one last time.

But her parents had made up their mind. Mia was not going to writing camp this year.

Mia was heartbroken. And today of all days too. It was Mia's birthday. She was 10. Double digits. But so far 10 seemed to be the exact same as 9. *For God so loved the world*, Mia thought. If that were true, why didn't He seem to love her?

Chapter Twelve

The family station wagon turned into the Maranatha Bible Outdoor Retreat Center around noon the next Saturday. Mia slept nearly the entire way. Snuggled tight in the back seat with Lucy gripped in her hands, Mia dreamt about writing camp even though she would never see it.

Momma had told Mia that she was not allowed to write anymore. Her pencils would be taken away, and all her paper too. She didn't take away her spy book though because Momma didn't know it existed. Even if she went in the desk drawer, she still wouldn't see it. Momma would have to dig all the stuff out of there, rubber matting and all. And Mia couldn't see her expending the effort to do that. Momma liked things to be done for her.

Momma told Mia that the Bible retreat would help her to refocus, and forget all the storytelling nonsense she was getting into. Mia didn't think reading the Bible would stop her from wanting to write, but she kept an open mind. Momma had been right about a lot of things in the past. Like when she said that she was going to get stung when she chased that bee last summer. Momma was correct. That darn bee got so mad at Mia swatting at it, that it turned right around in an angry huff and stabbed Mia with his stinger, right in her arm. Momma knew what was going to happen even before it did. Momma had EFP or whatever it was that helped you see the future. But this time, Mia wasn't so sure Momma was right.

Mia searched the campground through the car window. It looked the same as every other year. Red wooden cabins were scattered amongst large pine trees. To the right of the campground entrance was the large rectangular building the campers would worship in. It was made with white plywood walls. The windows took up half of the space, and worked on a pulley system. No glass was present, just screens. If you wanted air, someone would have to go outside and pull the pulley until the window flap lifted straight up in the air, exposing all of Jesus's disciples inside. Momma didn't like it when they opened all the windows at once during morning church. The sun was too low and the wind too little. She said things got smelly when that happened. Momma would say, when you're filled with the Holy Spirit and sunshine at the same time, well that's just too much for one body to handle. Your soul melts from the inside, expelling all the waste to the air. Mia liked it when the windows were open. It gave her something to look at outside when she couldn't keep her thoughts clear on the inside.

Daddy parked the car beside a large red cabin that sat smack dab in the middle of camp. That was the cabin Mia's family always got. It was referred to as the resident pastor cabin. Daddy was the pastor for the two weeks they were there. Many pastors took turns over the summer. Daddy got out of the car first and went to the office to pick up the keys. Momma gathered her stuff from the front and put things in an old shopping bag. She handed one to Mia and encouraged her to do the same in the back. Mia didn't really have anything to put in hers but she didn't want Momma to think she wasn't helping so Mia pretended to be busy packing and cleaning.

Daddy returned ten minutes later with keys. Mia sat on the ground, leaning against the big pine tree that shaded their cabin. She watched Daddy lift one suitcase and then another out of the car before he marched them through the cabin's front door. He was strong, her Daddy. He got that from all the boxes he lifted at his regular job at the warehouse. Daddy preached for the love of Jesus, but he worked the warehouse a few days a week for the love of his family.

Mia could hear Momma inside unpacking the boxes of food and kitchen supplies. Momma always did the cooking at retreat. Mia had two weeks where she didn't have to kill Daddy. Momma could.

Mia was half way through drawing a portrait of Lucy in the sand with a stick, when she was interrupted by a voice she forgot she would hear that day.

"Hi, Mia. Is your Father inside?"

Mia looked up at Frank and saw him standing above her. He was closer than she felt comfortable with. She felt bad that she no longer felt happy to see Frank.

"He's inside."

Frank nodded and walked away. As he passed in front of her, he kicked his foot out, sending sand flying to the heavens, erasing the picture of Lucy. Mia looked down at the mess. She looked up at Frank. He turned around and smiled. Mia didn't want to smile back but she knew it would be impolite. She gave Frank the best one she could before clearing away the sand to start her drawing again.

Mia felt sad for Frank sometimes. She had done something awful to him, and now he might go to jail forever. Aunt Colleen said it wasn't her fault, but Mia didn't know if that was true. Mia was the one who told her parents when Frank had warned her not to tell them. And he'd said that they would be disappointed. He was right. She was also the one who was too stupid to not know where babies came from. If she had known about that before, if she had just asked someone, she wouldn't have needed Frank to show her that night. Mia was embarrassed that she was so dumb.

And now Frank was mad too. She knew Frank didn't move the sand by accident. He was telling her with his foot just how angry he was. She didn't blame him. She was angry with herself too. Daddy was losing his best friend to jail, Momma was losing her mind to everyone, and Mia was losing her writing. She had no one to blame but herself. Mia knew better than to talk about what happened behind closed doors. That was just for her parents and the good Lord to know. Momma was the only one that was allowed to talk about it. And that was because Momma was so sad all the time. She needed to get her sad out to her friends. Momma knew how to tell the story right. Mia, sometimes though, wanted to get her sad out too. She just knew if she did, it would make Momma worse.

Daddy came out of the cabin with Frank. They were laughing and slapping each other's shoulders. Daddy looked over at Mia sitting in the sand. He steered Frank away from her. Daddy must have watched Frank kick the sand and didn't want to see her picture ruined again.

Mia watched them until they were out of sight.

"Mia! Don't stare," Momma called through the screen of the kitchen window.

Mia looked up to see Momma's scrunched up face looking at her. Mia nodded.

"And don't you go walking after them. You need to stay 500 feet or something to that effect, away from him at all times. Make sure you give him his space, you hear?"

Mia nodded again.

"Now I asked you a question, Mia. That deserves a proper response. I said, you hear?"

"I hear, Momma."

"Good. We don't want to go and get Frank in any more trouble than he already is."

Momma kept her eye on Mia a few moments before going back to washing dishes and counters. Mia didn't think there was any more trouble she could get Frank in. She just had to hang in a few more weeks and the court date would come. Mia would tell them all how she didn't mean to tell on Frank, that it was a mistake on her part. They were sure to understand. She would save Frank and make Momma proud and Daddy happy. Maybe Momma and Daddy would stop fighting with each other as well.

Mia finished her picture of Lucy then put her doll on the ground beside it. Perfect!

Mia took a few loose stones from around the yard and made a circle around her art like a picture frame. Satisfied that it would be safe, Mia picked up Lucy and went to the top of the cabin steps. She put herself right in front of the cabin door, turned around and started walking straight. She placed one foot directly in front of the other. She started to count the steps as she was walking. She had only got to two hundred and four before she was already in the far bush across from the cabin. Staying five hundred feet away from Frank when he visited her cabin was going to be a challenge.

Mia gave up by the two hundred and twelve mark. She had an idea of the distance just by what she had already accomplished. Instead, she walked around searching to see if Jason and his family arrived yet. She didn't see them. If they had arrived, they were hiding pretty well. She saw a few girls she knew from last year. Two of them she didn't like very much. Sandra and her best friend Jocelyn were mean girls. Last summer, every time Mia would pass them, they would say, 'there goes Mia Pratt, looking ugly, walking fat.' It wasn't very Christian like of them. Mia wasn't fat either. Grandma always told her that she was too skinny. Still, Mia didn't eat much the entire two weeks of camp last year, just in case.

By the time Mia got back to the cabin, Momma had hamburger macaroni on the table ready for them to eat. Daddy still wasn't back but Momma fed her anyway.

"Are you excited to be here?" Momma asked as she sat down with a plate of her own dinner.

"Yes, Momma," Mia answered with a mouthful of macaroni.

"Me too." Momma moved some food around with her fork but didn't stab any noodles to put to her mouth. "We have church tonight."

Mia liked nighttime church because all the kids were allowed to go in their pajama clothes.

"Can Lucy come?"

Momma said she could as long as she wasn't naked. Mia laughed at Momma's joke. Momma was so much funnier when she was away from home.

Mia and Lucy went to church without incident that evening and every evening for the next few days. Jason's family finally showed up, so it gave her someone near her age to sit with as well. They would often sit on the floor using the pew as a table, so they could colour fancy pictures for the guests. The whole camp experience was going great for everyone until Annie Carrington, or Mrs. C. as Mia called her, showed up with her brood 3 days later.

Mrs. C was a lovely lady that Mia adored. She didn't go to Daddy's church regularly on Sundays because she worked as a Veterinarian at her own animal hospital, and she often spent the night Saturday night with the sick pets that had to stay the weekend. She was always at retreat though, and always at church recitals at Christmas and Easter. She was tall and beautiful. Her straight shoulder length brown hair was always shining. She wore business attire most days, and stretch pants with t-shirts when she wasn't. When she walked into church all the parishioners would stare at her. Sometimes they would stare so long their jaws would even fall open. Mia had three pages of notes on Mrs. C. in her spy book. Mia found her interesting.

Mrs. C. smiled all the time. Except when she had to tell another woman in the church what they were doing wrong. Then she would squeeze her lips tight, and look at them a second or two, before relaxing and telling them something they often didn't want to hear. She always started these speeches by saying, "You know darling."

Mia practiced that squeezed lip look in the mirror many times but she couldn't seem to get the effect Mrs. C. could. Maybe when she was older she would. When her lips grew up.

Momma said she wasn't a fan of Mrs. C.'s but often, Mia would find Momma following Mrs. C. through the pews, chasing her down, just to say hello. Sometimes Momma couldn't catch her so she would just wave to Mrs. C.'s back. The tea ladies would give Momma a funny look and Momma would just shrug in response.

"I was busy doing important things and missed when she said goodbye. I was just trying to be polite," Momma would tell them. They would nod.

Mrs. C. told Momma her thoughts more than once. It never seemed to bother Momma to hear it, in the moment, but when Momma got home, she would yell and scream at Daddy about what a horrible wench of a woman she was. She would tell Daddy that he needed to remove her from the church. Daddy would just laugh and say, "Now Lee-Ann, that wouldn't be very Christian. She is a Lamb of God. Besides, she's rarely there."

Momma would walk away from Daddy in a huff mumbling something about a lamb that needed to go to the slaughterhouse.

Momma sat on the front porch watching Mrs. C. unpack her black truck while Mia sat in a chair and read the only book they had, the Bible. Every so often Mia would look up at Momma who never lost focus. She just sat there sipping tea, scowling, watching like a hawk. It wasn't until one of the other camper's husbands came over to help Mrs. C. that Momma finally spoke.

"That lady gets more attention than she deserves," she told Mia. "She reels them in with her hips. But you watch, Mia. She will reel them in, then kick them out with those clodhopper feet of hers."

Mia looked up from her Bible and over to Mrs. C.

"She's just getting help, Momma. Isn't that a nice thing to do?"

"Helping is nice, yes Mia. But what they are doing is not for the sake of helping. They want something else from Mrs. C. and they aren't going to get it. Not here at least. She's married."

"What do they want, Momma?"

"They want to do to her, what Frank did to you Mia. And that ain't proper."

Mia didn't understand. Why would they want to show Mrs. C. about where babies came from? She had 3 kids. Mia was pretty sure Mrs. C. already knew about babies. And Mia was 10. They were grown men, they should know that too. And, if it wasn't proper of them to do to Mrs. C. what Frank did to Mia, why was it okay that Frank did it to her? Adults made things so complicated. Mia wished she were smarter to understand how it all worked. She wanted to ask Momma about the difference but now wasn't the time. Momma had her focus on Mrs. C. and she didn't think she should ask her such a silly question just to help Mia with her dumbness.

"I think she's pretty. Maybe they do too," Mia finally answered.

Momma ran out of tea. She grabbed her cup and got up to head inside. She stopped at the doorway and pointed at Mrs. C.

"That's not pretty Mia, that's cheap. There's a difference. She didn't even bring her husband here with her. Ask yourself Mia, what kind of woman does that?"

Mia watched her Momma enter the cabin then looked back over at Mrs. C. who caught Mia watching. She smiled and waved a hello over. Mia waved back. Momma was wrong, Mia thought. Mrs. C. was definitely pretty and nothing about her looked cheap.

Chapter Thirteen

Jason knocked on the door a half hour before evening church was to start. Momma answered and began to speak, but Jason, being 5, just walked on by her, not waiting to hear what she had to say. Mia laughed. Momma laughed as well.

"Now, what can we do for you, young man?" Momma asked, following him around the corner to the table where Mia was sitting.

"I want to walk to church with you."

Mia looked up from her colouring and smiled. "Can he Momma?"

Momma looked like she might say no, but she didn't. "Well, I suppose that would be okay. Go and make sure it's okay with your Daddy, too."

Mia jumped up and went to the back bedroom where her Daddy was finishing getting dressed in his suit. Daddy always wore a suit and tie to God's house. Mia asked her Daddy and he said he was good with it and told her that if they really wanted, they could go ahead of him and Momma there. This made Mia even happier.

Less than 2 minutes later, both Mia and Jason were outside and on their way to the camp church. They were there so early, that the front doors hadn't even opened yet.

"Wanna play tag while we wait?" Jason asked.

"Uh, huh," Mia said. "I'll be it first. I will give you three seconds to start running."

Jason giggled and took off from the spot he stood. Mia counted out loud to 3 before she shot off after him. He was fast for a boy with legs half her size. Mia chased him through the big pine trees, around the large rectangular church, and over the rocks near the camp entrance. Jason twisted and twirled around every object he could see. Mia was thankful that she had pajamas on and not a Sunday dress. Momma would not have liked her running in that. She would have found a closet somewhere to put Mia in. Momma could get quite creative when she was mad.

Jason ran past the fork in the road that separated the cabins from the trailer park, and back over to the living area where they started. Mia decided she needed to pick up her speed and be craftier than his 5 year-old brain was able to match. When she saw him head to the right of Mrs. C.'s cabin, Mia darted to the left to cut him off. She was just about to round the back corner of the building when her shoelace got caught on a branch sticking out of a dead tree stump, forcing her to go flying high into the air. Mia landed down on her shoulder in a thunderous thump. Pain shot through her collarbone and straight into her neck. Mia screamed louder than she ever had.

Mia covered her mouth quickly with her good arm, in an attempt to muffle the sounds coming out. She looked around in panic. Did Momma hear? Momma didn't like it when Mia cried, especially when she cried from falling over her own two feet. She tried hard to get herself together but her shoulder hurt too much. Mia started to get up off the ground but struggled. Every move made the pain worse. She sat back down.

A noise came from her left. She looked over to see if it was an animal but it was Jason. Only a lock of his hair and half of his face was visible. He was hiding behind the back of the cabin, peeking over at her in fear.

"Are you okay, Mena?" He had the gentlest voice.

"I think so," Mia lied. "But I need help getting up."

Jason slowly inched his way from behind the cabin, and toward Mia. "How?"

"Just grab my good arm and pull. I need to roll onto my knees to be able to stand."

Jason nodded. When he was finally close enough to grab Mia, he reached out and took her hand.

"Not my hand."

Jason nodded again.

"Grab my arm. It's better for you to grip anyway."

Jason was awfully frightened for his friend. He seemed to be afraid to hurt her more. He hesitated a moment but then agreed. He reached out, took Mia's arm in his hands, and pulled with all of his might.

"Oooowwwww!" Mia screamed again, tears flowing forcefully once more. "Stop, stop, stop."

Jason's eyes widened. He stood frozen for only a moment before he took off, running as fast as he could, in the direction that took him the furthest way away from her.

Mia leaned back against the tree stump and cried. Momma was going to be so mad. Not only was she hurt, she was going to be late for church, she wasn't where she was supposed to be, and she had a rip in her pajamas the size of her knee. And now, she was going to have to wait until Momma noticed her missing and decided to come find her, before she had a chance to explain.

"Mia, what the hell happened to you?"

Mia jumped at the sound of the voice. How could Momma find her so soon? She didn't want to face her Momma just yet.

"Mia, let me help."

It wasn't Momma. Mia turned to see Mrs. C. heading towards her, with Jason lagging behind her, still quiet and looking scared.

Mrs. C. bent down to be eye level to Mia.

"You're hurt." She placed a soft hand on Mia's face and wiped away a tear.

At the feel of Mrs. C.'s hand on her skin, Mia melted. She cried so hard she could barely catch her breath.

"Oh Mia, sweetie." Mrs. C. wrapped Mia up in her arms and held her. Mia considered pulling away but she didn't want to. She wanted Mrs. C. to hold her. She wanted Mrs. C. to touch her. And she wanted Mrs. C. to say soft things. Mia stayed in the hug longer than she would normally want to be hugged but it took her that long to calm down and think clearly.

Mrs. C. kissed Mia on the head.

"Where are you hurt?"

"My shoulder," Mia answered and showed her the spot that ached. Blood was running right through Mia's pajama shirt.

"You're bleeding. We need to get you to the first aid medical building."

Mia agreed. Mrs. C. stood up and instead of grabbing Mia's arm she reached down and picked her up, full body, right from the ground to standing. Mrs. C. was a strong woman. Mia sighed with relief. Before this, getting up was proving to be quite hurtful.

"Can you walk?"

Mia nodded.

"Okay. Good."

The three started walking toward the front of the cabin.

"Let's go see Frank."

Mia stopped walking.

"I…I can't."

Mrs. C. looked at her curious.

"You can't?"

Mia shook her head.

"Why not, sweety? You're hurt. He has stuff to fix your cuts."

Mrs. C. didn't know. Mia guessed it was on account that she didn't go to church very often. No one had told her yet.

Mia debated for a moment if she should keep it to herself or not. She knew Momma would be mad if she told someone else, although Momma told everyone. But that was Momma. Momma had different allowances than Mia did.

Mia also worried how Frank would feel if he had another set of eyes looking at him. Mia didn't understand why Frank had to feel bad, but Daddy said he did. Daddy said that it hurt Frank to know that people might be whispering about him behind his back and staring at him as he walked by.

Mia knew that she couldn't be within a lot of feet of Frank. And Mrs. C. would not understand why unless Mia told her. And with all the kindness she was showing Mia, she knew she had to show her some kindness back.

"I can't be around Frank," Mia started. Wondering how much she would have to say.

"Your parents won't let you."

"No." Mia thought that was the easiest answer.

"Oh that's crazy. You're hurt. They won't mind."

Mrs. C. reached out for Mia's hand. Mia pulled it away.

"Good heavens child. Let's just go."

Mrs. C. started walking away.

"And the police, and court. They won't let me either," Mia said in a barely audible voice.

Mrs. C. stopped instantly, turning around slowly to look at Mia with that curious look she did before.

"The police?"

Mia nodded.

"Why the police?"

"I did something wrong, Mrs. C," Mia whispered. Embarrassed that she was going to have to tell Mrs. C. what had happened, she felt certain that Mrs. C. was no longer going to be kind to her because of her mistake. Mia considered running away but bumping into Momma while she was bloody and sore scared Mia more than Mrs. C. and the Frank story did.

"What did you do, Mia?" Mrs. C. asked in a softer voice, as she walked back over to where Mia was standing frozen.

"I let him show me how babies are made when he was babysitting me, and then I told on him, and now he's in a whole lot of trouble. Momma says I can't go within 500 feet of him, or else I will get him in more trouble."

Mrs. C. said nothing.

"I'm sorry, Mrs. C. I made a mistake."

Mrs. C. still didn't say anything for a long time, which made Mia very nervous. It wasn't until Mia started sobbing that Mrs. C. woke up from her quiet coma, snatched Mia up into her arms, and walked her straight into her own cabin.

Chapter Fourteen

Mia was sitting on top of Mrs. C.'s kitchen table, bleeding, waiting for her to return from the medical building with a first aid kit.

When they first went into the cabin, Mrs. C. sat Mia down on the table, kicked out all of her kids, as well as her non-kid, Jason, and asked Mia to tell her what happened. Mia was nervous, but she shared the whole story, all the way up to the part where Frank kicked the sand at her and ruined her picture of Lucy. Mrs. C. seemed to be angry, but she assured Mia several times that it wasn't Mia she was angry with. Mia wondered what Mrs. C. would say if she told her that Momma did those types of touches to Mia as well. Would she think Momma was at fault like she thought Frank was? Would that send Momma to jail like Frank might go? Mia was terrified of the thought. She couldn't send her Momma to jail. Daddy would be so sad. Mia decided to not tell her about Momma. She would ask another day. Maybe.

Mrs. C. kept saying to Mia that she couldn't believe Momma and Daddy would even bring her here, let alone not kill Frank with their bare hands. Mrs. C. was a lot like Aunt Colleen. Except Mrs. C. went on further to say that she blamed Momma and Daddy, and that they needed to go to the doctors because something was wrong with their heads. Mia asked her if they were sick. Mrs. C. said no, that it was just an expression. It wasn't a very good one, Mia thought.

After the whole story came out, and Mrs. C. calmed down, she attempted to help Mia take her shirt off so she could look at her shoulder. Mia's shoulder hurt so much, the shirt wouldn't separate from her body. Mia worried she would be wearing it until the end of time. But Mrs. C. had another solution. She went to the kitchen door and got a pair of scissors and cut Mia's pajama top from the neck, all the way down to the end of her sleeve. She took it off for Mia then slowly peeled the material away from the blood oozing out of Mia's shoulder. Mia winced in pain. She was thankful she was wearing an undershirt.

"Sorry sweetie, but it needs to be done," Mrs. C. said as she looked at Mia's shoulder. "Bruised and bloodied but not swollen. You should be okay. I need to go get the first aid kit. The one I have in my truck is only suitable for injured animals. Church has started which means Frank is gone. I'm going to sneak into his cabin and grab it. I will patch you up myself. Okay?"

Mia nodded.

"Then we are going to go have a word with your Momma and Daddy. I will explain why your shirt is torn."

Mia nodded again. She was thankful to have Mrs. C. to help talk to Momma about her shirt. Momma was going to kill Mia. She would give her a month in the closet at least, if not the whole summer. A day for every dollar Momma spent replacing her pajamas. It was bittersweet. The closet was scary. But some days, Momma was even scarier.

While Mia waited on the table, she wondered about what was going on in Momma's head at that moment. Was she sitting in church wondering what was taking Mia so long? Did Momma even know Mia wasn't at church yet? Or was she stomping around the campground looking for that rotten, no-good, daughter of hers? Mia couldn't decide. She just knew that none of the options were appealing to her. Either Momma was mad, or Momma forgot about her. Mia cried again just thinking about it.

The cabin door opened, saving Mia from her thoughts of Momma's rage. Mrs. C. had returned with a large kit in her hand. She opened it up and looked at everything inside.

"Okay, Mia. First, we are going to clean it, then I am going to put some of this lotion here on it," Mrs. C. explained, while holding up all the things one by one, that she was going to use on Mia's arm. "Finally, I will wrap it in gauze that you can keep on overnight. I will look at it again tomorrow if you want, or you can get your Momma to look at it. But I don't think I will need to give you stiches. It's just going to sting a whole lot."

"I would like *you* to look at it tomorrow, if that's okay?" Mia asked, worried she was asking too much. But Mrs. C. just smiled and said she would like to be the one to look at it too.

The washing of her cut hurt almost as much as the getting of the cut did. Mia cried when the cloth went over the wound for the last bits of dirt. Mrs. C. tried to be as gentle as she could but when she couldn't, she made sure to hug Mia lots. Gentle touches always made Mia feel nice in her heart. She didn't often feel big heart hurt anymore, or anger. She only felt sadness and sometimes fear. Her heart told her to block out most feelings so they wouldn't cause an outburst. Outburst never ended well for Mia. But gentle touches allowed her heart to feel good. She liked that. And when she found someone who would give her gentle touches and whom she wasn't afraid of, Mia felt happy. Even when she didn't think she should be happy. Mrs. C., Mia thought, was one of those people who could.

"Do you want me to patch it on top, or would you rather me wrap it all the way around your shoulder and under your arm pit?" Mrs. C. asked.

Mia was three words into asking for it to be wrapped around her shoulder when Momma came storming in the front door of the cabin, her face red, and a finger that was at risk of falling off, she was shaking it so hard.

"Mia Lee-Ann Elizabeth Pratt! You didn't show up to church, and now I hear you're hurt. Bothering Annie like this. What has gotten into you, child?" Momma didn't really want an answer to her question. She walked over to Mia and pulled her off the table.

"Ouch Momma, you're hurting my shoulder."

"I had to leave hearing the good Lords' message because of your incredible incompetence. You'll have to say sorry to me and Jesus tonight." She turned to look at Mrs. C. "I'm so sorry about this, Annie."

"Whoa!" Mrs. C. said as she stopped Momma from dragging Mia out of the cabin. "Your daughter is hurt. Let me finish wrapping her arm."

"She doesn't need wrapping. She is fine," Momma snapped back.

"How would you know? You haven't even looked at the injury. She's not fine. Look at her!"

Momma looked at Mia's shoulder. She pushed her finger into the cut to see if it would bleed more. It did.

"Ow!" Mia screamed.

"Oh, you shush child. You're just trying to get attention."

Mrs. C. grabbed Mia right out of Momma's hands and sat her back up on the table.

"Excuse me?" Momma asked not so politely.

"I need to wrap this properly or she will be screaming more. And it seems like you don't like her doing that. Give me 2 minutes, please."

Mrs. C. looked at Mia with sadness in her eyes. She mouthed the words I'm sorry to her. Mia nodded.

Mia wanted so desperately to stay with Mrs. C. Mia wanted to grab onto her and hug her tight. Beg her not to send her off with Momma. But she couldn't do that.

Momma stood back at the cabin door and tapped her foot on the wooden floor.

"Might I remind you that your PhD is in Veterinary Medicine so you can fix animals and not people?"

"I know exactly what my schooling is, thank you. I also know that I'm quite qualified to assess this cut and fix it properly."

Momma searched for an argument but found none.

"Well, hurry up then. The church ladies are waiting for me. Don't want them to think I went missing too."

"No, we wouldn't want that," Mrs. C. answered sarcastically. She had enough of Momma.

Mrs. C. took her time, more than she had taken before. Mia looked at her intently. She tried to figure out what was going on inside Mrs. C.'s head. Mia didn't know her well enough to decide.

"You okay, Mrs. C?" Mia whispered.

Mrs. C. smiled. "Just thinking of a plan, kid. Everything will be okay." Then she winked at Mia.

Mia nodded. A plan? What kind of plan? For what?

Mrs. C. finished wrapping Mia's arm, kissed her own two middle fingers, and gently placed them on top of the bandage.

"To help heal it," she said kindly to Mia.

Mia smiled back.

Mrs. C. picked Mia up and off of the table and walked her slowly over to Momma who was still standing at the door tapping her foot. Mrs. C. held Mia back so she was far enough away from Momma. Mrs. C. leaned in towards Momma's face a squeezed her lips tight. She tried to whisper but she wasn't very good at it.

"I know what Frank did to this little girl, and I know how you have done nothing to help her emotionally. You should be ashamed of yourself Lee-Ann Pratt. You're a sad excuse for a Mother. Making her feel like it's her fault. Shame on you! And bringing her here! Where he is. I don't even have words."

Momma looked Mrs. C. straight in the eyes. Momma spoke in a voice Mia had never heard before.

"You don't know my daughter or me. How dare you judge?"

"Know her? I don't need to know her to know what is happening to her is wrong. Grow a pair, Lee-Ann."

Mia thought Momma was going to jump over and bite Mrs. C. on the nose. Momma was so mad, she stuttered when she spoke.

"We-well, I never. Using that lan-lan-language here in God's land. I'm not the one that needs to be ashamed. No, I'm not!"

"And I'm not the one that needs this to stay a secret. Don't push me, Lee-Ann."

Mia looked back and forth from Momma to Mrs. C. unsure of who was going to snap first. Mrs. C. looked angry like she could choke Momma. And Momma looked like she wanted to tear Mrs. C.'s heart out with her fist. They stood there staring at each other before Mrs. C. relaxed her face and stepped back. She decided instead to focus her words on Mia. She crouched down to Mia's level again and spoke softly.

"Mia, if you need anything, anything at all, you call me, find me, anything you need to do to get to me and let me know. I will always help you. You understand?"

Mia looked up at her Momma and realized by her face that she couldn't answer Mrs. C.'s question. She just stood still and looked up at her Momma.

"I know you can hear me and you're afraid to talk. Just know I will always help you."

"That's enough!" Momma said as she grabbed Mia's arm and pulled her out the door. Mia looked back at Mrs. C. standing in the kitchen as Momma dragged her away. Mia wasn't sure, but it looked like Mrs. C. was crying.

Momma dragged Mia's half naked body across the campground and straight into their cabin. Momma didn't say much the whole walk, just mumblings about how Mrs. C. needed to mind her own business and get a life of her own. Mia spent most of the walk looking back at Mrs. C.'s cabin. She couldn't see her, but just looking at the cabin made her feel comforted.

Momma pulled Mia into her bedroom and roughly put another pajama shirt on her. Mia bit her tongue so she wouldn't cry in pain. She bit so hard she could taste blood in her mouth. But a little bit of mouth blood was a lot better than more outside skin blood which she was sure to get if she let Momma see her tears.

Mia already thought that Momma was going to punish her for telling Mrs. C. what she did but instead Momma just put Mia in bed for the night; lights out, with no nightlight. Mia could handle that. Momma left, said she was going back to night church and Daddy. She needed to pray to the Lord for an answer on how best to teach that Annie a lesson. She also told Mia that if she was smart, and loved her Daddy, she would tell him she was sick. Mia knew she wasn't smart, but she did love her Daddy. She would tell him what Momma asked her to. If Momma wanted her to be sick, then she was sick.

Chapter Fifteen

Mia didn't hear her Momma and Daddy come in from night church, nor did she hear her own terrified body making the bedposts shake as she fell asleep. But she did hear her Momma whisper her name in the middle of the night, when she came to get her from her bed.

"Where are we going, Momma?" Mia asked in her sleepy voice.

Momma didn't answer. She just pulled Mia up out of her bed, put a housecoat on her, and tucked Lucy into her hands.

"Momma?"

"Shhh! Mia, you're still sleeping. I'm not really here."

Mia wasn't sure what Momma was talking about. Mia was looking at Momma right beside her. She knew her eyes were fuzzy but they weren't that fuzzy.

"But Momma?"

Momma just shushed her again. She placed her hand on Mia's good shoulder and led her out of the bedroom and into the main room. Momma put her shoes on. Mia went to do the same but Momma said no. Mia didn't argue.

Momma walked her outside and down the path to the church. Momma took a hard right towards the forest and sped up as soon as she hit the tree line.

"Momma?" Mia couldn't see a thing in front of her. Momma didn't answer Mia, she just kept walking faster and faster. Her feet were starting to hurt from the rocks and twigs on the ground. They went deep into the forest before Momma stopped. She looked around frantically.

Momma pointed to a tree.

"You like that tree, Mia?"

Mia liked all trees so she said yes.

Momma led Mia over to the tree. She pulled Lucy out of Mia's hands and sat her on the ground leaning on the tree.

"See how Lucy is sitting? Sit like her. Right beside."

Mia did as she was told. Momma explained to her that the best thing to do when someone was lost in the forest was to sit down by a tree and stay still. Let people find you, Momma said. Don't go looking for them. Mia told Momma she understood.

"Good," Momma said. "Now I want you to do just that. I want you to sit here and stay here, until someone comes and finds you okay? Like hide and go seek. But you stay. Okay Mia? Stay here. Even if you hear the wolves."

"Wolves?"

"Just stay here Mia, okay?"

"But I'm not lost. You're with me."

"Oh, Mia. We are all a little lost child. Now just stay right there. You listening to me?" Momma's fake southern drawl was thick.

Mia nodded hesitantly. She didn't like wolves. She once saw a show on television about a man who got lost while hunting and a wolf chewed his leg right off. He had to get a wooden leg to replace it. Mia didn't want a wooden leg but Momma told her to stay, so that was what she was going to do.

Momma touched Mia's cheek.

"Goodbye Mia." Momma said, then she walked off into the darkness, back in the direction they just came from.

Mia waited to see if Momma was going to come right back, to make sure Mia was doing as she was told to, but Momma never returned. The darkness had taken her away. Mia held onto Lucy as tight as she could. She sure wished she had Mrs. C. there to hold onto too.

The first few hours passed rather quickly, but then time seemed to slow down. Mia had nothing to look at except trees, and she was bored with that now. Lucy's hair had been brushed with a twig Mia found nearby, and all but one rock near her had been thrown into the darkness. Mia was out of entertainment. She was also very sleepy. Her yawns produced tears that flowed down her face like rain. Momma said she had to stay there. She didn't say she had to keep sitting. Mia cleared some brush to the side of her until the ground was exposed and flat. She lay her head down, pulled Lucy in tight, and closed her eyes. The sounds of the forest were a lot louder with her eyes closed.

Mia had to do something to block out the sounds of breaking branches, and leaves moving in the wind. She rolled onto her back and looked up in the direction of the sky. A small clearing in the trees gave her a view of some stars. She counted eight of them. She studied them hard trying to determine which one was the largest. Mia couldn't decide.

After a while, Mia closed her eyes again and started singing to Lucy.

"Jesus loves the little children, all the children of the world. Red and yellow, black and white, they are precious in his sight. Jesus loves the little children of the world."

Mia repeated the song several times before she fell asleep. She dreamt of wolves. They were sitting with her, walking around her, and some would even come so close they would sniff her leg. Mia slept through it anyway.

Mia woke up to birds chirping. She opened her eyes. The sun had come out to play with her in the forest. The rays danced off the leaves and tickled her eyes. Mia was relieved to see the sun. But where was Momma? And the wolves? Mia checked her legs to make sure they were still there. She was thankful when she saw ten cold toes staring back at her.

Mia sat up, feeling slightly lightheaded when she did. She was hungry. She didn't have a bedtime snack last night since Momma sent her straight to bed. And she didn't have breakfast yet this morning because she was in the forest.

Mia's shoulder was paining.

Mia looked around. When were people coming to find her? What time was it? Did Momma get taken by the darkness? Mia had so many questions but she felt too dizzy to think of answers. Her brain was on pause. It was cold.

Sitting up made Mia colder. She decided to go back down on the ground in a curled-up position so she could warm up. Mia was grateful to Momma for reminding her to put on a housecoat. Without that, she would have been even colder. Lucy helped to keep her warm as well. Mia was so happy to have her with her.

As her head settled on the ground, finally in a comfortable position, Mia began to sing Jesus Loves the Little Children again. She only got a few verses in when her breath decided to start getting shorter. Her lungs were too cold to work.

She tucked her toes into the ends of her pajama pants to keep them warm, then wrapped her arms as best she could around her head. It was difficult with her hurt shoulder but she managed. She remembered Mrs. Gentry told the class one day that the best way to stay warm was to ensure your feet and head were covered as warmly as they could be. She said that most heat escapes your body from those places. She had to remember to thank Mrs. Gentry when she got back to school, she was right. It helped.

Mia felt something warm run down her face. She took her good arm and reached up with a finger to see what was causing that feeling. It was blood. She knew instantly it was from her shoulder cut. It had split open again when she stretched her arm up to her head. Blood didn't bother Mia. She has had a lot of it come out of her skin over the years. She has seen more blood then tears escape her body. Blood meant you were alive, Momma always said. Be thankful, dead people don't bleed.

Mia let the blood continue to roll down her cheek. It didn't bother her as much as the cold did. She tried singing one more time but words still wouldn't come out. Mia sang the song in her head instead. A few more verses in she heard her name being called from afar. But whose voice? She wasn't sure. She didn't really care. She was tired. Too tired to look up or call out. Mia just wanted to go to sleep. The cold was over taking her. She closed her eyes and drifted off. She wondered, if maybe, it was Jesus calling her name. Maybe it was time for Him to take her to Heaven.

Chapter Sixteen

"Mia. Mia!"

Mia could feel her body moving, shaking, but she couldn't tell why. Someone was moving her.

"I found her," the voice shouted to the air. "Mia!"

She opened her eyes as best as she could. Through a small crack in her one eyelid, she could see a teenage boy looking at her intensely. He was on his knees, his face close to hers. Jesus was a lot younger looking than she thought. And he got a haircut.

"That's a girl, open your eyes. Mia, it's me, Howey. Howey Carrington. Mrs. C.'s son. Everyone is real worried about you Mia. Your mother said you must have walked off in the middle of the night. Sleepwalking. The whole camp is out looking for you. Come on Mia, wake up! Let's take you back to your mother."

Not Jesus.

Mia's head felt pretty foggy. She was trying to understand everything that Howey was saying but she couldn't. Sleepwalking? Take her back to Momma? Why was Momma looking for her? Momma knew where she was. She brought her here.

Howey took Lucy doll out of Mia's arms, then gently pulled Mia up to her feet.

"Can you walk?"

Mia nodded although she wasn't sure if she could or not. Howie held Mia in one arm, and Lucy doll in the other. Mia put one foot in front of the other, and with Howey's help, she managed to get herself a few feet. But that was it. After 6 or 7 steps, Mia fell straight down to the ground. She couldn't walk anymore. Her eyes were going fuzzier as well. Mia had to sit down. She just wanted to sleep some more.

"Okay, Mia. We have two ways we can do this. I can leave you here and go get some help. Or, I can put your doll down and carry you back to camp. Which would you prefer?"

Mia wanted to tell him not to leave without her, that Lucy could wait to come, but she still had no breath for words. She just stayed still on the ground. She would have to take whatever option Howey thought was best. Mia was quite relieved when she felt Howey's arms wrap all the way around her, and her body lift from the ground. Bye Lucy, she whispered. She hoped she whispered. Maybe she didn't. So she waved at her doll instead.

Mia didn't really notice the walk back to camp with Howey. When she opened her eyes next, she was lying on a stretcher in the area just beside the camp church. An ambulance was parked nearby and two attendants were beside her. One was a lady who was talking calmly, saying Mia's name over and over. The other was sticking a needle into Mia's arm.

"Mia, keep opening your eyes. Thatta' girl. My name is Winter. I'm just going to put another blanket on you, okay?"

Mia nodded. She opened her eyes more now. She was warming up. She looked over at the male attendant who was poking her arm with a needle.

"That's Mike," Winter said. "He's starting an IV. We want to get some fluids back in your body. You look good Mia. We want to make sure you stay as good as you are now. Okay?"

Mia nodded again. Winter had a warm cloth to wipe down Mia's face.

"Looks like you got a bit of blood on your face from that cut on your shoulder. I'm just going to wipe it clean for you, okay?"

Mia agreed.

Winter looked away for a moment then returned her glance to Mia.

"Your Momma was worried sick about you. She's on her way over now, okay?"

Mia didn't want to see Momma. Mia was mad at Momma for leaving her in the woods. Momma could have found her easily. Unless Momma forgot where she placed Mia. Momma did that sometimes with her sunglasses. Maybe she did that with her too.

'Mia, my baby," Momma cried as she bent over and kissed her forehead. "I was so worried this morning when you weren't in your bed. Mia, honey, what am I going to do with you? Sleepwalking. You haven't done that before. Something or someone must have upset you before you went to bed."

"But Momma, I didn't…" Mia's voice was weak.

"Oh, don't talk sweetie. Save your energy."

"But Momma!"

"I said that's enough, Mia." Momma had that look on her face that meant Mia needed to shut right up, then and there, or Momma was going to get real mad, real quick. Mia stopped talking.

Daddy was the next to appear by Mia's side. He rubbed the top of Mia's head gently. Daddy seemed to be crying a little. Mia only saw Daddy cry once before, that was when his Mother died. Daddy was close to Grandma.

"Daddy."

"I'm so glad you're okay, Mia."

"She shouldn't talk much," Momma said to Daddy.

He nodded. He took his pointer finger and placed them to his lips.

"Shhh!" he said to her.

Daddy just stood there rubbing Mia's head. It helped Mia feel more awake.

"Mr. and Mrs. Pratt, the police would like to talk to you a moment," Winter said to Momma and Daddy. "We're just going to wait here a bit while we get some more fluids into her. I don't think we are going to need to take her in. Her vitals are good. She should be fine in a half hour or so."

Daddy nodded, and led Momma over to where the police were. They weren't gone for long before Mrs. C. came walking up to stand beside Mia.

"I'm just going to stay with her while her parents are talking. Mind if we have a minute alone?" Mrs. C. asked Winter.

"I don't know if that's okay. She's a minor."

"I'm a doctor." Mrs. C. pulled a badge out of her pack and held it up to Winter, sliding her first two fingers over the words Veterinarian Medicine as she did.

"Sorry, doctor. Take all the time you need. Do you need her vitals?"

"No. I'm not here on official duty. I trust that you are monitoring everything fine?"

Winter nodded. "We are. She's stable."

"Good. I'm just here for comfort."

Winter and Mike stood back.

Mrs. C. whispered in Mia's ear.

"I only have a moment, so you need to be honest. What happened, Mia?"

Mia wasn't sure if she could speak.

"Mia, you didn't sleepwalk did you? Did you run away? Did your Momma say or do anything to hurt you after you left my cabin last night? You can tell me sweetie. It'll be just between us."

Mia had heard the 'just between us' line before and had also learned not to believe it. Ever! Somehow, however, it seemed believable coming from Mrs. C.'s mouth. Mia shook her head, hesitant to use words.

"No, she didn't hurt you, no you didn't run away, or no you didn't sleepwalk?"

Mia looked her up and down. She seemed genuinely kind. Like it would be just between them. Mia was getting tired of Momma's lies. Mia didn't know what to do so she started with just a small amount of information to see how Mrs. C. reacted.

"I didn't sleepwalk."

Mrs. C. bowed her head. "I knew it." She reached down and lifted Mia up to a sitting position. She whispered so only Mia could hear.

"Did you run away?"

Mia shook her head.

Mia started to cry. She didn't want to tell on Momma, but she didn't want to lie to Mrs. C. either.

"Please don't ask me anymore questions," was all Mia could say.

"Son of a bitch," was her response. Mia was taken aback by Mrs. C.'s language. Right there at Bible camp, Mrs. C. cursed. Jesus would not be happy with that. "I knew I should have kept you with me last night. I should have told that Momma of yours to go nail herself to one of those empty crosses we have in that church."

Mia didn't think Mrs. C. was really talking for Mia's sake, but she tried to look like she was listening anyway. She nodded every once in a while, looking back behind her to make sure Momma wasn't over hearing the things she was saying. The things Mia was nodding yes to.

"Mrs. C.," Mia's words brought Mrs. C. out of her rant.

"Yes."

"Mrs. C., Can…" Mia feared finishing. She couldn't be brave. She wanted to ask Mrs. C. for a hug but she was worried she would say no. She also wanted to ask her to hold her hand. Mia never wanted anyone to hold her hand.

"Are you afraid to talk to me?"

Mia didn't answer. She looked over and saw her Momma still talking to the police. She looked at Winter as well, who took Mia's look as a sign that they were done. Winter walked back over to where Mrs. C. and Mia were and asked how they were doing.

Mrs. C. answered and said that they were okay. Then as if she knew what Mia was going to ask, Mrs. C. looked at Winter and asked, "Can I pick her up if I am careful about the IV?"

Winter said it was okay.

"Is it okay if I hold you for a bit?" Mrs. C. asked. But before Mia could answer, Mrs. C. had picked her up tightly in her arms, swaying her side to side. Mrs. C.'s hair smelt like shampoo. Mia was happy. Comfortable. Safe. Mia held her back. She whispered into Mrs. C's ear, "Momma walked me out to the forest and left me there last night."

Mrs. C. squeezed Mia so tight she thought her stuffing was going to fall out.

"Thank you for being so brave, Mia. Thank you!" she whispered back. "I love you."

"I love you too, Mrs. C." And for the first time in forever, Mia felt those words for real.

Chapter Seventeen

Winter checked Mia's IV. She was gentle on Mia's hand, so Mia didn't mind the intrusion.

"Looks like your parents are done with the police. They are headed back here now."

Mia looked up and over at her Momma. When Momma saw that she was in Mrs. C.'s arms she shook her head. Mia knew the safe hug needed to come to an end.

"Momma's going to be real mad that you are hugging me. Hugs are for the weak."

"Let her be. I can handle your Momma. I'm not ready to let you go yet."

Mia wasn't ready to let go either.

"Please don't tell Momma I told you," Mia pleaded.

"I'm not sure I can make that promise, Mia. You need more love than your Momma is capable of giving. I might need to make sure that happens."

"But Momma loves me lots, she says. She just ain't good at showing it."

Mrs. C. just squeezed her tight again. "No she ain't."

Momma got to them in lightening time, beating Daddy by about six yards.

"Put her down immediately," Momma demanded quiet enough so that no one could hear.

"Why I'm just comforting your child Lee-Ann. She was in the woods all night after all. From what? Sleepwalking you said." Mrs. C. did the opposite of Momma. She spoke so everyone could hear.

"That's right. The child sleepwalks. Has all her life."

"I'm sorry. I didn't know if she was allowed to hold her or not." Winter chimed in. No one listened.

"She hasn't slept walked before!" Daddy responded. "This was her first time."

"Oh, Richard. You're such a man. She has been doing this since she was 5."

Daddy looked confused but he didn't argue. Nobody argued with Momma, except Mrs. C. Momma walked closer to Mia and put her arms out.

"Come to Momma, baby."

Mia didn't want to but knew she had no choice. She pushed away from Mrs. C. and held her arms towards her Momma. But Mrs. C. pulled her back in tight and twisted so that Mia's back was to Momma. Mrs. C. placed her hand on the back of Mia's head to hold her in stronger.

"She is staying with me until she has the go ahead to be okay."

"Excuse me! That is my child, give her to me!"

Winter tried to step closer again but the two women wouldn't let her in. They were too busy competing with each other. She stood still and watched.

"No. I will not give her to you."

Momma stomped her foot. She and Mrs. C. stared into each other's eyes for many moments. So many moments that even Daddy expressed discomfort.

"I thought her being a doctor would make it okay. I'm sorry. Do you want me to call the police over?" Winter asked Momma.

"No!" Momma answered Winter quickly.

"What's going on ladies?" Daddy interjected.

"Why don't you tell him, Lee-Ann?" Mrs. C. asked.

"Tell me what?"

Mia was afraid. Instant fear rushed through her body. "Please don't tell," she quietly re-asked Mrs. C.

Both ladies stood silent.

"Would someone tell me what is going on here?" Daddy asked one more time, getting frustrated.

"Nothing dear," Momma responded. Annie and I are just two Mommas worried about this little girl here. Why don't you go and make sure the crowd knows everything is alright?"

Daddy looked at the two ladies for a moment then nodded. He walked behind Mrs. C. and looked at Mia.

"You okay? Feeling better?"

Mia nodded.

"Okay. I'll be back in a moment."

Mia nodded again. She found herself running her fingers through the back of Mrs. C.'s hair. It was soothing. It felt as soft as it looked.

Daddy walked away and left the two ladies to fight over Mia. Mia didn't like being in the middle like she was. She would have preferred to be somewhere else, but only if Mrs. C.'s hug came with her.

"So how did she get into the woods last night?"

"I told you how," Momma answered.

"I don't believe you."

"What did Mia say? Did she say otherwise? Because she is lying if she did."

Mrs. C. took a step back from Momma. "Mia didn't say anything to me. She won't talk."

Momma seemed to believe Mrs. C.

Winter awkwardly walked away from the two ladies and busied herself with her medical bag.

"Of course, she didn't talk. Because that's what happened."

Mrs. C. just laughed. "Lee-Ann darling, kids don't just sleepwalk and go that far on their own when they never have before. Dragging their doll behind them, with a housecoat on. If she were really sleepwalking, she wouldn't have been conscious enough to do those things. Shall I bring those facts up to the medical and other professional help that we have here?"

Momma spit with anger when she said the next sentence. Mia could feel it on her back. Without even seeing them, Mia knew the shade of black her Momma's eyes just turned.

"Annie *dear*, you may be right. You may not be. But one could assume that if you were right, and a child doesn't just walk out to the forest on her own, that it may be because someone upset her mother very much the night before, and that mother may have been wanting to send out a warning. Mess with me, the child suffers."

Momma then moved closer to Mrs. C. and spoke in the ear that Mia wasn't pressed against.

"Back off, or Mia will get hurt more. Now give me my kid."

Mrs. C. had no response. She kissed Mia on the side of the head three times. She whispered into Mia's ear, "I'm so sorry." She kissed her again then handed Mia over to Momma. Momma snatched Mia up and instantly put her back down on the stretcher. Winter walked over to Mia and checked her vitals.

"You can go now. We have her in good hands," Momma said.

"I have no proof of anything. Keep it that way. Because if one mark comes on that child and I see it, or one more time her life is at risk, I promise you, you will dislike me even more."

Mrs. C. didn't look like she wanted to leave but she did. She looked from Momma to Mia and back again then walked away slowly. Once she was about 30 feet away, her slow walk turned into a run. Mia wanted to be running away with her.

Mia was released from the paramedic's care within 20 minutes of Mrs. C. leaving. They wanted to take Mia into the hospital for observation after all but Momma said that it wasn't necessary. They weren't happy about that, but Momma was boss of them too, it seemed. Mia had to speak to the police officer for a moment, but once she did, he and the paramedics left. Momma took her back to the cabin for some rest. Mia expected Momma to say something to Mia about Mrs. C.'s accusations but Momma didn't. She was nice to Mia. Brought her hot chocolate and a cookie in bed, sat with Mia while she ate, and even tucked her in under the covers before she left. Mia didn't understand why or how Momma had changed so much just over night. It was like a different woman.

Mia slept right up until Momma called her for dinner. Mia sat at the table and gorged on chicken, fried leftover spaghetti, and broccoli bites. She was so hungry. Mia couldn't remember the last time she ate anything other than the hot chocolate and cookie Momma gave her that morning. It felt like days. Mia loved camp food. She loved fried spaghetti the most. Momma would take last night's pasta and put it in her black heavy frying pan with lots of butter. It was delicious. Mia would smear it with so much ketchup it almost made the dish a soup.

The other thing about camp food that Mia liked was that Momma and Daddy let her have as many helpings as she wanted. Apparently, gluttony was not a sin at Bible retreat. Mia had just dished herself another scoop of spaghetti when there was a knock on the door.

"Well who would come visiting at dinner time?" Daddy asked. Momma just shrugged.

Daddy got up to answer the door. Mia could hear a familiar male voice talking to him but wasn't sure who it was. Daddy finished his conversation and shut the door. He returned to the kitchen carrying Mia's doll. Mia noticed her and squealed.

"Lucy!"

Mia jumped out of her seat and ran to fetch Lucy from Daddy. She held her tight. Lucy stunk but Mia didn't care. She thought Lucy was gone forever. Mia was used to losing favourite toys. They were always taken away. But Lucy was one doll she wanted to keep forever. She was happy to have her back.

"Howey just brought it by. Good kid that boy. His mother raised him right."

Momma gave Daddy a look of distaste.

"I'm not sure what you and Annie got going on, but that kid is a good one. You can't deny that. He found our daughter and then went back and found her doll. That boy will be a great gentleman someday."

Mia wanted to agree with Daddy but she didn't. She returned Lucy to her bedroom like Daddy asked, then came back and finished her spaghetti. After dinner, her and her parents picked up a little so it was easier to pack up in the morning when they were getting ready to go the day after. Daddy even played two games of checkers with Mia before bedtime. After the second game, and Mia's fourth yawn, Daddy had suggested that Mia go back to bed and sleep some more. He said her body was probably really tired after spending the night outside. He said he was going to sleep on the couch that night so if she were to sleepwalk again, he would hear her. Momma told Daddy that he didn't have to do that, but he just said it was okay. That Jesus hadn't told him yet that he could be with Momma in the biblical sense since she betrayed him with Frank, so it didn't matter that he wasn't in the bed that night. Momma left the room in a hurry. Daddy just smiled at Mia and kissed her on the head.

"Go to bed, little one. Everything is alright."

Mia believed Daddy. She said goodnight and went into her room. She changed her pajamas before getting under the covers. She snuggled herself in, happy to be warm. She turned on her flashlight for a nightlight and grabbed Lucy. As she rolled over onto her side she heard a crunching noise coming from Lucy's sweater pocket. What was that? Mia sat up and pulled her flashlight closer. She reached into Lucy's pocket and pulled out a piece of paper that was stuffed inside. She couldn't read it very well in the dark so she directed her flashlight on it. The note was from Mrs. C. It read:

Mia, here is my number at home. Call me anytime you need me. ANYTIME. You are loved. ~ Mrs. C.

And under the note was her phone number. Mia smelt the paper. It smelt just like Mrs. C.'s shampoo. Mia tucked it back into Lucy's pocket. That night she slept better than she ever had. Mia was loved by someone. It was in writing. And a person willing to write it out for the world to see *has* to be a person who means it.

Chapter Eighteen

Mia spent the first day back from camp in the lawyer's office with Momma. Mia had to tell the lawyer, Mrs. Walsh, all about what happened at Frank's house, in her own words. She felt a bit uncomfortable telling the whole story again with Momma right beside her even though Momma already knew everything. Mia just didn't like Momma hearing it again. Mia felt gross when she said it in front of her.

The meeting in the lawyer's office took about two hours. Once Mia was finished telling her story, they went over what was going to happen on the day they went to court next week. Mrs. Walsh told Mia that she wouldn't have to stay in the court very long, just come in, tell what happened to the judge and then she could leave. She did tell Mia that Frank would be in the room, but that Mia didn't have to look at him. Only to point and say to the judge that he was the one she was talking about. But Mrs. Walsh promised she would tell Mia when that was happening and she wouldn't have to remember to do it on her own.

Mrs. Walsh also told Mia that Frank would probably be very upset and that that was okay. It wasn't her concern to take care of his feelings. She just needed to say things exactly how they happened. Mia said that she understood.

Momma then asked Mrs. Walsh about something called an impact statement. She said she wanted to give one. Mrs. Walsh said that that wouldn't be possible, that it didn't really fit into a trial like theirs. Momma didn't think that was proper but she couldn't argue with a lawyer. She knew more about the law than Momma did, so Momma let it go. She said that at least Jesus knew just how difficult this whole situation had been on her, and if she couldn't tell the judge then maybe Jesus would in his sleep. Mia wasn't sure Jesus worked that way but the same rules applied for her as it did for Momma. She didn't argue. Momma knew more about Jesus than Mia did.

On their way home from the lawyers Momma told Mia that they should plan a big turkey dinner for Frank, just in case he was sentenced to jail after court. Momma said that the food in jail would be awful, and he should have one more taste of delicious food before he went away. Mia wasn't sure Frank would want to come over on account that they were the ones that made it so he might go to jail, but when she suggested that to Momma, Momma just replied that Frank knew that they had to call the police, and he knew where he went wrong. Frank was sorry, she said, and was going to change to be a better man. She said that Daddy wanted Mia to forgive Frank just as Jesus forgave the Roman Soldiers who crucified Him. If Jesus could do that, Mia could certainly forgive a man who just touched her. Mia didn't know if she should forgive him or ask for forgiveness herself. It was all very confusing.

Momma pulled into the parking lot at the grocery store and parked real close to the doors.

"You'll need to come in with me, child. If you're going to cook a turkey, you will need to make sure it's a size you can lift in and out of the oven."

"But I've never cooked a turkey before, Momma."

"Well it's about high time that you did," was all Momma said. She grabbed her keys, her purse, and hopped out of the car. Mia followed.

Momma said it was a sign from the Lord that the turkeys were on sale that day. Jesus was telling her that her decision was right. Momma was proud of her smarts.

Mia lifted cold turkey after cold turkey, only dropping one on the ground in the process. It was the biggest one, and the coldest. Mia wished she had brought her winter mittens with her. Momma said the one she dropped was almost 18 pounds of meat. When Mia went to lift the large turkey back up off the ground she accidentally kicked it instead, sending it sliding down the aisle floor to the egg section at the end of the store. Frozen turkeys were quite slippery, Mia realized. She ran after it but it was too heavy to carry back all the way so she just kicked it back to where Momma was standing with her arms folded across her shoulders. Momma was not impressed.

After that, Mia would only lift them over the bin so if they fell, they wouldn't go far. It took a while to find one that was both big enough to feed everyone, yet small enough that it wasn't too heavy to lift. When Momma and Mia agreed on the final bird, Mia put it straight into the cart.

"Well hello, Lee-Ann," a voice said from behind. "Planning a big dinner, are you?"

It was Henriette Larouche from church. Henriette was one of Momma's tea friends.

"Oh, you know, just a nice turkey dinner for my family and a friend. You know how I love to cook for my loved ones."

Mia looked at her Momma quizzically. Momma ignored her.

"Well, be careful when you cook it. You know Leo, Janet's husband? Well they cooked a turkey just a few months ago for Easter and she didn't clean it properly, and wouldn't you know it, the whole family got sick with salmonella. Most of them recovered, but that Leo is a big boy. He just ate and ate that turkey. He was so sick he ended up in the hospital for 5 days. Poor Janet. She felt so bad. Leo almost met our maker and Lord Jesus Christ that week. But just like an Easter miracle of his own, Leo rose from the near dead and survived. Praise be to his name."

"Amen, for that," Momma replied. "Our Lord is good."

"That He is. That He is."

Salmonella? What was that? Mia had never heard of that before. When she and Momma got to the car after getting all the ingredients for the dinner fixings, Mia asked Momma.

"Oh, it's just a poisoning that can happen when eating unclean or uncooked meat. You'll just need to make sure you clean it proper beforehand, and cook it well. I'll give you my recipe book. If you follow that, everything will be fine. That Henriette is a drama queen anyway."

Mia didn't think the word poison was fine at all. That sounded rather awful in fact. She would definitely kill Daddy with poison. No thank you, she thought.

Momma didn't give her any more information than that about salmonella so Mia worried about it all the way home.

Daddy was sitting in his recliner when they arrived.

"How did the lawyer's appointment go?"

Momma explained the meeting to Daddy while Mia unpacked all of the groceries. They were still talking by the time she put the last item in the fridge. Mia pulled out Momma's Holiday Recipes Made Easy cooking book and found the recipe for cooking a turkey. It said nothing about salmonella or on how to clean the bird, just that you had to. Maybe Aunt Colleen would know? She was coming over later that night to talk to Daddy about something. She would ask her then.

Mia took a few more moments to find recipes on how to make turnip and stuffing. They both looked easy enough. Mashed potatoes she already made many times, so she didn't bother finding a recipe for that.

Momma called her to the living room to speak with her and Daddy. Momma said she told Daddy about the dinner and he agreed that it was a good idea, but that if Mia wasn't comfortable around Frank, she could leave and go upstairs with her plate after she finished cooking. They said they would make an exception for her on this occasion. Besides, Mia wasn't supposed to be around him anyway. Mia thanked them both and said she would like to go upstairs. She knew this now. She knew she would have no appetite sitting at the table looking at Frank's sad face.

They decided to do dinner Friday night. That was three days away. The court day was the Monday after that weekend.

Momma told Mia that she didn't have to cook that night so Mia went upstairs and listened to music. She pulled out her journal and read over some of her previous entries. She hadn't added anything in weeks and that bothered her. She wasn't being a very good spy. She was a spy on vacation. She wondered if she could go out with Abby for a while, but knew the answer would be no.

Instead, Mia just continued to read it all from the beginning. She didn't make it to the end before she heard a knock on her bedroom door.

"Knock, knock," Aunt Colleen said as she opened the door. "Can I come in?"

Mia plunged her book back into the drawer. She debated leaving it just on top but knew she couldn't. She lifted the mat and hid it under as she always did. It didn't matter if Aunt Colleen noticed, she wouldn't tell anyone, that Mia was certain of.

"How's it going, kiddo?"

Mia jumped up and ran to her aunt, landing in her arms for a big hug.

"Better now," Mia answered.

"Man, I missed your hugs."

Aunt Colleen went down to her knees and hugged Mia again with a full body press hug. Mia giggled at her aunt's excitement

"Were you writing?" Aunt Colleen asked.

"Ya, just in my journal. But don't tell Momma you saw it."

Aunt Colleen pretended to twist a lock on her lips and throw away an imaginary key. "Your secret is safe with me."

Mia smiled. She knew it was.

"Getting ready for writing camp?"

Mia's smile faded. She hadn't told her aunt the bad news yet. School ended and then Bible camp happened. There was no time to call her.

"What's wrong? That doesn't look like a camp-ready face."

"I'm not allowed to go to camp. Momma and Daddy said no." Aunt Colleen's face scrunched up with concern. Mia told her more. "I got in, but at a cost. Mrs. Gentry said that I had a mystery angel pay for my camp and Momma got mad. She said we weren't a charity case. That I couldn't accept it."

Aunt Colleen stood up. She looked angry.

"Are you kidding me?"

Mia shook her head.

"Mia, I love your parents but there is something wrong with them. What is going on in their heads? You listen to me: you will go to that camp. I will make sure of that. You stay here and give me a moment. Don't come downstairs. I'll be right back. Got it?"

"How are you going to get them to say yes?"

"Don't worry, I'll think of something. I'll lie if I have to. Make them want you to go. Just don't worry, okay? I got this."

Mia nodded. "But Aunty…"

"Yes?"

"Be careful. Momma gets really mad when it comes to writing camp."

Aunt Colleen nodded. "Your Momma gets mad over everything it seems."

Aunt Colleen left and Mia considered staying put like she was told but she couldn't. She needed to listen to what was going to happen downstairs. She was worried for Aunt Colleen. Mia's only hope was that Momma never got fist angry when Daddy was around. So maybe Aunt Colleen would be okay. She settled herself at the top of the stairs. Aunt Colleen had already started talking to Daddy.

"But Richard, she loves to write. How could you say no? She worked hard to get into that school."

"Stay out of it Colleen."

"That's my niece Richard. I can't stay out of it. She has had a rough year, with everything Frank did. She deserves this."

"You heard my husband," Momma's voice finally chimed in. "Stay out of it."

"Lee-Ann, look at you. You're tired. You could use a break too. Imagine all the stuff you could do if you didn't have to worry about being a mom for a few weeks. It'll be great for you."

"That is true," Momma agreed. "But still, we aren't a charity case."

Mia could see Aunt Colleen pacing back and forth. She got a glimpse of her every time she stepped to the right.

"Okay, I'll tell you."

"Tell us what?" Daddy asked.

"I was the one who paid for her to go to camp."

"You what?" Momma said in an outside voice.

"I know. I should have told you, or asked you but I wanted to give it to her as a graduation present but then I forgot to tell you and her. You know me, half a brain."

Mia couldn't see Momma's face but she could definitely see the lamp as it flew across the room and hit the wall right next to Aunt Colleen's head. Aunt Colleen ducked out of the way just in time.

"What the hell was that for? You're fucking crazy," Aunt Colleen yelled at Momma. "Richard?"

"Now settle down ladies."

"Don't tell me to settle down," both Momma and Aunt Colleen said at the same time. And as if the double voices had weight, Daddy fell into Mia's view, landing on the couch.

"Richard, are you okay?"

"Just tired. That's all."

Daddy sat there and caught his wind. Momma gave him her attention.

Mia wanted to rush down the stairs to hug her Daddy and shelter Aunt Colleen from Momma's wrath. But when she stood up to do so, Aunt Colleen noticed her and subtly shook her head no. Mia sat back down.

Momma turned her attention back to Aunt Colleen.

"How could you do that without asking? The nerve!"

Aunt Colleen opened her mouth to yell, but instead she apologized. She said she was sorry, that she really meant to ask them first, and when that failed, she meant to tell them right away, but she got distracted.

"Well, I'm not sure about all of this," Momma said. She left Daddy's side and picked up the lamp. There was silence for a long time. Finally, Daddy spoke.

"I think we should let her go, Lee-Ann. The money is already spent. We could use the time here at the house to fix it up without Mia underfoot. We could have a mini-vacation maybe. It is summer after all."

"That sounds lovely, Lee-Ann. Just the two of you, spending some time together away. I can even take her to the camp. I will be heading out that day for a vacation, myself."

More silence. Mia couldn't stand it anymore. She got up from her perch on the stairs and walked back to her room. If she couldn't participate in the conversation or cover Aunt Colleen, she had to leave. She would sit and wait in her room where interrupting the adults wasn't as tempting. Mia was not good at practicing her patience.

Minutes later she heard footsteps down the hall. The door opened up. Mia waited to see who it was before she spoke. Thankfully, it was Aunt Colleen.

"Well?"

Aunt Colleen just smiled.

"Really?"

Aunt Colleen nodded. Mia jumped and grabbed Aunt Colleen's arms. They jumped up and down, in a circle, smiling and laughing. Mia was very happy. Mia was going to writing camp.

Chapter Nineteen

Mia woke up happy that morning. She was so grateful to Aunt Colleen for talking her parents into letting her go to writing camp. She danced around her room some more, thinking of all the wonderful stories she was going to write over the two weeks. Or maybe just one really amazing story, she couldn't decide.

Her dance of excitement didn't last very long. Soon after getting up, she remembered that she had to cook a turkey in just two days and she still didn't know what salmonella was. All of the chaos surrounding writing camp the night before made her forget to ask Aunt Colleen all about the mysterious poison. She sat and thought for a while about how else she could find out. If she was at school, she could ask her teacher, or an office assistant. Or she could go down to the library and see the librarian. But school was out for the summer. It wasn't an option.

"The library," she said out loud to no one. How could she not have thought of that yet? She could go to the library downtown. Maybe Abby would go with her.

First, she ran downstairs and asked Momma if she could go out for a while with Abby. Her mother said it was fine. It was the summer, school was out, and Mia's chores were done until suppertime. Mia then ran upstairs and knocked on the wall that was connected to Abby's bedroom on the other side of the semi-detached home. Three knocks: one slow, then two fast. That was their signal to meet downstairs. She hoped Abby was in her room at the time.

Mia ran down to the basement and waited at the hole. She waited for what felt like an eternity, but finally Abby showed up.

"Sorry, I had to go to the bathroom first."

"That's okay," Mia said. "I need to go to the library. Want to come?"

Abby said she did, and 5 minutes later the two girls were outside, and headed to the building that held all the answers that Mia was seeking.

It didn't take them long to get halfway across town to the library. It was a straight bike ride down Main Street with just a turn at each end of the ride. The girls walked in the front door, passed the turn-style, and stood still, looking at all the books. It was quiet inside. Like no one was there. But people were. Mia could count at least five just from the doorway. She wasn't sure where to start on her search, so she waited at the counter to talk to the librarian. When the librarian walked over, Mia asked her where to find books on salmonella.

"Salmonella? I don't think we have any books specifically on that topic. It's not a very long one. Your best bet is to use the encyclopedias."

"Where would I find those?"

"In the back on the far wall. Do you have a library card? You need that to get anything from the library?"

Mia said she didn't. She asked if she could get one but the librarian told her that she would need a parent or someone over eighteen to sign her up. Then she would need them to be there with her to go inside. Mia tried to explain to the librarian that she just needed to read a little bit about salmonella, that she could write it down, and didn't need to take the book out, but the librarian wouldn't budge. Rules were rules, she said. Mia was under twelve. She needed a guardian with her.

Mia and Abby left the library and sat on the curb just outside. Mia picked up a loose rock that was on the ground and tossed it onto the road.

"I'm sorry Mia. What did you need that book for, anyway?"

"I have to cook a turkey and I don't want to kill anyone."

"Oh!" Abby replied. "I wish I was old like you. I'm not allowed to cook."

Mia just shrugged in response. She liked cooking and hated it at the same time.

"Will your Mom come and get you a library card?"

Mia shook her head. "Probably not."

"My mom might. I can ask her?"

"That's okay. If she tells Momma or Momma finds out, I will be in trouble."

Abby nodded. Mia knew Abby understood.

"It's too bad that you don't own any encyclopedias. Then you wouldn't need the librarian or a way around her rules."

"I know."

Mia sat and sulked for a little longer thinking about what the librarian and Abby had said. Encyclopedias. Encyclopedias. No, she didn't own any, neither did any of her family members, but she did know someone who did. Frank! Frank had every letter of encyclopedia you could need. How was she going to get in to see the books though? It wasn't like she could ask him to borrow one. Nor could she knock on his door and stay there to read them. She had the 500 feet rule that she couldn't break without her parents with her, and besides, Frank didn't need to know that she was worried about killing him now, especially after she was already possibly sending him to jail. She also didn't want to be alone with him anymore. She knew he just made a mistake, and was trying to get better, be better, but she was still worried that he would try to teach her something else. She didn't want to see his ugly penis again. Maybe he and Jesus could make that better too while they are working on Frank's inner parts.

"You're quiet." Abby broke Mia's thoughts.

"Just thinking."

"Bout what?"

Mia didn't want to tell Abby but she knew she had to. Mia needed Abby's help. She couldn't go to Frank's alone.

"I have an idea. But it means our biggest spy mission yet. Are you ready for that?"

Abby's smile said she was ready.

"I know someone who has encyclopedia's but we can't let him know we need to read them."

"That's going to be hard."

Mia knew she had to break into Frank's house when he wasn't there. She was going to have to do it that night after dinner when Daddy had his Bible study. Frank was sure to go to it. He often did. Mia was going to have to be brave.

"I know. And dangerous. Maybe even illegal. Can you handle that?"

Abby looked down at her toes a few moments. She seemed nervous.

"Oh, please Abby! You won't need to do any of the illegal stuff, you will just need to be a look out for me. It won't be that hard. Please?"

Abby looked up from her toes and looked into Mia's eyes.

"Okay. What do we need to do?"

Dinnertime seemed to pass incredibly slowly. Mia's knee shook under the table as she waited for her parents to finish their food. Mia took no time finishing her plate. She ate her hamburger and soup in record time. Momma made a comment about how hungry she was, Daddy laughed at how much she must have enjoyed her own cooking. Mia agreed to both. Daddy was the last to finish. His last bite of burger was barely in his mouth when Mia grabbed his dishes from under him and brought them to the sink.

"In a hurry, tonight?"

"Yes! I'm tired and looking for bed."

Mia suddenly realized that her rush to get through dinner was a futile effort. She still had to wait until her parents went to Bible study. Mia cleaned the dishes, put the food away, and turned off most of the lights. She went a little too far in her effort when she turned off the dining room light while Momma was sitting at the table reading the bills. Momma yelled at her to turn them back on and she did. Mia then retreated up to her bedroom and waited.

By 7 p.m., she heard Momma yell upstairs that her and Daddy were heading out. She said they would be back around 10 p.m. Mia rushed downstairs and said goodbye then watched through the door window until the family car was out of sight.

She went back upstairs to her room and changed into all dark clothes; she wore jogging pants and a hoodie. She threw her hair back into a ponytail, and slipped the hood over her head. She looked and felt like a burglar. Mia was ready. She grabbed all of her pillows and placed them underneath her blankets to make it look like she was still in her bed. She wasn't sure it would work if Momma or Daddy came in, but she saw it once on television in an after school special and thought it wouldn't hurt to try. Last, she went to the wall that connected to Abby's room and did their secret knock.

Going back downstairs she noticed something she hadn't earlier. Daddy had his pillow and blanket set and waiting on the couch for his return. Was he spending the night on the couch again? He must be.

Mia headed to the door. She looked out one more time to make sure her parent's car hadn't returned. Satisfied that they were gone Mia put on her shoes and headed out, making sure to grab the key for her bike as she went. Mia stood in the fresh night air and breathed in deeply. Mia, again, felt the twinge of excitement, for breaking one of Momma's rules.

Chapter Twenty

Abby came out shortly after Mia.

"My parents are sound asleep. That was easy to get past them." Abby boasted in a whisper as she unlocked her own bike.

"Good. Thanks again Abby."

Abby patted Mia on the shoulder. The two girls didn't need any other words.

Mia and Abby biked their way through the dark streets of town. It was Mia's first time riding a bike this late. She really wished she had a light for the front of her bicycle. They were about three blocks away from home before she remembered the flashlight in her pocket. They pulled over on the side of Newton Road, and Mia grabbed it out of her hoodie pouch. She clicked it on. It didn't give much light but it gave some. More importantly, it let cars know that they were there. Before they started biking again, she said a little prayer to Jesus to keep them safe, just in case. Hoping that He didn't mind that she was asking for help while she disobeyed her Momma. Abby must have appreciated the prayer too because when Mia was done, Abby said Amen.

The girls turned onto the street where Frank lived. It was hard to find his trailer amongst all the houses since it sat back so much, but she eventually did. Frank's car wasn't in the driveway. She felt lucky. She thought about Momma and what she would say in this case. Momma would claim that this was Jesus telling her that she was doing the right thing. But Jesus didn't speak to Mia like He spoke to Momma. Jesus ignored her, like most other people did. Or maybe she just didn't listen for Him. She was bad at listening.

Mia and Abby parked their bikes in a bush and walked over to the doorstep.

"How are we going to get in?"

"His key should be..."

Mia bent down and reached under the trailer steps for the Mason jar she knew would be there. Frank hid his extra key inside of it. Mia knew this because he told her once. He was babysitting her and she had to come over when he wasn't going to be home. He told her where it was and said she could let herself in. Mia was sure he didn't mean it for a time like this, but she knew he would be grateful if she didn't kill him with salmonella as well. Frank would never know how close his untimely death had come.

She found the Mason jar and pulled it out. The key was exactly where it should be.

"Got it!" Mia exclaimed louder than she should have.

She stuffed the jar back under the steps and paused to make sure no one was on the street. Seeing that it was clear, Mia stood up and unlocked the door. Abby stood right behind her. Mia turned to face her friend.

"Okay, I'm going in alone. I need you to keep watch and make sure he doesn't come home while I'm inside."

'I'm not going in?"

"No. It's too dangerous for both of us to be here. I need you outside."

Abby looked disappointed. Mia tried to make her feel better.

"You have the important job. The one that gets us in and out safe."

Abby nodded.

"Can you still caw like a crow?"

Abby nodded again.

"Good. If you see his car come back, make sure you caw really loud. But not so he hears you, just in case he figures out it's not a bird. Do it once you see his car coming. So, sit in a bush where you can see down the street. You know?"

Abby looked around. She pointed to a bush near the end of the driveway.

"How about there?"

"Perfect!"

Abby ran off to the bush and situated herself down low. Mia waited until she was still before entering the trailer. His trailer still smelt of fish.

Mia got straight to business. She walked over to the shelf with all of the encyclopedia's. Q, R, S, she found the one she needed. She pulled it out and sat down on the couch in the main part of the trailer. She thumbed through the book until she found salmonella. It read:

Salmonella

Salmonella is a type of food poisoning caused by Salmonella Enterica bacterium. There are many different kinds of these bacteria. You can get salmonellosis by eating food contaminated with salmonella. Most common ways of getting salmonella poisoning are through unclean foods such as poultry or beef, as well as through fecal matter of animals. Symptoms include nausea, vomiting, tiredness, abdominal cramps, diarrhea, and fever. To avoid salmonella, make sure you wash your food well and cook until you have reached a safe internal temperature.

Mia read on a little more. She was looking through some of the pictures when she heard a loud caw coming from the outside. The caw got louder and louder, and a little frantic until it stopped. Silence. Mia jumped from her seat and looked out the window. Frank was home. Not only that, Frank was already out of his car and headed into the trailer. Mia had no time to leave. She could feel her heart beating in her chest. What was she going to do? Mia searched the room for a place to escape but there was none. It was a trailer. There was only one door to go out of and Frank was on the other side of it.

Mia grabbed the book and darted under the couch. She pushed herself back as far as she could against the wall. Mia held her breath as she saw Frank's feet enter the trailer. What would he do if he found her there? Why wasn't he still at the Bible study? Did he go, or did this mean her parents were home as well?

"You're losing it Frank," he said to himself. "Door unlocked, leaving on all the lights again."

Mia didn't think he knew she was there. She listened to Frank drop his keys on the counter, and take his coat off. He walked to the fridge and opened up a beer. He took a big drink of if before sitting down on the couch Mia was under. He burped loudly. Mia had to stop herself from laughing at the sound that came out of his mouth. Mia always found burps funny.

Frank's boots were inches from Mia's face. She could smell the stink of dirt and oil coming off of them. Then she saw Frank's hands come down toward the floor as he untied his laces and kicked his boots off, one at a time. She wished for his boots back. Frank's socks smelt even worse.

Frank continued to drink his beer on the couch, while Mia stayed underneath praying that he wouldn't catch her. What if he did? Would he try to touch her privates again? Would he yell at her? Tell Momma and Daddy what she had done. She was more afraid of that than anything. Was Abby okay outside? What if he caught her, would he hurt her?

Mia wanted Frank to go to bed so she could leave but he didn't move anywhere. He stayed there for almost an hour.

Finally, Frank got up, locked the door, and went into the bathroom. Mia heard the shower start so she squeezed herself out from under the couch. Quickly, she made her way over to the door. She unlocked it, twisted the handle, and pushed. The door wouldn't open. She tried the lock again, back and forth. She twisted the handle and pushed. Still nothing. Mia leaned on the door with all of her might but it just wouldn't open.

She looked out the window. Maybe Abby could open the door from the outside. She knocked on the door lightly hoping Abby would hear. But nothing moved in the darkness. Mia looked over to the bush where their bikes were hiding; Abby's was gone. She had left. Mia felt a moment of relief, then anger. Her friend had left her. Mia was alone.

Mia tried the door again.

"Come on you stupid thing," Mia said to herself. When the door wouldn't open on the fifth try, she searched the edges. What was making it stick? Mia looked up and noticed that there was a lock at the top of the door as well. Way beyond what Mia could reach. She attempted to jump for it but she was too short. She looked around for a chair or a stool. He had no furniture that wasn't nailed to a wall. Maybe a stick would help, she thought, but she couldn't find one of those either. She lifted newspapers up, books, and tools. Nothing was long enough.

Mia listened for the shower. It was still going but she knew it wouldn't be for long. She needed out. Panic was starting to set in again. If she got caught, she would be in so much trouble. Mia didn't know what was worse, being caught by Frank, or by Momma. Or heaven forbid, being caught by both.

Chapter Twenty-One

The water stopped running. Frank's shower had ended. Mia placed herself back under the couch. Frank came out of the bathroom naked. It was everything she could do to not vomit. She was regretting her decision to go to Frank's trailer.

Frank got himself dressed in boxers, then walked back into the kitchen area. He pulled down a package of bread from the top cupboard, pulled two pieces out, placed them on the counter then put the loaf back into the cupboard. He moved to the fridge, pulled out lunchmeat and mustard. Frank made himself a sandwich. He ate the whole thing before he put the lunchmeat and mustard away. He turned off the kitchen light and was headed for his bedroom when there was a knock on the door.

"What the hell?" Frank shouted. "It's late."

Mia hoped it was Abby coming back to get her.

Frank turned the light back on and walked to the door. He unlocked all of the locks on the door and opened it up.

"Annie?"

"Hi Frank, I'm so sorry to bother you so late, I need your help."

Frank looked at her quizzically, but opened the door wide enough for Mrs. C. to walk in.

"With what?"

"I was driving in the area, dropping off medicine to one of my sons at a sleepover just on Talon street over there, he forgot to take it with him and he needs it for his allergies."

Frank nodded as she talked.

"Well my truck seemed to die not long after I left their house. It's a blessing it died right here in front of your place. Being a washer and dryer mechanic guy, I thought you might be able to help me get it back up and running."

Frank chuckled. "The inside of a washing machine is a lot different from the inside of a vehicle."

"Is it? I didn't think it would be that different. Huh!"

"It's quite different Annie."

"Oh!" Mrs. C. played with a loose strand of hair that hung from under her hat. She twisted it in circles. Frank watched her. "You think you can try anyway? Maybe you'd recognize something under the hood." She stepped a little closer to him. She was acting cheap again, like Momma said she did around men. Mia didn't like how close she was to Frank. She was scared he would hurt her. Mrs. C. didn't seem nervous at all.

Frank smiled. "Of course!" he said. "I'll take a look and see if I there's anything I can do."

He asked her to hold tight while he looked for his keys to get the tools from his car. When Frank left to his bedroom, Mrs. C. whispered Mia's name.

"Down here." Mia answered, surprised that Mrs. C. knew she was there.

Mrs. C. looked down at Mia with wide eyes. She put her finger to her lip to tell Mia to stay quiet. Mrs. C. walked down the small hall toward Frank's room and stood watching him dig through old pants to find his keys.

"They are here somewhere," Frank mumbled.

Mrs. C. looked over at Mia and motioned for her to leave. Mia pulled herself out from under the couch, put the book back on the shelf, and left the trailer, escaping back into the night. Mia ran to the bush where her bike sat. She wanted to leave but she couldn't with Mrs. C. still inside. Mia had left her with Frank of all people. Mia started to feel rage. If Frank hurt Mrs. C., it would hurt Mia more than anything he could have done to Mia herself. Mia couldn't leave until she knew Mrs. C. was safe.

Frank's front door opened.

"Thanks Frank. I knew I could count on you. Sorry again for such a late hour."

Frank got his tools out of his car and followed Mrs. C. to her truck parked on the side of the road. She opened the front door and pushed the button to make the hood pop up. Frank opened it up and looked around underneath.

"You see anything?"

"I just started looking."

"Oh, sorry."

Mia watched it all from the bushes. She was afraid to move or breathe. Mrs. C. was looking around to see if she could see Mia. Mia tried to get her attention but couldn't. It was too dark.

"I don't see anything, maybe your fuel pump needs a jolt."

Frank grabbed the back of his wrench and smacked it down hard on something under the engine. It was loud. Mrs. C. jumped. She pointed to the engine.

"Isn't that cylinder thing the fuel pump?"

Frank looked up at her. Mia couldn't tell what expression he was making because his back was to her but by the look on Mrs. C.'s face, it wasn't pleasant.

"I know that woman! I was just trying to check something else first."

"I assumed you knew what you were doing, I was just wondering about the parts. I don't look at a lot of car engines you know. I know animals inside out, literally, but not cars."

"That's okay." He hit another part under the engine. "Now go try and start your truck."

Mrs. C. went to her driver side door, opened it, and put the keys in the engine. The truck started right away. Mrs. C. got out and thanked Frank. Frank shook her hand. He held it longer then Mrs. C. liked. She pulled her hand from his in a forceful way. Frank gave her an awkward smile.

He turned and went back to his trailer.

Mrs. C. watched the closed trailer door for several seconds before calling out to Mia. Mia quietly exited the bush. Mrs. C.

walked over, grabbed her bike, threw it into the back of her truck then motioned for Mia to get in the front. Mia did.

They didn't speak until they were several blocks away from Frank's trailer. It was as if they were both worried he would hear them if they did. Mrs. C. pulled the truck over to the side of the road. Once in park, she leaned over and grabbed Mia by the arm.

"You scared me. You could have gotten hurt. What were you thinking? If your friend Allie…"

"Abby."

"Abby, whatever, if she didn't almost drive her bike straight into my truck tonight, bawling her eyes out with fear, spilling every secret she has ever had in her entire life to me, you might still be in there!"

Mia was taken aback by the tone Mrs. C. was using. She didn't know what to say. She made Mrs. C. mad. Mia needed to explain.

"I needed to look at his books, and the library wouldn't let me look at theirs, and I can't give everyone salmonella. I just can't. Let me go."

Mia pulled her arm in attempt to loosen Mrs. C.'s grip.

"What? That doesn't make sense." Mrs. C. let go of her grip on Mia. "I'm sorry. I was scared. You scared me. I love you Mia, you can't be doing stuff like this. Take a deep breath and tell me again. Only with more information."

"You shouldn't love me," was all Mia could address. "I hurt people."

"No Mia, you don't."

"I do. I just hurt you. Look how upset you are."

Mrs. C. put her head back against the headrest. She paused a moment before she spoke.

"You didn't hurt me, Mia. I was scared. You were in a dangerous place tonight. I want you safe. Do you understand the difference?"

Mia nodded. "I think so. I was scared when I was waiting outside and you were still in there. I was afraid he was going to hurt you. But I wasn't mad at you. Is that what you mean?"

Mrs. C. smiled. "Yes. That is exactly what I mean. Now, slower, tell me how you ended up there tonight."

Mia told her everything, everything except for the fact that the dinner was for Frank. She didn't think that would go over well with Mrs. C. She told her about the turkey, about making dinner, the library not giving her a card, Frank's key, Abby's help, and the lock she couldn't reach from the top of the door. Once her story was done, Mrs. C. asked Mia that next time, instead of going to Frank's house, or being anywhere near him, if Mia could maybe call her first so she could try to help her solve the problem. Mia agreed. Mia asked her a question back. She asked Mrs. C. what really happened to her truck, if it really broke down. Mrs. C. said no. She was hoping that Frank wouldn't ask her to start it when he first went out. Mia said Mrs. C. was brave. Mrs. C. laughed. She said that she was probably more stupid than brave but she would take the compliment.

They sat in silence for a moment before Mrs. C. started the conversation again.

"You okay?"

Mia nodded. "I just have another question."

"Shoot."

"Why are you being so kind to me? You don't really know me. Why did you come tonight?"

"That's two questions."

"Sorry."

Mrs. C. laughed, "I'm only kidding. Let's see, I'm kind to you because I like you. You deserve kindness. I'm not kind to everyone you know?"

Mia nodded agreement although she felt bad for it after. She didn't mean to agree to Mrs. C.'s comment about not being kind to everyone.

"I came tonight because I heard you needed help. You were alone and needed a friend. I can't imagine you ask a lot of people for help?"

"I used to. But Momma scares them too much."

"I will help you. Call me anytime you need to. Do you still have my number?

Mia nodded.

"I will ask questions, but you don't need to answer them. It makes me mad that others haven't helped. You know, Mia, your Momma needs help too. And that's not a kind of help you can give her at nine."

"I'm ten now."

Mrs. C. cocked her head to the side.

"My birthday was just before camp. When school was ending." Mrs. C. nodded. Mia continued. "I try to help Momma, but I'm not very good at it. I make things worse."

"Mia, you are nine, er, ten. She needs adult professional help. Does your Momma ever hit you?"

"No!" Mia responded quickly. Then she paused for a moment. She was lying to Mrs. C. and she didn't like it.

"Mia, are you sure?"

Mia didn't know how to answer this question. So many things ran through her mind in such a short amount of time. Would she be in trouble if she said yes? Would Momma get in trouble? Would Mrs. C. feel like she needed to stand up to Momma and get hurt by her? And worse, what if she told Mrs. C. and Mrs. C didn't do anything. What if she just walked away and left? Mia couldn't handle Mrs. C. leaving like the others did. She was one of the only ones that made Mia feel safe. Mia was starting to really like that feeling.

"I need to go now."

"Wait. Not yet."

"My parents will be home soon. I will get in trouble if they know I'm gone."

"They're already home."

Mia's heart sank. "How do you know?"

"When I was dropping off Abby, their car pulled in the driveway."

"Oh, man." Mia smacked her head back against the seat. Momma was going to be mad.

"Maybe I can bring you home and help explain, or help you lie, or distract them while you sneak in?"

"No. Momma will get more upset if she sees you."

Mrs. C. and Mia looked at each other. Both deep in thought trying to figure out a way for Mia to get in safely. They seemed to be coming up with nothing.

"Well, this is what I figure. Your parents either already know you snuck out and are now waiting angrily for your entrance, or they went to bed without checking and have no clue. Either way, I believe your fate for tonight is set. So, will you stay with me a little longer? Give me thirty more minutes? I would like to show you something at my animal hospital. It won't take long, and I will have you back here in good time. Maybe it will help you. Maybe it will give them more time to fall deeper into sleep so you can sneak back in safely. What do you say?"

Mia liked the idea of spending more time with Mrs. C. and she was right, her fate was most likely already set.

"Okay."

Mrs. C. smiled. She put her signal light on and slowly merged back onto the road.

"Great! Let's go meet a dog named Sanchez."

Chapter Twenty-Two

The truck pulled up to a large brown brick building. The sign out front read Carrington Animal Hospital. Mia had walked by the building many times over the years but never wandered inside.

Mia followed Mrs. C. up to the entrance of the building and watched as she unlocked the door and turned on only one of the lights. Mia entered behind her. Mrs. C. shut and locked the door.

"Follow me."

Mia did as she was told. They went through an examination room and into the back. When they got to a large white door, Mrs. C. pulled out another key from her pocket and unlocked it. She turned on the lights and within seconds, sounds of barking and one really loud meow filled the room. Mia couldn't help but giggle with excitement.

"These are our resident animals. We have some dogs, a cat, and an iguana named Pete staying with us."

Mia looked at all the animals in cages. She hated seeing them locked up but understood it was necessary. Like how sometimes it was necessary for Momma to lock Mia up. Sometimes it was safer that way.

"Do they live here?"

"For now. Some are here because they are sick and we need to make them well. And some are here because they have no home. Like Sanchez. Come meet him, I think you will like him."

Mrs. C. walked to a cage at the end of the row. She opened it up. Sanchez was a small dog. He seemed happy to see Mrs. C. come. She opened up his cage and patted his head a few times before picking him up. She turned and faced him towards Mia.

"Mia, meet Sanchez."

"Hi Sanchez," Mia said as she reached out to pet him. Sanchez showed his teeth while moving his body away from Mia, cuddling into Mrs. C. tighter instead.

"He's nervous. He is afraid of people."

"He isn't afraid of you?" Mia responded.

"No. But it wasn't always that way. It took him a long time to get trust in me. I had to tame him. Do you know what that means?"

Mia shook her head.

"Well, taming means trust. It means being able to cultivate a relationship, or friendship in where both people, or living things in this case, come to slowly trust each other. It's getting each other to believe that they don't have to be afraid that the other will purposely hurt them, or leave them. They are connected together. That isn't always as easy as it sounds. Especially if they have never experienced a safe person before."

"Oh!"

Mia looked at Sanchez sitting in Mrs. C.'s arms. He was mostly light brown in colour, with a few patches of white. He had a lot of chunks of hair missing from his body. Sanchez was also missing a leg.

"What happened to his leg?'

"I had to cut it off. He was hurt and if he kept his leg, he would have died. I fixed him so he wouldn't."

"You cut his leg off?" Mia had never heard of someone doing that.

"Yes. In surgery. I'm a doctor for animals remember?"

Mia nodded.

"I had to, to save his life."

Mia wanted to hold him so bad. He was incredibly cute. She reached her hand out slowly but then changed her mind. She didn't want to scare him. She hadn't tamed him yet. She wasn't sure how to.

"How does someone tame a dog."

"Well, every dog is different, just like every person is different. You just need to show Sanchez slowly that you won't hurt him. Here, give me your hand."

Mia hesitated. For a brief moment, she thought about giving Mrs. C. her hand but she found herself too afraid.

"Will you take my arm instead?"

Mrs. C. agreed. She grabbed Mia by the wrist and slowly pulled her hand closer to Sanchez. Sanchez looked at Mia's hand, then at Mia. At his own pace, Sanchez reached out his nose and took a sniff. His nose was wet on her finger. She giggled. Her laugh scared him and he brought his nose back.

"That's the first step. Good job."

Mia smiled.

"How did he hurt his leg?"

Mrs. C. stood back up and placed Sanchez back in his cage. She shut the door. Mia noticed that the cage had his name on it. Underneath his name the sign read: Maltese, 7 months.

"Sanchez belonged to some owners that shouldn't have had a dog. Some people aren't good at taking care of other living things."

Mrs. C. sat on the ground and patted the floor to have Mia sit down beside her. Mia did. She leaned back against an empty cage.

"Sanchez had owners that weren't very nice to him. They said mean things to him, hit him, and locked him up for days without food or water when he wasn't behaving. He was a puppy, he didn't know how to behave. That was their job. To teach him what was proper. When they didn't teach him that, and he did puppy things, they punished him for it."

"That doesn't sound very nice."

"It wasn't nice. And one day Sanchez got into a bunch of grocery bags that his owners left on the floor. He made a big mess trying to get at as much food as he could. Sanchez was starving. His male owner got so mad at him that he did the unthinkable. He took Sanchez outside and shot him in the leg."

Mia gasped.

Mrs. C. nodded in agreement to her response.

"How did you get him?"

"How did we get him here at the clinic?"

Mia nodded.

"His owners had a friend over who witnessed the whole thing. She was horrified, so she left their house, picked up Sanchez's bloody body from the yard, and brought him straight here. We called the police."

"You did?"

"Yes."

"What happened to the owners?"

"One went to jail and both were fined."

Mia sat in silence. She didn't know what to say. She looked back up at Sanchez who was now resting calmly watching them sit on the floor. Poor dog, she thought.

"Dogs deserve better."

"I agree. And so do children."

Mia looked at Mrs. C. confused.

"You see Mia, it's like some parents. They just don't know how to be a Mommy or a Daddy. They do the best they can, and that's great, but when the best they can do still hurts the little one they are in charge of, they need to be stopped. Stopped before it gets too bad."

Mia started thinking of her own parents. Did they need to be stopped? Would they go to jail or be fined if someone tried? She didn't want to look at Mrs. C. anymore. Mia felt uncomfortable.

"Sanchez needed to be loved. He needed to play, and cuddle, and all the stuff puppies are supposed to do. Just like you. You need those things too. I don't think you get them."

Mia started to protest but Mrs. C. stopped her.

"Don't worry, I'm not going to do anything tonight. I could be wrong and I know it, although I doubt it. You haven't told me everything yet. Not as much as I would like you to at least. But I wanted to tell you this. If you ever need more love and cuddles and play time, I am here. If you need things at home to stop, I am here. And if you can't tell me, then please tell someone. Anyone. You're going to need to let someone tame you one day. You're a good kid Mia. You don't deserve to be hurt."

Mia really wanted to get out of there now. She didn't like the conversation that was happening. She wasn't sure how they got from the dog to her but she didn't like it. She wanted to tell Mrs. C. that she wasn't getting hurt at home but that was a lie. She was getting called names, and getting hit, and being locked up. Just like Sanchez was. Could that be as wrong as what Sanchez's owners did to him? But Momma didn't mean all the things she did. She didn't want to hurt Mia. And Mia was a wimp. She cried easily. And that wasn't Momma's fault either. If she told Mrs. C., would she understand that? Momma said nobody would understand that she did it out of love. Momma said Mia would just look like a bigger idiot than what she already was. Mia didn't want Mrs. C. to think that way of her. Mia was so confused. She started to feel awful all over.

"I think I should get back home before it's too late."

Mrs. C. sighed quite heavily then agreed.

"Okay Mia, we can take you home."

Mia got up from the ground and gave Sanchez one more look. She no longer wanted to tame that stupid dog. It was its own fault that he got so hurt and Mia didn't want to be around anything that stupid anymore.

Mrs. C. pulled up to a curb a few doors down from Mia's house.

"Are you okay? You're pretty quiet."

"Yes."

Mia looked at her house for signs of movement. She saw nothing. All the lights were out. Mrs. C. noticed that too.

"Looks like they went to bed."

Mia agreed.

"That's a good sign. It means that they don't know you were out."

"Or they don't care."

"Or that." Mrs. C. said in an exhausted whisper.

"You sure you don't want me to come with you?"

"I'm sure."

Mia thanked Mrs. C. again for finding her at Frank's house, and for bringing her to the Animal Hospital. Mrs. C. said she was happy to and reached over and gave Mia a hug. Although still upset, Mia decided to nestle in a little like Sanchez did, and Mrs. C. responded by wrapping a second arm around her and kissing her head. Mia's thoughts were more jumbled than they had ever been before.

She said goodbye then grabbed her bike from the back of the truck. Mrs. C. said she was going to stay out on the street until she saw Mia's lights flicker on and off to say she was safely in her room.

Mia promised she would signal Mrs. C. when she was there. Before Mia walked away she paused and took one last look at Mrs. C. Quickly and quietly she shared, "The turkey dinner I'm making is for Frank!"

Mia ran off home.

Mia locked up her bike, noticing that Abby's bike was back and locked up too. She was still a little mad at her friend for leaving her.

Mia unlocked her door and quietly stepped inside. Daddy was sound asleep on the couch. Mia reached her room, and flickered her lights on and off to signal to Mrs. C. She looked out her window and waved as the black truck drove away. Slightly satisfied with her accomplishments, Mia reflected on her night. She and Abby had made it out alive, and she was no longer going to poison her family at Friday's dinner. And Mrs. C. had helped her. No one had ever stopped someone from hurting her before. On top of all this, Mia broke one of Momma's rules and got away with it. Mia couldn't help but feel good about that, about all of it. She had outsmarted both Momma and Frank. Mia was going to be okay. She wouldn't lose her leg like Sanchez. The last thing she thought of before going to sleep was Mrs. C. words: "you are a good kid Mia. You don't deserve to be hurt."

Chapter Twenty-Three

Mia got up early on Friday to take the turkey out of the sink. It had been sitting in there all night to thaw. She was pretty confident that she knew how to make sure the turkey didn't hurt anyone, so she set about cleaning it in the morning before anyone else was awake. She wanted to make sure she had time to reach all of the bird's crevices.

She took the turkey out of its wrapping, and filled the sink with warm water. She placed the turkey back into the sink and looked under the cupboard below for the dish soap. She held it up to the light. It said anti-bacterial. Perfect, she thought. Mia placed the soap on the counter and pulled out all of the bird's insides. She wasn't cooking those today although she had a recipe for them. She just couldn't manage it all on her own.

Once it was cleared out, she grabbed the bottle of dish soap and squeezed a little more than a quarter of the bottle on the outside of the bird, and another quarter of the bottle on the inside. She placed the soap back under the cupboard and began scrubbing. She washed the breast area, the wings, the legs, and the thighs. She then moved to the inside. She could feel the ribs of the turkey. It was an odd feeling. Feeling a bird from the inside out was not a pleasant experience. Soon she felt satisfied that all of the spots were washed well so she rinsed the soap off. She rinsed, and rinsed, and rinsed. Bubbles were everywhere. She laughed a bit at this. Bet this turkey never saw a bubble bath in its future?

It took Mia more time to rinse the soap off than it did to put it on and scrub it in. She hoped she got it all. She placed the turkey in the empty sink and cleared the soap from the one she was using. She pulled out the roasting pan, put the turkey in, and grabbed the stuffing from the fridge that she had prepared the night before. Confident she was doing it right, Mia filled the bird's middle until she could fill it no more. Momma showed her the day before where the pins were to keep the turkey's body closed. Momma said to make sure it was closed tight. Mia wouldn't want the stuffing coming out mid cook. It would be like the parishioners at Daddy's church when they were filled with the Holy Spirit. Their stuffing spewing out for all to see, whether they wanted it to happen or not. Momma said Daddy didn't mind it in his church, but wouldn't want it to happen in his kitchen. Mia agreed.

Mia placed the bird in the oven then washed her hands. That was in the book many times. MAKE SURE YOU WASH YOUR HANDS WELL WHEN HANDLING POULTRY. Mia used another quarter of the soap on her hands and the counter. No one was dying today.

Mia knew she had about four hours before she had to worry about prepping anything else for dinner. Daddy liked an early supper when they were big like this, but early only meant around 3 or 4 pm in the day. It was only 9 a.m. Mia decided she was going back to bed for a little while. Maybe read a book, or have a snooze. She took one last peek at the turkey, then shut off all of the lights and headed up to her room.

Mia looked up at the ceiling thinking about Mrs. C. She wondered if Mrs. C. only liked her because she was bored. She had three boys at home and no daughters. Did she just want a girl in her life? Mia didn't think that would be so bad, she wouldn't mind having Mrs. C. mother her from time to time. She wouldn't tell Momma that, though, but she didn't think she would have to. Mia wondered other things about Mrs. C.'s intentions as well. Like, did she just hate Momma and want to stick it to her? This would be a good way. If that were the case, Mia would have to stop telling her things so she didn't get revenge on Momma then leave when it was done. Mia didn't know what the truth was. She was really great at figuring people out but Mrs. C., she was a mystery. Why did she care? Mia has told some people what happens at home before, like teachers and friend's parents and such, but they didn't think it was a big deal. Nobody did. Mia didn't anymore either. She reminded herself that it wasn't that she had it so bad. She had a good life. Momma and Daddy did love her. She just wondered why they never said they loved her, rarely touched her in ways that made her feel okay, or never told her what she was doing right. Maybe that was Mia's fault. Maybe she didn't do anything right, so there was nothing to talk about. But other big people complimented Mia, like some teachers, some friends, some friend's parents; a lot of the same people who thought of her complaints as nothing. It was all so confusing. Was she a good girl or a bad girl? She couldn't figure the answer out on her own, and no one told her proper. At least not until recently.

The thing that confused Mia the most was how Momma and Daddy blamed Mia for things that Aunt Colleen and Mrs. C. said weren't her fault. Like Frank's lesson, or Momma's anger, or Daddy's illness. Who was right? Was Mia so bad or was Momma? Mia felt one way one minute, and another way the next. She decided to push it out of her mind for now. All this thinking was making Mia sleepy. Mia decided to take a nap.

Mia woke up to the sound of Momma giggling. It was the laugh that she used when she was trying to get Daddy to pay attention to her in the bedroom. Mia could hear them through the walls. Momma kept tickling Daddy and Daddy kept asking her to stop. He wasn't laughing at all. Momma tried and tried but Daddy would have none of it. Momma finally started yelling and told him that Jesus wasn't being fair to her. That if Jesus really cared about her and Daddy, he would tell Daddy to get his head on straight and start paying more attention to the wedding vows he said in the Lord's house of all places. Daddy yelled back that Momma shouldn't talk about Jesus that way. Momma didn't care. She slammed the door on Daddy then yelled through the wall that if Daddy weren't going to touch her then she would just have to touch herself. She and Jesus would have a good time in the bathtub. Mia didn't understand that at all but Daddy did. He yelled names at Momma that Mia didn't even know existed. Except the last one Mia kind of knew: betraying bitch. Daddy then stomped all the way down the stairs and out the front door. Silence only fell on the house for a few moments. Soon Mia heard the running of water in the bathroom and cries from Momma's heart. Daddy had made Momma sad. Mia left her room to go check on Momma. When she opened her door, she could see Momma curled up like a puddle on the bathroom floor. Sobbing into her nightgown.

"You okay, Momma?" Mia asked softly.

Momma turned around and looked up to see Mia standing in between the doorframe. Momma stared at Mia. Glared even. She took a deep breath in.

"Fuck you, you little bitch. You ruin everything. Everyone!" She screamed the last part so loud her voice cracked. She quieted down for the next words out of her mouth. "You are not loveable. You were supposed to die in that forest." Then Momma reached out and shut the bathroom door so Mia could see her no more. Mia was the next puddle of sobs to fall that morning.

Chapter Twenty-Four

Mia allowed herself to cry for a few minutes then she stopped. She wiped her tears away, cleared the snot from her nose with her pajama sleeve, and got up. She changed into some nice yet comfortable clothing, and brushed her hair. She looked in the mirror. She looked ready for the day. No one would know she had been crying.

Mia left her room and headed downstairs. It was time to check on the turkey. Mia opened the oven door to a wave of delicious smelling heat hitting her in the face. It smelled and looked amazing.

She went to the drawer and grabbed the baster. She opened the oven again and started drawing juices from the bottom of the pan up into the tube. She drizzled the liquid over the main part of the bird. As she moved around to the back she could see something bubble up from the leg. Mia didn't know what it was so she pulled the oven door open fully and slid the roaster out. By the leg, there were a few small soap bubbles forming. She must have forgotten to rinse a bit of soap off the bird.

Mia pulled out the roll of paper towel, pulled one off, and wiped as best as she could around the area. Mia thought she got it all. She placed the turkey back into the oven. She looked at the recipe book briefly, found the recipes she needed, and started preparing the rest of the food. Within 2 hours, she had the potatoes, turnip, peas, and carrots peeled and in pots waiting for her to start the stoves. She didn't need to do that until 2 pm. It was only 1.

Mia went upstairs to check on Momma. Momma had finished her bath and was getting dressed. She had stopped crying. Mia watched through Momma's slightly opened bedroom door. She loved watching her Momma get ready. She looked so beautiful when she felt good about herself and she always felt good when she was dressing up nice for someone. Tonight, it was for Frank.

Momma opened her armoire and looked at all of her options. She moved them all around, holding a few up, one at a time, to her body. She would rock back and forth in front of the mirror, forcing the dresses' bottom to sway with her. She did this for many items until she decided on a pretty navy-blue dress with pink flowers that showed a lot of Momma's skin when on. When she bought it, Daddy was very happy, although he said that she couldn't wear it to church. He made a joke about the assistant pastor not being able to handle it, and Momma laughed.

Once Momma had her dress on, she sat in front of her mirror to do her powder and her eyes. Momma looked in the mirror. Mia felt Momma's eyes hit hers.

"Well come in, child. No use peeking at me like a creeper."

Mia was happy to be invited in. She pushed the door open and sat on her parent's bed. She looked at her Momma in awe. Momma's hands, the body part Mia usually feared the most, seemed so gentle and small when she put on her makeup. Mia stared at them for the entire time Momma did her powder. Mia wished to be closer to her Momma.

Momma's movements were slow, and graceful. Powder hit the air in a great cloud of dust. The smell was a mix of musk and chalk, so clean, so gentle. Mia couldn't help but smile. Momma was so beautiful.

Mia inched closer to her Momma when it was time to put mascara on. Momma laughed and smiled at Mia's curiosity.

"Want to try some on?" Momma asked.

Mia couldn't believe her ears. Momma's attitude sure did change after her bath.

"Yes please."

Mia moved to the very corner of the bed. Momma moved closer to Mia too.

"Close your eyes."

Mia closed her eyes. The feel of the brush tickled Mia's face. She giggled. Momma giggled with her. Momma blew wind on her eyes when she was done. Mia didn't have to look in the mirror to know that she was almost as beautiful as Momma now.

"All done. Be careful not to rub your eyes or cry. Beauty has no power against sadness. You get one or the other."

Mia nodded. She wasn't going to cry today. Not now.

Momma picked up her perfume bottle to spray it on herself. Mia excused herself before she did. The smell would have taken Mia's happiness away.

Mia was just settling down at the table to kill the last half hour before she had to cook, when Aunt Colleen came through the door. She had a paper in her hand that she needed Momma or Daddy to fill out. Momma had to do it, since Daddy wasn't home from his tantrum yet. Momma came downstairs and sat with Mia and Aunt Colleen at the table.

"What are these forms?" Momma asked.

"They are for Mia to go to camp. Permission forms."

Momma looked up at her curiously. "How come you have them?'

Aunt Colleen explained that because she paid for Mia to go to the camp that they figured she would be able to get them to Momma and Daddy easiest. So, when the writing camp called, Aunt Colleen said she would go pick them up and bring them to the house. That was what she was doing now. She said she was going to bring them back signed on Monday. Momma said okay, she looked at the papers carefully, then signed on all of the lines she needed to. Mia thanked Momma with a hug. Momma even sort of hugged her back.

"Want to stay for dinner?" Mia asked Aunt Colleen.

"I'm not sure we have enough Mia. It isn't nice to invite someone over to dinner then not feed them. You should have checked first."

"It's okay, Lee-Ann. I don't think I could anyway. Thanks for the offer though, Mia."

Mia tried to hide her look of disappointment from both ladies. She had hoped that Aunt Colleen would stay so that she could eat at the table and not have to focus on Frank. Mia knew she could go up to her room if she wanted, and she liked that idea at first, but now that today was here, she was kind of hoping to stay downstairs with everyone else. It was less lonely. With Aunt Colleen at the table, she could have done that. But with her leaving, Mia knew she probably would have to eat alone upstairs.

Momma got up from the table and went to the couch. She picked up a Woman's Day magazine that she had been reading, opened it to the page she left off on, and immersed herself into the story. Mia went into the kitchen, with Aunt Colleen in tow.

"Are you cooking dinner tonight?" Aunt Colleen asked surprised.

"Uh, huh. I even put the turkey on myself."

Aunt Colleen didn't say anything for a bit. Mia thought she must have been too impressed for words. Aunt Colleen lost her words sometimes. Mia filled in the silence by telling Aunt Colleen everything she planned to cook, and how she knew how to cook it. She showed her Momma's recipe book.

They were just discussing how she didn't need a recipe for mashed potatoes when the door to the house opened. Mia could hear the sound of her Daddy's shoes coming through, but she wasn't sure of the other set coming in with him. Not until she heard Frank's voice. Mia bowed her head. Although she feared him less, she still didn't like being around him. She couldn't look at him without seeing his penis in her mind. And that made her stomach upset.

Daddy rounded the corner of the entrance way with Frank in tow, hugged his sister hello and introduced him to his friend. It took a moment for Aunt Colleen to register who Frank was, but once she did, Mia thought she could have knocked her over with a feather. Aunt Colleen's mouth hung wide open. Aunt Colleen refused to shake his hand. Daddy was unimpressed. Mia was sure he was about to say something to Aunt Colleen about it, but Momma interrupted before he could.

"Well hello Frank!" Momma said. She ignored Daddy, just walked straight over to Frank and helped him with his sports coat.

"How are you today?" Momma hung it up. Aunt Colleen was still watching in anger. Momma finished with the coat then walked back over to Frank. She smoothed his shirt with her hands and giggled.

"You're looking particularly handsome tonight, Frank." Momma's tone was concerned. "How are you doing?"

"I'm okay," he answered. Momma walked him to the living room, arm in arm, in front of Daddy. Daddy just watched. He joined them after a few moments.

Aunt Colleen looked over at Mia with big eyes.

"Momma said she wanted to cook him one last nice meal in case he goes to jail on Monday," were the only words Mia could find to explain.

"Excuse me?"

Momma had said people wouldn't understand them still loving Frank, especially people who don't know Jesus's work yet. So, Mia wasn't surprised that Aunt Colleen was struggling with understanding. Mia didn't really understand herself, and she knew Jesus. Well, not personally, but in her heart. Daddy said that counted.

Aunt Colleen sat down on the floor and leaned against the cupboard. Mia sat down beside her. "What is your father thinking, Mia?"

Mia shrugged.

"I can't believe they are asking you to sit down to dinner with that man after what he did. And to cook for him? *You* cook for that freak! That makes no sense. No sense at all."

"It's okay. I did him wrong. I need to fix it. I'm sending him to jail."

Aunt Colleen looked Mia in the eye and whispered in a strong yet quiet voice.

"Stop saying that! He did wrong, not you. You did nothing. He is a perverted freak that should be in jail. You aren't sending him there, he sent himself there. You understand that?"

Mia didn't but she nodded like she did. Aunt Colleen seemed quite sure of herself and Mia didn't want to argue with that kind of confidence.

"Stay here a moment." Aunt Colleen got up and went into the living room to where the other adults were. Mia stayed real still so she could hear. She was worried about what Aunt Colleen was going to do. But all Aunt Colleen said to Momma was "I would like to stay for dinner after all, Lee-Ann, if that's okay?"

Mia didn't hear Momma's reply, but she must have given one. Aunt Colleen entered the kitchen a few moments later and sat back down on the floor.

"Are you staying for dinner?" Mia asked.

"Yes."

Silence.

"You okay?" Mia asked. She hated when people lost their words.

The doorbell rang. Aunt Colleen went to answer the door. Before she rounded the corner, she looked at Mia.

"I'm okay. I just wish I had more balls to stand up to your mother and father."

"He's my Daddy. Jesus is my Father. And you do stand up to them. But why would you have to today?" Aunt Colleen rolled her eyes then headed to the door. Mia thought she was getting it. People didn't think Frank should be around her, yet Momma and Daddy did. Something was wrong about them wanting that but she couldn't understand what. Mia was uncomfortable around Frank, and up until recently she felt nervous around him, but that was her fault. Why did all of the people she liked see it differently? Why didn't Momma and Daddy see it the way they did? Adults were so messed up.

Aunt Colleen returned to the kitchen with Mrs. C. behind her.

"Someone is here to see your daddy. Just a minute, baby." Aunt Colleen put up her one-minute finger as she said that, and walked Mrs. C. to the living room where Daddy was. Mrs. C. winked at Mia as she walked by. Aunt Colleen returned moments later.

"Mia, he shouldn't be here. Besides, he is not supposed to be within 500 feet of you. Even the law knows he shouldn't be here."

Mia looked to the living room. Why was Mrs. C. here? Was she telling Momma and Daddy about their conversation? About going to Frank's trailer? Mia was concerned.

"But, if I can't stop them, and neither can you, then I will stay here with you. We will do it together," Aunt Colleen added.

Mia wrapped herself around Aunt Colleen's arm. They sat there for a few moments. Quiet. Interrupted only by the cries of Mrs. C. coming from the living room.

Mia looked in fear. What happened to Mrs. C? Did Momma hurt her?

Mia and Aunt Colleen got up and walked closer. Mrs. C. was crying into Daddy's shoulder.

"I'm sorry Pastor Pratt. I didn't know where to go and the good Lord told me to come here. To you! That you would give me comfort. I just need to be in the presence of the Lords' followers. Please tell me I can stay for a while."

"Sure," Daddy replied. He looked to Momma pleading with her to understand. She just shook her head. "There, there Annie. I'm here. We're all here. Stay as long as you need. In fact, Mia is cooking us a lovely dinner tonight. Please stay for it."

Momma stayed silent.

"If that's okay, I would love to. Thank you, Pastor Pratt. Thank you!"

Daddy nodded. He looked at Momma. She glared at him.

"I'll go help Mia in the kitchen. Then I'm not in the way of your company and at least I'm helping. The Lord didn't tell me to come here and do nothing. He just said to come here. Thank you again."

Mrs. C. looked at Momma and smiled. "Thanks to you too, Lee-Ann. I'll just be in there with your daughter. Making sure everything is safe in the kitchen." When Mrs. C. turned around, her tears were gone.

Mrs. C. smiled at Mia. Mia didn't know what was happening. Aunt Colleen did. As they walked through the dining room toward the kitchen, Aunt Colleen whispered.

"I'm Colleen. I don't know who you are but I think you may be my new best friend."

Mrs. C. reached out her hand.

"My name is Annie. Annie Carrington. Mia has talked about you. We are here for the same thing I think."

Mia looked back and forth between Aunt Colleen and Mrs. C. They seemed to like each other.

"For Mia?"

"For Mia.

Returning to the kitchen, Aunt Colleen was the first to look around and gasp.

"Mia, are those soap bubbles coming from your oven?"

Chapter Twenty-Five

Mia ran to the oven. What was happening? There were bubbles on all edges of the oven door. Big rainbow-coloured bubbles. Bubbles everywhere.

"Oh, no!" Mia cried.

"What the hell?" Aunt Colleen asked.

"It's from the dish soap," Mia tried to explain as she opened the oven door. A flood of bubbles flew out of the heated box and danced all around her feet. Mia tried stomping them out as they landed.

"Dish soap? From the pan or the oven? I don't understand."

"From the turkey!"

"The turkey?" Mrs. C. was confused too.

Mia grabbed a cloth from the counter and started wiping quickly.

"Oh, Momma's going to be so mad."

Aunt Colleen and Mrs. C. seemed frozen still but Mia had no time to explain further.

"Momma's going to kill me!" Mia gave both ladies a pleading look. "Please help me?"

Lucky for Mia, they didn't ask any more questions. They grabbed a cloth and started wiping. The three worked hard at cleaning the mess, and they almost got away with it. They would have, if Momma hadn't decided that that was the time she needed to go into the kitchen and give Mrs. C. the what for.

"What in Jesus's name is going on in here?" Momma cried from the doorway. She rushed over to the oven to look. She slammed her fist against the stovetop. "The turkey!" Momma stood up and faced Mia. "Mia Elizabeth Pratt!"

Mia backed up against the wall. Aunt Colleen and Mrs. C. stepped between Momma and Mia.

"Now, Lee-Ann, take it easy." Aunt Colleen spoke first. She must have noticed Momma's veins popping out of her forehead as well.

"Don't you tell me to take it easy. I paid good money for that turkey and now it is ruined. Ruined!" Momma ripped the cloth out of Mrs. C.'s hand and started wiping the bubbles up. "This is awful, just awful."

Mia couldn't do anything but watch. Mrs. C. stood over with Mia, protecting her from the oven and from Momma.

Momma tried, with Aunt Colleen's help, for several minutes to clean the turkey up. She didn't give up until she heard the answer to her question of what in God's name made all of the bubbles. Said that even if she did get all of the bubbles to go away, the turkey would still taste like soap. Mia tried to tell Momma how very sorry she was but Momma didn't want to hear it. Mia should have known better. Aunt Colleen suggested that maybe leaving a 10-year old to cook a turkey dinner all by herself may not have been a good idea, but Momma didn't want to hear that either. Momma stood and stared for a moment. Mia saw Momma's thinking face on. Momma was good at solving problems. Mia looked to Aunt Colleen for some advice. Aunt Colleen just shrugged. So did Mrs. C.

"Okay, you have peas, turnips, carrots, and potatoes to cook. The turkey and stuffing aren't edible. There are pork chops in the freezer, cook those. We will eat it with the rest of the stuff. Colleen, can you go to the basement and grab the pork out of the big freezer?"

Aunt Colleen agreed right away and headed downstairs.

Once she was gone, Momma leaned in towards Mia. "I will never forgive you for this. You really do ruin everything child. But we have company so I will deal with this, with you, later. How could you do this to me, Mia? It is such an important night for Frank. Understand?"

Mia nodded.

"Whoa!" Mrs. C. interjected. She grabbed Mia by the arm and slid her behind her body as much as possible.

"If I were you, I would be very afraid." Momma said to Mia and Mrs. C.

Mia was afraid. Afraid for so many reasons. Momma didn't have to tell her to be. She could see in Momma's eyes that this was different than the other times she messed up. Momma was mad and Mia was going to pay. Mia knew Aunt Colleen and Mrs. C. weren't able to help her this time. She even thought this was bigger than something Jesus could help with.

The pork chops and vegetables were cooking nicely and set so that dinner could be served at 4 pm. Once Momma left the kitchen, Mia asked Mrs. C. why she was there and if she was okay from her crying earlier.

"I had a feeling that I needed to be here. I'm glad I came. What the hell is he doing here? Your parents are really a piece of work."

Mia put her head down and walked to the sink.

"Mia, I can't help you if you don't tell me what is going on."

Mia wanted to respond two ways. First, she wanted to tell Mrs. C. everything. But second, she wanted to just nod and not have a conversation at all. She wished Mrs. C. didn't need Mia to say the words. The less Mrs. C. knew, the safer she was. The safer Mia was as well.

"Are you okay? You were crying with Daddy?" Mia changed the subject.

Mrs. C. said she was. She knew she needed something to make Daddy say yes to her staying.

"I don't know what to do here, kid. This is new territory for me. I'm just going with my gut. Something isn't right in this house."

Aunt Colleen, who had been listening to this conversation the whole time, agreed with Mrs. C.

"I'm lost on what to do too."

The two ladies stood close to Mia.

"Do they hit you Mia? Beat you? I don't want them to but if you told me they did then I have something I can use to help you. My hands feel tied."

Mia knew what that meant. If Mia said yes, they would call the police. The police would either do nothing as they had before, making Momma and Daddy angrier with Mia, or they would pull her out of the house and make her live with strangers. That hadn't happened yet, but it did to her friend George at school.

Mia asked if the conversation could stop for the evening. Both Aunt Colleen and Mrs. C. agreed that it could as long as Mia agreed to talk about it on another night. Mia said she would. They moved on, making sure the dinner was ready and the table was made.

Momma gave Aunt Colleen her usual seat at one end of the table, and sat beside Frank instead. Mia was happy that she wasn't the one that had to sit beside him. Mrs. C. sat on the other side of Mia, between her and Daddy. The talk over dinner was a lot about church and the Holy Spirit. Daddy and Frank also talked a lot about people from Bible retreat. Daddy talked about Mr. Hansford, and how some of the other men at church saw his car at the racetrack many days of the week. Daddy wondered if he wasn't maybe wandering from his faith a little. Aunt Colleen asked why it wasn't okay for someone to love God and horseracing at the same time. Daddy just laughed it off and said that she wouldn't understand until she lived a life of Christ. Aunt Colleen said she didn't want a life with Him if Jesus wouldn't help her out with her prayers when she went to the track. Mrs. C. found that funny. She told Daddy that she agreed with Aunt Colleen. She didn't understand why going to the racetrack every now and again wasn't okay with God. Daddy said that it just wasn't and that they would have to trust him on that.

Mia tried to eat as much as she could, but she wasn't that hungry. Seeing Frank's face right in front of her as she put potatoes and turnip in her mouth made her not want to eat it. Her stomach was angry again. Mia pushed her food around her plate from side to side, trying to place it in an order that looked like she had been putting a lot of it in her belly. She tried many different positions for the food but none of it really worked. Momma and Daddy didn't seem to be paying attention to her anyway. Momma was mostly focused on Frank. In fact, no one said a word to Mia until Mia's elbow knocked her spoon onto the floor and Aunt Colleen told her that she needed to pick it up. Mia got off her chair and reached under the table to grab it. She looked up at everyone's legs. Momma's hand was on Frank's thigh, squeezing it. Frank's legs jumped when Momma squeezed tighter. Mia found it very odd.

"What are you doing down there?" Daddy asked. Mia bumped her head on the table. Daddy's voice startled her. His voice must have startled Momma too, because as soon as he spoke, Momma removed her hand from Frank's leg.

Mia returned to the table. "I dropped my spoon."

Momma gave Mia a look of concern but then focused back on her company. Aunt Colleen reached over and touched Mia's arm. "You okay?"

Mia nodded. She went back to pushing her food around her plate.

The food went rather quickly during dinner. Everyone was real hungry. As soon as the last person dropped their fork to show they were done, Mia got up and collected plates and brought them into the kitchen. Aunt Colleen helped her with the bowls of leftover food. There wasn't much. A few spoonfuls of turnip, and half a bowl of peas was all that remained. Mia cleared the plates and put them in the sink to soak. The peas and turnips she left on the counter. The turkey went straight into the garbage.

Mia went in and wiped the table off while Momma, Daddy, Frank, Mrs. C., and Aunt Colleen sat at the table talking. Mia didn't think Aunt Colleen looked particularly interested in what they were saying, because she kept looking at her watch to see the time.

The adults talked for some more time before Daddy excused himself to the washroom. Aunt Colleen and Mrs. C. returned to the kitchen, leaving Momma and Frank alone in the dining room.

"Need some help with the dishes?"

"Sure," Mia answered.

The ladies rolled up their sleeves and warmed up the water in the sink. Mrs. C. pulled out the dish soap and poured some into the running water. Aunt Colleen giggled at the sight of the soap.

"Is this the soap you used?"

Mia nodded.

"You must have used a lot?"

Mia nodded again, laughing a little this time as well.

"It was full when I started cleaning. I didn't know how much to use."

Aunt Colleen's eyes popped. "Full?" She busted out in a fit of laughter. Mrs. C. joined her. Their laugh was so strong that Mia couldn't help but join in. Aunt Colleen's eyes watered. She even had to cross her legs so she wouldn't pee herself.

"You crack me up, kiddo."

Mia, still laughing slightly, just shrugged.

Momma called for Mia to bring her wine and glasses. Mia did so. Daddy still hadn't returned from the bathroom. Mia put a glass in front of Momma and Frank, and one near Daddy's empty chair.

"Need me to pour?"

Momma gave Mia a strange look. "Of course, I do. Seriously child."

Mia realized it was a silly question. Momma never poured her own wine, besides, her hand was back onto Frank's leg again and wine needed two hands to be poured. At least for Mia it did.

As Mia finished pouring Daddy's glass, Frank looked to Momma with a serious look.

"I don't think this is a good idea, Lee-Ann."

"Oh, Frank," Momma laughed. "It's just a little red wine."

"That's not what I meant."

"Prison can get awfully lonely, Frank."

"Lee-Ann! We can't."

Momma paid no more attention to what Frank was saying. She turned her head and started drinking from her glass. She must have squeezed Frank's leg really hard at that point, because he jumped up with a loud ouch that went from his mouth to the ceiling.

"Damn it, Lee-Ann, stop it!"

Momma didn't like to be spoken to in that tone, Mia knew that for certain. Momma looked at Frank with a terrible pause.

"Excuse me? How dare you." Momma threw her wine right at Frank.

Mia stepped back to the entranceway. Daddy walked in from the other side.

"What's going on in here? Frank, you're wet!"

Momma had no words. Frank spoke some for her.

"Your wife seems to have been a little clumsy, and spilt her wine all over my lap. Just an accident really, no big deal." He looked over at Momma before continuing. "It's probably best I head home now and change. Do you mind giving me a lift back, Richard? I can show you that new used washer and dryer I just acquired at the same time. If you're interested, it's yours."

Daddy agreed to do so.

The adults went into the kitchen to say their goodbyes. Aunt Colleen claimed that she would have to leave too. She bent down and whispered to Mia, asking if she was okay now that Frank was leaving. Mia said she was.

Momma and Frank had a near silent goodbye. He thanked her for the meal then walked out the door. She just nodded. Aunt Colleen gave hugs then left as well. Momma went back to her wine. Mrs. C. looked at Mia who was still in the kitchen.

"I'm going to head out too. Just for the record, Frank wasn't who I was worried about. It's your momma that scares me. Can I leave you here alone with her?"

Mia nodded.

"Why am I asking you this? You're going to tell me yes no matter what, aren't you?"

Mia stayed silent.

"What do I do Mia?"

"You can leave."

"Are you just saying that?"

Mia shook her head. Mrs. C. stepped back.

"I don't mean this in any way that means ill towards you, but I don't trust what you are saying to me right now. Your Momma looks quite sad, and your Daddy seemed upset when he left. I have a feeling that they hurt you more than you are telling me."

Mia thought about that for a moment. Thought about what Mrs. C. was saying. How she knew so well what was going on. Except for the part about Daddy. He didn't hurt Mia that much. He only hit her a few times and he hit with an open hand. Open hand hits only sting for a few moments. Momma hurt. She used her fists. But Mia didn't want anyone else to get it tonight. So, she needed Mrs. C. to go. It wasn't safe for her.

"I'm okay tonight. I promise." Mia lied.

Mrs. C. looked at Mia for a moment then agreed.

"You know where to find me if that changes. I'll be here in a heartbeat."

Mia nodded.

Moments later, it was just Momma and Mia, alone in the house. Mia thought about Aunt Colleen, and Mrs. C. and how maybe she shouldn't have told them it was okay to leave. Mia, looked at Momma. She was afraid of her. But Momma surprised her. She didn't yell, she didn't give Mia a look of hate, nor did she even start to cry. Momma just sat down at the dining room table and drank Frank's glass of wine. Then she drank Daddy's glass.

And when that was empty, she asked Mia to pour her some more. Before long, Momma had the bottle nearly done.

Mia sat on the living room couch and watched Momma through the doorway for some time, waiting for Momma to crack. But she didn't. She did start laughing around her 5th glass though, and that made Mia a lot more comfortable. Deciding it was safe to go upstairs, Mia stood up.

"Goodnight, Momma."

Momma turned her head from her wine for the first time since she sat down.

"What's good about it, Mia dear?" Momma asked so politely that it caught Mia off guard. Mia didn't have an answer for her Momma that she thought Momma would accept so she just stood still and silent.

"Eh? What was so good about this evening?" Still polite.

Mia didn't know if Momma was messing with her or not. Mia just shrugged.

"Well shrugging's not an answer child. You answer my question."

Mia panicked.

"Some things went okay. Frank enjoyed his dinner, Daddy had fun. And even Aunt Colleen and Mrs. C. liked it."

Momma snorted out of her nose then took another sip of wine.

"Some things went okay," Momma said in a mocking voice. She wiped her mouth with the back of her hand. "Nothing went okay! The turkey was ruined, the pork chops were dry, and your Daddy talked only about church. And don't get me started on your nosey Aunt Colleen and new friend Annie, who weren't even invited to be here." Momma wasn't being polite anymore.

"Mrs. C. came to see Daddy."

"If you believe that, you're dumber than I thought."

"I invited Aunt Colleen."

Mia knew as soon as she said it that, that was the wrong thing to say. Momma's face went red and her lips squeezed together real tight.

"No one asked you to invite anyone!" Momma yelled. "You're a child. It's not your place to invite someone to a dinner I paid for. And that Colleen, she is so rude to your Momma, and you don't care. Don't care at all about my feelings. You're so selfish."

Momma was right about Mia not being old enough to invite company to stay.

"I'm sorry Momma."

Momma stared at Mia. She drank down the last half of her glass of wine in one swallow then poured what was left of the bottle in her glass. The air went out of Momma in one loud sigh.

"You should be."

Momma looked at the table then back up to Mia. She had a big smile that Mia couldn't understand.

"Come here, my baby."

Mia didn't want to. She was confused by Momma's change in mood. First, she was happy, then angry, and now happy again.

"I said come here, Mia."

Mia did as she was told. Momma tapped her hand on her knee and told Mia to sit down on her lap. Mia hesitated but did so. Momma never wanted Mia that close to her.

Momma started to rub Mia's back. She rested her head against Mia's arm and started to hum. Momma hummed the first three verses of her favourite church song, while she rocked them both back and forth. By the second verse, Mia was more relaxed in her Momma's arms. She even began to smile as well. Momma finished the song then drank some more wine to wet her throat again. Momma took one finger and slowly rolled it down Mia's back.

"Tell me Mia, why is your Momma so unattractive?' Momma's voice was drunk.

"You're not unattractive, Momma!" Mia exclaimed in surprise.

"Well, you see, I must be. Your Daddy don't wanna do his husbandly duties with your Momma no more, and Frank doesn't either. No man wants your Momma, Mia. And well, since they seem to both like you very much, they both think you're attractive, I was wondering if you could tell me what you got, that your Momma don't have?"

Mia didn't really understand the question. "What do you mean Momma?"

Momma reached up and slid the hair from Mia's face back behind her ear. Momma looked into Mia's eyes softly. Mia felt uncomfortable. She wanted to break the look with Momma but couldn't. Momma put a finger up to Mia's lips and gently pulled her bottom lip down.

"Why does Frank want to show you how to make babies, but doesn't want to show Momma? Do you think you're prettier than your Momma, Mia?"

Mia shook her head. "No Momma. I'm not pretty."

Momma smiled at Mia, still not breaking the stare. Mia continued to talk. She didn't know what else to do.

"You already know how to make babies, Momma. You made me."

Momma laughed at what Mia said. Mia didn't realize she was making a joke. She laughed too, so Momma didn't know that Mia didn't get her own comedy. Momma stopped laughing abruptly, grabbed Mia by the back of the hair, and kissed her on the lips. Momma took a deep breath in through her nose, pulling Mia's hair harder from the back. Mia didn't like the feeling. Mia wanted it to stop. But she couldn't tell Momma that, even if her lips were free. Momma's lips tasted like alcohol.

Momma pulled away, paused, made her eyes real big then kissed her again. Mia wanted to cry but she held it in like the good girl that she was.

Momma stopped the second kiss. She pushed Mia off her lap and onto the floor. Momma had her angry face on.

"I don't get it. Why does he want you, and not me?" Momma didn't seem to need an answer for her question, so Mia didn't give her one. Mia wanted to get up but didn't know if she was allowed to. Instead, she crawled a few feet away from Momma. Momma started talking again, but not to anyone in particular.

"A woman has needs. A woman has desires. Daddy said his vows before our Lord, and promised to take care of those needs. Your Daddy is a hypocrite, Mia. He's a fucking hypocrite, not as perfect as you think he is. Nope, not at all. I need certain desires filled. And if he doesn't, then Momma needs to go elsewhere. You know what I'm talking about, Mia?"

Mia knew enough to nod and that's it.

"So, Momma tried going to Frank. He seems to not have any concern over who it is that he tries to get into bed. But he wanted you, pfft! He didn't want me!"

Mia was trying hard to follow what Momma was saying, but she couldn't.

"Is it Momma's fault, Mia?"

Mia shook her head. She knew that answer as well. Nothing was ever to be Momma's fault. Mia crawled back a few more steps. Momma saw her do it and shook her head back and forth. She made a t'sking sound with her mouth. Momma stood up, walked over until she was standing above Mia.

"You'll have to do."

Mia didn't like the look on Momma's face. Mia scrambled quickly to get out of the room but Momma used her feet to stop her. Mia tried again. Momma reached down and grabbed Mia by the ankle and dragged her into the kitchen.

"That hurts Momma," Mia cried. Momma didn't seem to hear her.

"Momma, stop!"

Without stopping, Momma dragged Mia through the front entrance and toward the front door. Mia's shirt had lifted up and her back was starting to feel the burn of the floor. Was Momma going to throw Mia outside? Mia was hoping she would. The one thing that wasn't outside, that was inside, was Momma. And Mia needed away from her. But Momma just locked the door and dragged Mia back to the kitchen.

"Momma, what are you doing?" Mia screamed. She never screamed at Momma but she was feeling like she had to. Momma wasn't responding to Mia's talking voice. Mia's back felt like it was on fire.

"Momma, stop!"

"Stop screaming child. The neighbours are going to hear."

Mia always listened to Momma, but not this time. Momma was different. Momma was not Momma. Mia screamed louder, hoping maybe the neighbours would hear.

"I said shut up!" Momma held Mia's ankle tighter. Mia couldn't break free. She wiggled and wiggled but all that did was cause her head to hit the floor several times. Momma looked around the kitchen. She opened the knife drawer but didn't find what she was looking for.

"Where is the tape?" Momma said to herself. Mia knew where it was but wasn't about to tell.

Momma looked over at the counter. She picked up the bowl of peas and smelt them. Momma laughed.

"These will do."

She took the bowl and dragged Mia back to the dining room. Momma placed the bowl of peas on the floor. She dropped down to her knees.

"What are you going to do Momma?"

"If I let you go, will you stay still?"

Mia nodded. She just wanted her leg free. She didn't want to get it cut off like Sanchez needed his off.

"What are you going to do Momma?" Mia asked again. Momma didn't answer either time.

Momma let her ankle go but Mia was still trapped. Momma crawled on top of Mia, full body, and swayed her weight from side to side. Mia started to cry. It hurt. Her body and her heart burned deep inside.

Momma reached over and grabbed a handful of peas.

"Open up."

"Open up wha…" Just as Mia said the words, Momma shoved the entire handful of peas in Mia's mouth. Then another handful, and one more after that. Momma was quick. Mia couldn't breathe through her mouth.

"Now maybe you will shut up?" Momma started swaying harder on top of Mia. Mia spit out a few peas but Momma placed her hand tightly over Mia's lips to stop the majority from coming out. Momma's hands were no longer the beauty they were to Mia that morning. Now they were cold and heartless looking. Mia couldn't open her mouth. Momma grabbed the kitchen table leg with her other hand. Her grip on the table seemed to make her sway harder and faster. Mia flinched, causing some peas to trickle down her throat. Mia was going to vomit.

Feeling desperate to breathe, Mia reached up with her only free hand and scratch Momma's eyes but Mia's nails were too short to do anything substantial. They just rubbed Momma's face. Momma let go of the table leg long enough to force Mia's free arm under Mia's back with her other trapped one. The pain in Mia's spine increased.

"Now when you are done chewing all of those lovely peas baby, this will be over, and there will be no need to scream. You understand, sweetheart? This won't take long. Just a little special time with Momma."

Mia nodded frantically. Taking deep breaths in and out of her nose as tears escaped her eyes without permission.

Momma pulled Mia's pants down, then lifted up the bottom of her dress. Mia had no fight in her to stop it.

"If you were good enough for Frank, then you are good enough for your Momma. Be good for me like you were for him."

More peas trickled down her throat. Momma rocked harder now. The pain was almost unbearable. Momma placed her head down beside Mia's. She could hear Momma breathing heavy into her ear. Momma's pelvis hit Mia's pelvis over and over again. Momma began to moan when her pelvis became wet. Mia concentrated hard on chewing up all those peas as fast as she could. She wanted this to be done. But there was no room in her mouth to chew and the more she tried, the more the peas fell down her throat instead. Mia started to slip into unconsciousness. The last thing she heard before the room went dark was Momma scream to God, and Mia together. "Oh, God, thank you Mia, thank you for wanting your Momma to be happy."

Chapter Twenty-Six

It was Monday. Court day. The day Mia had been dreading all weekend. Momma was going to be so sad to see Frank go to jail, if that was what happened.

Mia sat in the lawyer's office waiting for Momma to come out of the bathroom. They were early for their pre-court appointment so Momma decided to freshen up instead of sitting on one of the hard, brown chairs. Momma said the chairs were slightly more comfortable than sitting on a hot fire rock from hell, and nothing else. She said her bottom wouldn't be happy with her if she sat in one for the half hour they had left to wait. She still had to sit in the God-awful court benches all afternoon. Momma said her butt would be halfway home, without her, by dinner, if she sat in the hard, brown chairs as well, now.

Mia found it awful to sit on them too, but she did it anyway. Her ankle was pretty bruised and that made standing hard. Unfortunately, her back was also still sore from Friday night. It had been sore all weekend. She'd had to lie on her belly just to be able to sleep. She couldn't see her skin behind her, but she was sure it was red and angry. But in the end, a sore back was a lot easier to deal with than a busted ankle. Mia couldn't even put her good shoe on all the way that morning, since her ankle decided to thicken up like a watermelon. Mia wanted to get a doctor to check it out but Momma told Mia that if they did, they would have to lie to the doctor, and that wouldn't help Mia get into Heaven. Momma said people can't lie at hospitals on account of all their cameras and recorders.

Mia thought back to what had happened on Friday. She was so thankful for Daddy to have pulled the peas out of her mouth as quickly as he did. He popped one finger into her mouth and scooped them all out. At least that was what Mia was told. Truth be said, she didn't remember it that well at all. She remembered Daddy calling her name. "Mia, Mia!" He said it over and over again until she opened her eyes. Then when Daddy sat her up, she vomited on his good pants. Not just a little either, but a lot. There were green mushy peas all over his clothes. Mia apologized but Daddy said he didn't mind. That he was just so happy that she was okay, and that her little game of 'shove as many peas into her mouth as she could' didn't get her seeing Jesus faster than Daddy was ready for her to see him.

Mia didn't know that game, or why Daddy had said that she played it, so she asked him. Momma interrupted his explanation with tears, saying that Mia should have stopped the game when Momma asked her too. That Momma was so scared for Mia. And how thankful Momma was that Daddy came home before Mia stopped breathing forever.

Once Mia was done vomiting, Momma sent Daddy upstairs to go clean himself up. She waited until Daddy left the room before she told Mia that she would have to not tell Daddy what happened because it would make him very sad to think that a little 10-year old good for nothing girl had to do a job that he was meant to do. Momma reminded Mia that Daddy just saved her life, and that it would be a terrible blow to him to think that Mia was trying to replace him in his role in the family. She said Daddy might even not want Mia around anymore. He might kick Momma and Mia out of the house forever, and they would have to live alone in a shack, by themselves. Mia didn't want to hurt her Daddy, and even more, she didn't want to live alone with Momma. She loved her Momma, but sometimes, loving her hurt an awful lot.

Momma made Mia say thank you to her for her quick thinking in getting Mia's pants pulled back up before Daddy saw them down.

Mia was grateful that Daddy never saw her back either. She didn't know what to tell him if he did. It was a good thing for Mia, that Daddies sometimes got too busy to pay attention. Mia spent the rest of the weekend hobbling around, making dinners to freeze so Momma and Daddy could eat while she was away at writing camp. Making several servings of shepherd's pie, spaghetti sauce, and lasagna took up most of her weekend, so Mia had no time to answer any of Daddy's questions, if he thought of any to ask.

The big wooden door to the lawyer's meeting room opened up, bringing Mia back to Monday. She saw Mrs. Walsh walk out with another man who looked very lawyer like too. He was just as tall as Mrs. Walsh, and shared her short haircut, but he had brown skin instead of white. Mrs. Walsh thanked him for something, shook his hand, and said goodbye. She smiled and looked over at Mia.

"Where's your mom?"

Momma was still in the bathroom Mia explained. Mrs. Walsh nodded and invited Mia into her meeting room. Mia wasn't sure if she should go in without Momma, or go check on her in the bathroom. She looked at Mrs. Walsh, then at the ladies' room door.

"Momma's been in there a long time."

Mrs. Walsh gave Mia a look of concern, and then smiled.

"I'm sure everything is okay, but why don't I go and check on her just in case?"

Mia agreed that that was a good idea. She got up and limped into the meeting room to wait for Momma and Mrs. Walsh to return.

The meeting room was full of books, shelves and shelves of them. They started near the floor and went all the way up to the ceiling. There was even a small ladder that Mia guessed was used to reach the really high ones. The books looked like encyclopedias. Mia thought about Frank's shelves of books. Boy would he be jealous of this collection, she thought.

Mia walked to the wall on the far right. She took her pointer finger and rubbed it along the spines of all the books on the middle shelf. The books felt smart. They smelled old. Wise she thought. Smart and old always meant wise too. She was just about to pull a book out to look at it, when Momma and Mrs. Walsh came into the room. Mrs. Walsh was helping Momma. Momma looked like she had been crying. Momma sat down with Mrs. Walsh's assistance.

"Mia, can you come have a seat with us?" Mrs. Walsh asked. Mia obeyed and sat beside her Momma. Mrs. Walsh continued talking. "I was just telling your mom that we have some good news. Looks like you won't need to be going into the courtroom at all this afternoon. Your mom was so happy, she started to cry."

Mia looked over at Momma, she was crying again. Mrs. Walsh spoke directly to Mia.

"I just had a meeting with a gentleman named Mr. Sanderson. That was the gentleman you saw leaving my office. You remember him?"

Mia nodded but didn't speak.

"Well, he is Frank's lawyer. Frank pleaded guilty this morning. He doesn't want to go to court. So, this means that you are able to go home. Does that sound good Mia?"

Mia nodded again. No court? What did that mean for Frank, and why did Momma cry harder when Mrs. Walsh said the word guilty? Mia wasn't sure if she could ask or not.

She looked at Mrs. Walsh hoping she would read her mind, but she didn't.

"We just have to sign a few papers, then that's it. I'll get in touch with you Mrs. Pratt, by the end of the day, and let you know what the ruling is."

Momma was too upset to speak. Mia had questions. What was a ruling?

"Mrs. Pratt, do you wish to have a moment alone? I can take Mia for a walk?"

Momma told her that she would like that very much, so Mrs. Walsh stood up, waved Mia to follow her, and the two walked out of the meeting room together. They heard Momma wail as they left.

"Why is Momma so sad?" Mia asked.

Mrs. Walsh walked Mia over to the God-awful chairs again and sat down with her.

"You're limping. I figured a seat is better than a walk."

Mia thanked her for that. Mia wanted to tell her that she needed better chairs in the waiting room, but decided it was none of her business.

"I think that your Momma is sad because she is so relieved that it is over and you don't have to go up on the stand and relive that experience again. Mommas do that. They worry so much for their babies that it makes them sick. And when they don't have to worry anymore, they get it all out by crying."

Mia sat and listened.

"Mia, do you have any questions for me?"

Mia was hesitant. She took a few moments and looked around the waiting room, then bowed her head down until her face felt hidden.

"Maybe a few."

"Okay, what are they?"

Mia kept her head down. "What is a ruling?"

"Good question. A ruling is what the judge decides is the outcome of the case. In incidents like this, the ruling also comes with a sentence. So, for Frank, since he pleaded guilty...you know what that means right?"

"Yes. That he said that he did something wrong." Mia knew what guilty meant, she just didn't know if Frank was guilty or not. But he must be, if he said it himself.

"That's right. The judge will make an official ruling, when Frank declares his guilt in court, to legally find him guilty. Then, she will give him a sentence. A sentence is what the judge thinks his punishment should be for the crime that he committed."

"Oh!" Mia didn't know what else to say.

"Does that clear it up?"

Mia nodded. Mrs. Walsh asked if she had any other questions. Mia had one more.

"Does this mean Frank is going to jail?"

"Yes. It most likely does."

"Oh!" Mia wasn't feeling very intelligent with all of her oh's, but she didn't know what else to say.

"Then that's probably why Momma is crying. She likes Frank a lot."

Mrs. Walsh leaned in closer. "Mia, she likes you a lot."

"I know," Mia said. "But she likes Frank more. She told me. He's not as stupid as I am."

Mrs. Walsh did a funny thing with her eyebrows. She looked like she was going to say something but forgot what it was. She didn't have time to remember either, because Momma came out of the meeting room and said she was ready to go. She thanked Mrs. Walsh for all of her help, and then walked past them and to the exit. She called back to Mia to follow. Mia stood up. She remembered her manners and thanked Mrs. Walsh as well.

Mrs. Walsh grabbed Mia gently by the wrist. Mia looked down, looked at Mrs. Walsh before pulling her arm away.

"Mia, is everything okay? Like at home?"

Mia nodded. "Everything is fine, Mrs. Walsh," she answered. "Just fine." But for the first time in her entire life, she knew how far that was from the truth. Things sure didn't feel fine anymore. Everything hurt: her ankle, her back, her legs, her head, and her heart. Mia just wanted it all to stop. She wanted to scream. She wanted to say that it wasn't feeling okay. But she didn't.

"Thanks for asking, though."

Mrs. Walsh nodded. "Take care, Mia."

Mia limped over to the steps to catch up to Momma. She took one look back at her lawyer. Mrs. Walsh was still watching Mia. Mia waved. She wished that she was brave enough to tell her the truth and ask for a hug, but she wasn't. She was just a cowardly girl, and nothing would change that. But a hug, a hug would have been really nice. Mia turned around and ran up the steps as fast as she could, pain and all. She needed to get far away from Mrs. Walsh before she did ask for kindness. And before she had to hear Mrs. Walsh say no thanks.

Chapter Twenty-Seven

Mia started packing her clothes for writing camp. Aunt Colleen was picking her up at 6 pm. Mia couldn't wait to get away from Momma and her sadness. It seemed Mia just made that sadness worse.

Aunt Colleen was set to come later because they didn't know how long court was going to be that morning. They made a 6 o'clock pick up deal, hoping that it would all be over by that time. Since there was no court, Mia was home by noon. She had called Aunt Colleen to see if she could come earlier, but no one answered. She left a message on her answering machine.

Daddy was home. He took the day off from work for the court date but he didn't end up going with them. He woke up feeling pretty sick in the stomach. He was also having trouble seeing. Momma said it was his diabetes acting up, and the stress of his best friend Frank being in court made him feel worse. Mia understood that. She woke up feeling pretty sick in the stomach from the court date as well.

Mia opened her drawer and grabbed two bathing suits. She wasn't sure if there would be swimming at writing camp, but figured, since it was on a lake, that she might as well be prepared. She brought two so she had a backup. She also packed shorts, some long pants, t-shirts, and a few sweaters. Last, she went into her desk drawer and grabbed a few pens, and her two writing books. She debated for quite some time whether she wanted to bring her spy book with her or not, but in the end, she decided to take it. Even though it was hidden well and she knew Momma wouldn't find it, she still felt better knowing it was with her.

Mia looked at her full suitcase with satisfaction. She was ready to go. She just needed to add her toothbrush from the bathroom. She wasn't too concerned with adding this before she closed her case because she put it in the outside zipper. She liked to have it handy just in case something got stuck in a tooth, or if she ate something she didn't like and needed the taste out of her mouth.

She sat down on top of her suitcase and pulled the zipper shut. It was a challenge. Her clothes exceeded the available space to put them in, but she managed. She placed the luggage on the floor and headed to the bathroom.

The aroma of grilled cheese sandwiches wafted up her nose as soon as she opened up her bedroom door. It reminded Mia that she hadn't eaten yet that day. Her stomach had been too upset in the morning. She grabbed her toothbrush first, so she wouldn't forget, then headed down the stairs to have some lunch. She was almost at the bottom step when she heard the phone ring. Mia jumped the last stair, hoping it was Aunt Colleen on the phone. She wanted to get to it before Momma. But when Mia jumped, she landed on her sore ankle, and crumbled to the floor in agony. It was everything Mia could do to not burst into tears from both the pain, and the sound of Momma answering the phone with a perky hello. She stayed on the floor and listened to Momma's conversation. She could tell right away that it wasn't Aunt Colleen. It was Mrs. Walsh calling about the ruling.

Momma said a lot of *oh no's*, and *I understands*, with a few *uh huh's* added in. She ended the conversation with telling Mrs. Walsh that she was grateful for her call and all that she had done to help, then hung up the phone with a furious crash.

"Mia!" Momma yelled loud enough for Mia to hear from upstairs, if that had been where she was. Mia slowly got up to her feet, went to the stairs, and made stomping sounds on the last two steps so Momma would think she was just heading down. After she made enough stomps to account for all the stairs, Mia rounded the corner to the dining room and greeted Momma. Momma was crying. Daddy was comforting her.

"What's wrong Lee-Ann? What did she say?"

"Oh, it's awful," Momma said, waving her hands in the air like she was shooing away flies. "Just awful."

Mia watched Daddy console Momma's tears, waiting to hear what the awful news was. Momma gave Daddy a run for his money in the tears department, but finally, she sat down at the table and took a deep breath.

"That was the lawyer. Frank has been sentenced. He is going to jail because he pleaded guilty."

Daddy sat down beside her. He now looked sad as well. Momma placed a gentle hand on his arm. Daddy placed his other hand on top of hers. Mia stayed back and just watched.

"For how long?" Daddy asked.

"Six months. Mrs. Walsh said that because he pled guilty, and because there was no penetration, that he didn't have a high sentence. So that's good, but I feel so guilty. I feel so guilty that I said anything. You were right, Richard, I should've listened to you and let the Lord handle it, not did my own thing. Look what I did."

"It's not your fault Lee-Ann. Frank did do something wrong. It's his fault too."

Momma nodded.

"Well, six months isn't that long. With good behavior, he will be out in no time. That's how it works. It'll be okay. Don't feel guilty. Just say a few prayers to the Lord, saying you're sorry, and you'll be forgiven."

Momma agreed to do so. Daddy encouraged her to start one then and there, and Momma did. Daddy held her hand and started praying with her. He started speaking in his church language, putting his free hand up to the sky as to get God's attention. Momma prayed for forgiveness and love. Mia wondered if she needed to pray for both of those too. Mia also wondered what the word penetration meant, and if she had done that, if it would have made things better for everyone. Mia felt really dumb, and mean. She upset a lot of people by this. Mia wanted to run far away from it all. But she couldn't. Not with a busted ankle, and not with the smell of burning grilled cheese coming from the kitchen.

Mia spent the afternoon in her room. She tried calling Aunt Colleen a few more times but she still wasn't home. Mia remembered that Aunt Colleen said that she was going on a trip for a few weeks as well, that was why she could drive Mia to the camp. Mia thought that maybe Aunt Colleen was out buying what she needed to go away.

Finally, at 5:45 pm, Mia heard the front door open, and Aunt Colleen's voice talking to Daddy. Mia jumped off of her bed, grabbed her suitcase, and took one last look over her room. It was clean, and put away. She was ready to leave.

Aunt Colleen was at the fridge picking out some snacks when Mia reached the main level of the house.

"Mia, is that you?"

"Uh huh!" Mia said. She had no breath for much more than that. It was a heavy suitcase, and Mia was injured from head to toe.

Aunt Colleen met her in the dining room and helped her the rest of the way.

"You're limping?"

"She fell out of a tree." Momma, coming from the kitchen, answered for Mia.

Aunt Colleen accepted the answer without any questions. Mia let it go.

"Do you have everything you need?"

Mia said she did, but then remembered she was wrong. She told Aunt Colleen that she needed one more moment, and took off back up to her room. Moments later she returned with Lucy. She couldn't go to camp without her favourite doll.

Aunt Colleen packed the car up while Mia said goodbye to Momma and Daddy. It only took them 10 minutes to get it all done, and get on the road. Mia was headed to writing camp.

"Want a snack? They're in that bag."

Mia looked down and saw a small white plastic bag full of treats. She was hungry. Not only did she miss breakfast, but she missed lunch too. Burnt grilled cheese was not appealing. She also lost her interest in lunch when she found out that Frank was headed to jail.

Mia looked into the bag and found a honey bun, her favourite snack. She asked Aunt Colleen if she could have it and Aunt Colleen said yes.

"I have something to tell you."

"What's that?" Mia asked with a mouth full of food.

"It's about writing camp."

"I'm still going, right?" Mia became concerned.

"Yes, of course. But you aren't going alone."

Mia tilted her head not understanding. Who would be going with her?

"Do I have a friend from school going?

Aunt Colleen shook her head. "No. But you will have a friend there."

Mia pulled out the last of her honey bun and licked her fingers clean while she thought about whom the friend might be.

"Who?" She asked before shoving that last bite into her mouth.

"Me! I've been there all day."

Mia smiled.

"Really?"

Aunt Colleen explained more.

"When I went in to pay for your camp, I also signed up as a volunteer. I'm going to be with you for the whole two weeks. If that's okay with you of course?"

Mia beamed. "Of course, it is!"

Aunt Colleen nodded. "Really? I thought it would be fun. You've had a rough week. I wanted to make sure these next two are the most fun they can be for you. We'll do this together."

Mia loved the thought of having her Aunt Colleen at writing camp with her. It would make the moments she wasn't writing much more fun. She liked having people she loved near her. Mia giggled loudly.

"That's awesome!"

"I thought so too," Aunt Colleen agreed.

Mia looked down at the bag of treats. She was still hungry but wasn't sure if having another one would cause her to break the 'gluttony is a sin' rule.

"Go ahead, eat whatever you want. I bought them for you. Have it all."

Mia looked up. Aunt Colleen's attention was bouncing back and forth between Mia and the road.

"Are you sure? Wouldn't that make Jesus mad? I'd be eating more than I need."

Aunt Colleen's lip sucked in on the corner.

"Oh, child. You don't think Jesus is watching your every move, do you? He's got bigger things to worry about than what junk you're eating on this road trip."

Mia frowned.

"Auntie, he watches our every move. He's good that way. Plus, I know better. So, if for some reason his head is turned in a different direction in this moment, it's still wrong and I know it. It would be a sin. And I would be disrespecting him."

"Oh Mia, he doesn't watch your every move."

Mia was saddened by this thought.

"Yes, he does."

"No, no he doesn't. That is just a fear tactic given by fear-driven church goers."

Mia felt like she could cry.

"If he isn't watching all of the time, then I'm not safe all the time? He won't protect me. Will that happen? I can't do it by myself."

Mia knew that bad things have happened to her, but she always figured that that was because Jesus wanted them to happen to her. That's what Daddy said. That if bad things happened it was because Jesus wanted her to experience that pain. It was His will. That had always comforted her. It made her feel safe. What was supposed to happen was happening. There was a bit of comfort in that.

Aunt Colleen pulled the car over to the side of the road. She looked Mia so deeply in the eyes that it made Mia unsure whether she should turn away, or keep her ground.

Aunt Colleen placed her head against the steering wheel, still looking at Mia, and gave a loud sigh.

"No, Mia. If you need protection, Jesus will help you. Always. So, will people around you."

"But you just said…"

"Mia! I said that he isn't watching everything you put into your mouth. He isn't counting your every bite, honey. He won't judge you if you have a day now and then where you eat a few more snacks than normal. If you did it every day, that would be different. But you don't. What I meant was that, Jesus would understand. It will be okay."

"Are you sure?"

Another loud sigh from Aunt Colleen.

"Yes, yes I'm sure. Now don't worry so much about doing right or wrong. You're a good kid, Mia. You do right all the time. Stop being so hard on yourself."

"I'm mostly bad," Mia admitted with shame.

"That's just not true, Mia," Aunt Colleen countered.

Mia didn't agree but she nodded anyway. She was pretty hungry. As Aunt Colleen started driving again, Mia slowly reached down and picked up the bag. She looked inside. There was a bag of ketchup chips, a chocolate bar, some sour key candies, a banana, and an orange pop. Aunt Colleen sure knew what she liked. Mia grabbed out the pop, the sour key candies, and the bag of ketchup chips. She put the rest of the goodies back down on the floor.

"Thatta girl. Eat!"

Mia winced as she sat back up. Aunt Colleen noticed.

"You must have fallen pretty hard out of that tree!"

Mia ignored her aunt's comment.

Mia was still concerned that she was eating too much but Aunt Colleen seemed convinced that it was okay. So, she dug right in.

As she popped open the bag of chips she asked Aunt Colleen one more time, the question that she seemed to be avoiding.

"So, why does bad stuff happen sometimes? Is it because Jesus is watching someone else? Or because it is His will to let it happen?"

Aunt Colleen looked at Mia softly.

"Bad things like what Mia?"

Mia wasn't sure how much of that question to answer.

"Things that hurt your heart and body?"

"Like what Frank did?"

That was part of it, so Mia agreed.

"Listen honey, that didn't happen because Jesus wasn't watching you."

"So, he watched that?" Mia's pain in her stomach returned.

"No, that's not exactly it. This is what I believe, anyway. Jesus, or God, they don't watch horrible things that happen to people and just let it happen. He can't fix or stop everything. There are some evils in the world that are too great. But Jesus stays with you through it. He makes sure you are not alone. So, although He can't stop it, he is right there, protecting your heart from as much of it as He can."

"Like a friend?"

"I guess you can say that. He is always there for you to talk to, and to give you comfort. God is love, Mia. He's there, here, whatever, to give *you* love."

"You sure?"

"I believe so."

"You know a lot about Jesus, even though you tell Daddy you don't."

"Your Daddy and I just see Jesus differently, that is all. And that's okay. I believe in Jesus, to be truthful, I just don't believe in organized religion."

"Organized religion?" Mia asked.

"That's a conversation for another day. I'll just say this. Some people try to make Jesus into what they want Him to be, instead of letting Him just be who He is. People use religion, and Jesus, as a defense mechanism to make them feel better about their life, instead of just living their life and being thankful for what they have. They use him to justify their sins. Some also use religion to control other people's movements and feelings. I don't believe in that. You know?"

"Does Daddy use Him to control others?"

"I feel that he does."

"Oh!" Was all Mia could reply. Truth was, she needed more time to think about what Aunt Colleen was meaning. This conversation was the opposite of everything she ever thought. She liked the idea that maybe Jesus didn't want her to be hurt. That the pain wasn't His will. She even liked the thought that maybe, just maybe, someone out there felt sad with her too.

Was her Daddy wrong in his thinking? Mia filled her mouth with a handful of chips as she considered what Aunt Colleen had said.

"Okay, enough of all this religion talk." Aunt Colleen interrupted Mia's thoughts. "It's giving me the heebie-jeebies. We still have quite a drive ahead of us. Let's get this vacation underway."

Mia opened her window a crack as they picked up speed. She could feel the wind blowing in against her face. It felt good. This all felt good. Mia felt a sense of freedom. Mia felt in control.

Darkness had fallen by the time they reached the camp. A large Bristol board welcome sign was nailed to a tree at the entrance of the camp. It had pink and blue balloons taped to the sides. Mia wished she had her camera out of her suitcase to take a picture. Although, she also knew that the darkness outside would not make for a good photograph and if she used the flash it would just reflect off of the window and cause only a yellow image to show up. She knew this from the time her family took a weekend trip to see Mia's Great Aunt. Mia used a whole roll of film in the car while driving, and nothing showed up, just yellow pictures. Except the one she took of Daddy driving. That turned out because there was no window between the flash and Daddy's face. Mia was sad when she got her pictures developed. She had her heart set on a full album of memories. She even bought a book to put them in. But when she opened up the envelope from the film store, there was only one picture worth putting in the book.

Daddy tried to cheer her up by saying the yellow spots were angels that wanted their portraits done too, and that the pictures were proof that Mia had many angels by her side. Mia found out that that wasn't the truth when she went back the next day and asked the man at the film store about the spots and he said they were reflections of the flash off of the glass.

Mia could take pictures tomorrow when she was out of the car.

Aunt Colleen pulled up to a large building and explained to Mia that it was the registration office. She told Mia that she just needed to go in and check what cabin Mia was in and that she would be back in just a moment. Aunt Colleen was already inside when Mia realized that that meant that Mia was sleeping in a different cabin other than the one Aunt Colleen was in. Mia asked her to confirm as soon as she got back into the car.

"I sleep in the volunteer cabin. It's a large cabin with a bunch of separate rooms. All the kitchen volunteers stay there. But it's adults only. All the kids, the writers, they stay in other cabins that have one large room full of bunk beds. I think there are 10 campers per cabin, plus of course a volunteer to watch over you all. I registered as a volunteer late so I didn't get to have a cabin with campers. I'm working in the kitchen."

"Oh." Mia wasn't quite sure how she felt about being away from Aunt Colleen. On one hand, it was okay, since Mia didn't even expect her to be there anyway. On the other hand, Mia was looking forward to spending a lot of time with Aunt Colleen, and bunking with her would have been really nice.

"It'll be fine. You'll have lots of fun. And you'll be with kids your own age, not your old Aunt," Aunt Colleen joked as she steered the vehicle down a short narrow dirt road to a parking lot full of cars.

She parked the car and they got out. Aunt Colleen opened the trunk and grabbed Mia's suitcase.

"What do you have in here?"

Mia laughed. "A lot!"

"Feels like it. Let's go find cabin four. That's where you are staying."

Mia was thankful that Aunt Colleen had some idea of where she was going, because it was dark. The trees that surrounded the cabins blocked out the light of the moon, leaving nothing to show the way through the woods. Mia didn't like dark woods anymore. Not after what happened at the Bible retreat. Aunt Colleen had a flashlight. She was quite smart.

They reached cabin 4. An outside light was shining by the screen door, and inside Mia could hear a volunteer reading a story out to the campers.

They climbed the stairs, and Aunt Colleen knocked once on the door, then opened it and held it for Mia to head in first.

"Hi! We're a little late getting here, but I have one more camper for you today. This is my niece, Mia."

Mia looked over at the woman reading the book. She was short and stout. Her hair seemed long, but Mia wasn't sure because it was in a bun. The woman smiled, closed the book, and wobbled over to greet Mia.

"Hi! I'm Ellen. I'm your cabin volunteer. Come on in, Mia."

Mia did as she was told. Ellen showed her which bunk was left, the bottom one of a bed that was right beside the door. Aunt Colleen placed her suitcase on the bed and told Mia that she would see her in the morning. Mia didn't want her to go but she didn't tell her. Aunt Colleen kissed her on the cheek.

"Tomorrow I'll show you where my cabin is. It isn't far from here. Sleep well, sweetie."

Mia nodded again then waved to Aunt Colleen as she walked back out to the darkness.

"Put your suitcase under your bed for now, and come and join the circle. We have a little bit of story left before lights out."

Mia did as she was told. It was just a little less than a half hour later that Mia found herself tucked into the bottom bunk of her bed. She had forgotten to change into her pajamas like the other girls had so she slept in her clothes. She was so tired and sore that her clothes didn't bother her at all.

Chapter Twenty-Eight

Mia was walking with her group to the first class of the day. All the girls in cabin 4 had the same schedule. They were together all day and evening, for the entire two weeks. The others came on Sunday, so they had already been through one day of classes. Mia was behind due to court. But she didn't want to tell any of them that even though they seemed like a nice bunch of kids.

It was a bit of a hard morning. Mia got up, still in her clothes from the night before, and wondered where they went to change. She pulled her suitcase out from under her bed, and looked around the room for the bathroom. There were only two doors in the entire cabin. One that led to the outside, and another that led to Ellen's bedroom. Where was the bathroom?

Mia put one foot on her bed and lifted herself up to see over the top bunk. A young blond girl, around her age, was sitting up there tying her shoes. Her chest badge said her name was Kelly.

"Excuse me, where is the bathroom?" Mia asked shyly.

"Down the laneway," Kelly answered.

"Down the laneway? Like outside?"

Kelly nodded.

The bathroom was outside? Mia's only experience with camping was at Bible camp, and their cabin had a bathroom inside.

"So, our cabin's bathroom is outside?" Mia said to confirm.

"Yes, it's shared by the whole campground. The showers are there too."

Mia slowly brought herself down to her bunk. She looked around. Everyone was changing where they were standing. Mia was torn. She didn't want to show her body, especially with the marks on her back. But she didn't want to stand out from the crowd either. Quietly, she tucked herself into the far corner of her bunk and changed as quickly as she could. Watching, to make sure no one was paying any attention. No one was.

Now, walking with the group, she felt a bit more at ease. They were headed to theatre writing class. She knew this because she asked Kelly to show her a copy of their class schedule. It was a 2-day cycle. Day 1 had creative writing and poetry, and day 2 had theatre plays, and writing for fun or journaling.

She felt creative. She felt ready. She was happy that her ankle was feeling a bit better. Her limp was almost unnoticeable now.

The classroom was warm. There were many windows that faced the lake, allowing the sun to come in and heat the room. The girls filed into the classroom one by one. Mia took a seat that had Kelly sitting behind her, and a young caramel skinned girl in front of her.

The teacher waited until they were all sitting down quiet before he got up from his desk to speak. He welcomed everyone to day two, and explained the rules of the classroom. The rules weren't hard. No chewing gum, the garbage was under his desk for when we ignored him and chewed gum anyway, no goofing around when people were trying to work, walking around was okay if it helped you feel creative, and most importantly he said, no making fun, or teasing anyone about anything they were writing or sharing with the class.

Once he finished the rules, he wrote his name on the chalkboard. It was different than regular school. In regular school, teachers wrote their names with a Mr. or a Mrs., and then their last name. In writing school, the teacher, this teacher, just wrote Kirk.

"Welcome to theatre class. This class will be a little different than all your other classes. In this class, you won't be writing your own piece of work, but we will all be writing a theatre piece together."

There were a few moans from the class, but mostly excitement. Mia liked the idea of trying to work with a group of girls to create one story.

"Now, we need to work hard on this. At the end of the two weeks, at the closing banquet, we will be performing it in front of everyone. The other 3 classes will be performing theirs as well. I had four topics to choose from, but because you guys are the third class to be here, there are only two left. They are timely topics. Your options are: the coming of fall, which we will see in just a few months, or a solar eclipse, which we will be seeing some time next week."

Kirk looked around the room. Everyone was quiet. A redheaded girl in the far corner of the room broke the silence by asking what a solar eclipse was.

"Great question," Kirk answered. "What is your name?"

"Jennifer."

"Jennifer. Excellent." She smiled at his enthusiasm over her name. Kirk continued. "Jennifer a solar eclipse is when the Moon passes in between the Sun and the Earth, causing either a partial or a full blocking of the Sun. Next week, we will be having a full solar eclipse. You will notice, it will get dark as night during the day."

The class thought the idea of this was pretty cool. There were a lot of oh's and ah's. Mia didn't find it as cool. She didn't oh or ah. She didn't like the idea of darkness during the day.

The class naturally chose the solar eclipse theme and Mia had no choice but to participate and pretend like she was excited.

The rest of the class time was spent on researching what a solar eclipse might look like, and how they were going to create that into a 6-minute play that others might want to watch.

When class was over, the group headed to the dining hall for lunch. Mia was happy to see Aunt Colleen there. She tried a few times to go up and talk to her, but Aunt Colleen was pretty busy with all the lunches she was trying to deliver. She was so busy in fact, that Mia didn't even hear Aunt Colleen's voice until she walked by with some lunches, and gave Mia heck for picking out all of the peas in her pasta salad. Mia couldn't eat peas anymore. The taste, the feel, the smell, any and all of it made her sick. It reminded her of what happened with Momma. Mia didn't like to remember that night. Mia wished that night never happened. She wasn't one to ignore her Aunt and what she asked of Mia, but this time she would have to. Mia was not eating her peas.

Mia really enjoyed the rest of the week. In her creative writing class each student was responsible for writing their own short story during the two weeks at camp. The 3 best would end up in the program the night of the banquet. For journaling class, the students were going to learn how to write for fun. Writing with no rules. Mia liked rules, but she also liked journaling already so maybe it wouldn't be that bad.

The fourth class was a poetry class. Mia liked making things rhyme. Chantal, her teacher for her poetry said that the top 4 student poems would be read out loud to the entire camp, the night of the banquet. Mia wanted this in a bad way. The thoughts of everyone hearing something she wrote excited her.

Mia also made a lot of notes in her spy book during the first week. She wrote about the people she was spending the most time with like her Cabin Volunteer, her favourite teachers, and the bunkmates she seemed to talk with the most.

<u>Ellen</u>
Short lady, a little chubby
Looks like a librarian with her hair
Funny
Wakes up early
Doesn't like messy beds
Eats bananas like ice cream, licks the sides before she bites it

<u>Kelly</u>
Sleeps above me
Blond hair that is long and always brushed
Really likes boys
Says barbies are for babies, so are dolls
Is 12
Has an older brother who has a lot of friends visit
Her older brother is a singer

Kelly says he knows Donny Wahlberg
I don't know if she likes me or not
She is sometimes mean

<u>Jennifer</u>
Red hair
Funny
Laughs at Kellys jokes a lot even when they are bad

<u>Donna</u>
Caramel skin
Never eats
Really nice

<u>Kirk</u>
Theatre teacher
Tall
Needs to eat more
Snorts a lot
Jumps on desks when talking loud
Runs through camp every morning
Cute

<u>Chantal</u>
Poetry Class
Brown hair past shoulders
Glasses sometimes
Likes to rhyme
Eats a lot of candies
Cussed in class on the first day

Mia liked almost everyone so far. She was having fun. Mia only had moments of sadness at night when she was in the silence of her own bed. Her sadness came not from missing Momma, but from not missing her. Mia knew that Momma would be so broken hearted if Mia told her that she barely thought of her at all. Daddy too. Mia liked being alone. Not that Mia wasn't alone before, she was. But that was usually when she was locked in the closet for the day, or left alone at home while her parents went out. This was different. This was alone, but with others. This was alone, but not in trouble. This was alone, but with no fear of when someone would return and what mood they would be in when they did. This alone was an alone that Mia could handle. Besides, Aunt Colleen was there with her, kind of. Mia didn't get to see her much at all, but the weekends were free weekends. No classes. Some kids who lived close were planning to go home, while others could stay and enjoy the beach, and the campfires. All the volunteers stayed the weekend. Aunt Colleen promised Mia that they would spend a lot of time together then. She told Mia that she didn't need to cook on the weekend, she just had to supervise supper hour. They had weekend volunteers to cook. That gave Aunt Colleen all day to play with Mia.

Saturday morning Mia woke up energized. She put on her bathing suit, her shorts, her t-shirt, and her flip-flops and put her hair up before she headed out to see her Aunt. They were going to go swimming, which was good because Mia was beginning to smell. She hadn't showered since she got to camp. She spent her evenings working on her stories and besides that, she was too shy to shower in front of everyone. It was a wide-open space, with no curtains between the showerheads. Mia didn't want anyone to see her ugly body.

She stepped outside of her cabin. The sun seemed to be on fire more than usual that morning, and even though the wind was quite strong, it was hot. It reminded Mia of her Daddy's car heater. She loved nothing more than to get into the car on a winters day and blast the heat straight into her face. Daddy would complain that it was killing the car battery, but Mia did it anyway, at least for a few moments. Cold shivers felt a lot like nervous shivers. Mia preferred to be warm. It was comforting to her. Like this strong morning warm wind was comforting as well.

Aunt Colleen was sitting on her cabin steps, sipping a cup of coffee, when Mia walked up to get her. Mia sat down beside her.

"Hey kiddo!" Aunt Colleen blew on her coffee before taking a small drink.

"Hi," Mia answered. Mia liked listening to people sip on their coffee. To hear the slurping sound people made when they could only take a little sip because it was too hot made her giggle. She couldn't imagine herself wanting to drink anything so hot that she could only take a few short slurps at a time. Adults were weird.

"Look at the butterfly over there."

Mia looked to the railing that Aunt Colleen was pointing at. A beautiful butterfly, either golden yellow or orange, Mia couldn't tell, was sitting only a foot from them.

"She's pretty!"

"She is. She's been here all week. I think she may belong to this cabin."

"Really? We should name her then."

"Good idea. Any thoughts?"

Mia closed her eyes and pictured the butterfly in her head.

"Tulip!"

"Tulip?"

Mia nodded. She thought tulip would be a good name for the butterfly.

"Tulip." Aunt Colleen nodded as she said it the second time. "I could get used to that. Good name."

Mia smiled. Aunt Colleen liked it. Mia looked at the butterfly.

"What do you think? Is Tulip a good name for you?"

Tulip fluttered her wings in response. Mia gasped.

"I think she likes it too!"

Aunt Colleen laughed. "I think you're right."

Mia sat and watched Tulip for a few moments while Aunt Colleen drank more of her coffee. Aunt Colleen eventually broke the silence.

"Are you having fun?"

Mia nodded.

"What's your favourite class so far?"

Mia thought about it for a moment. "I like them all. I don't have a favourite."

Aunt Colleen laughed. "That sounds like a good week then."

Mia agreed.

"When do I get to read some of your writing?"

Mia wasn't sure about letting Aunt Colleen read her writing. The last time someone read something she wrote was the writing camp assignment for Mrs. Gentry and that didn't go well at all. It caused a heck of a mess.

"I don't really like to let people read my stories," Mia admitted.

"Interesting. So why do you write them?"

Mia shrugged. "For me, I guess."

"Don't you ever want to write a novel, or a play, or a movie?"

"Yes."

"Well, you're going to have to let people read it then."

"I suppose so." Mia thought for a few moments. "Our play we write will be presented at the banquet, and the top students in poetry class will have their poems read out loud that night. And the short stories, if they're good, will make it into the program as well. Maybe, if I'm good enough, you can read something then."

Aunt Colleen could take bigger sips of her coffee now that it was a bit cooler. Mia found a leaf on the step. She lifted it closer to her face and looked at the veins. The leaf had plenty.

"Okay, but if you change your mind, or would like to practice showing people your writing, you know where to find me. I would love to read it. And if you want, I won't tell a soul that you let me."

Mia smiled. She placed the leaf on her Aunt's knee. "Deal. If I decide to."

"If!" Aunt Colleen repeated back. "Got it! No pressure."

Tulip fluttered over and rested on Mia's lap.

"Want a picture?"

"Yes, please!"

Mia slowly reached for her camera and passed it to Aunt Colleen.

"Say cheese!"

Mia crouched closer to Tulip and said cheese.

"Thanks!"

Aunt Colleen smiled and handed her back her camera. Mia gently ran her fingers over Tulips wings. They were soft.

They didn't say much while Aunt Colleen finished her coffee. Once she swallowed the last drop, she stood up, and walked to her cabin door, taking the leaf Mia left on her lap with her.

"I'm just going to bring my cup back inside and grab my bathing suit. You hungry?"

"No."

"Me either. We will eat after swimming. Be right back."

Mia was going to wait outside but Tulip left, so she stood up and followed Aunt Colleen into the cabin.

"I can wash your cup. You go get changed'."

Aunt Colleen placed the cup on the counter and headed upstairs to her room. Mia went to the sink and started washing. They had dish soap, but no towel. She looked under the sink. No towel there either, but they had a drying rack. Mia pulled it out, washed the cup then placed the cup in position to dry. She looked around the cabin. It was big compared to hers. The walls were made of wood. The furniture was scarce, only a love seat and a recliner. The windows had no curtains. They had a bookshelf full of books and binders in one corner, and a small boxed television in the other. The television had bunny ears on top of it, with a healthy stash of tin foil wrapped all around the antenna.

Mia turned the television on to see if it worked, and it did. It was snowy. Mia reached for the antenna and moved it back and forth.

"Don't bother. I've been trying all week to get a clear picture and haven't been successful." Aunt Colleen startled her.

"Oh. That's not good."

"Tell me about it. I'm missing my shows. But that's okay. Let's go swimming."

Mia held the door open for Aunt Colleen who had her hands full with two towels, and a beach ball.

The beach was small, just enough for a few people. Lucky for them, there was no one else there yet. Aunt Colleen spread the towels out like blankets, and took off her shirt and shorts. Mia did the same.

"You ready?"

Mia nodded. "Last one under water is a dirty rotten egg."

Mia took off running. Aunt Colleen followed behind her. Mia laughed as she ran across the sand.

"Mia, wait!"

Mia ignored her. She kept running. Her feet hit the lake.

"Mia, stop!"

Mia knew Aunt Colleen's tactics. She was trying to make her stop so she could run past and win. Mia wasn't falling for it. Not this time. She was smarter than that. Aunt Colleen knew that too because she increased her running speed. She was almost at Mia's side.

"Mia! Stop right now. I mean it!"

Mia laughed as the water hit her belly. It was harder to run now that the water was that high. It was rough. Waves were splashing at her. And just as a wave came flying into Mia's face, she felt Aunt Colleen grab her wrist and whip her back. Aunt Colleen dropped down to Mia's level and grabbed her around the waist. Mia stopped laughing. Aunt Colleen had a terrified look on her face.

"What's wrong, Auntie?"

Aunt Colleen held her waist with strength.

"Mia, what the hell happened to your back?"

Chapter Twenty-Nine

Mia was caught off guard. How could she forget about her back? She felt the floor burns every time she moved. Every time she put a shirt on. Every time she sat back on a chair. She knew there was always a day that the pain of an injury stopped getting her attention, but normally she would still remember to hide it. This time, she was different. She knew better than to wear clothing with no back to it.

She wanted to say something to Aunt Colleen, but she had no words. Should she tell her the truth? Should she lie? She didn't know. All she could do was stand there in the water letting the waves hit her back. The moment was painful inside and out.

Mia couldn't handle Aunt Colleen's look anymore. She turned away, looking out at the water in the distance. She pulled her arm from Aunt Colleen's hand and swam as fast as she could get away.

Aunt Colleen followed.

"Mia, stop!"

Mia couldn't. She had to think this through first.

Telling the truth meant Mia might get Momma in trouble, and make Momma go to jail like Frank did. And Daddy would then lose both his best friend and his wife. He would really hate Mia after that.

Telling a lie would mean that Mia would never see Jesus. She would never go to heaven. But Momma had made her lie before. Was she already not going to heaven? Or was Aunt Colleen, right? Did Momma and Daddy tell her all of this stuff to control her, using Jesus to do so? Mia's heart hurt. And her arms began to burn as much as her back.

Mia had to decide what she was going to say quickly. Aunt Colleen was starting to cry-scream, and if Mia didn't talk soon, she would be crying too. She could already feel the pain in her cheeks, the pain you get before you burst into tears.

She kept swimming even though her arms told her not too.

She looked back. Aunt Colleen had stopped swimming. She was just moving her arms and legs back and forth in the same spot to stay positioned where she was in the lake.

"Mia, I can't swim anymore. Come back."

Mia slowed her swimming. She turned to look at Aunt Colleen. Aunt Colleen still hadn't moved. Mia decided to stop too.

"Mia, come back. Please!"

Mia wanted to, but she still didn't know what to say. She muttered the first thing that came to her mind.

"We're going to have a solar eclipse next week. Did you know that?"

Aunt Colleen laughed. Then the laugh turned back into tears. Harder, stronger droplets.

"What happened to your back, Mia?"

Aunt Colleen wasn't giving up the question. Mia wasn't giving up the answer.

"That's when the Moon goes between the Sun and Earth, and it blocks out the light. It means it's going to get dark in the daytime."

"What happened to your back, Mia?"

"I don't mind it getting dark in the daytime. Kirk says it won't get as dark as night, but pretty close."

"Mia?"

"He says that it will only last a few minutes, and maybe not happen again in this part of the world, for many more years."

"MIA?"

"We are making a play on it too. You will get to see it at closing banquet. We are not sure…"

As Mia opened her mouth to finish her sentence, a large wave of water hit her in the face.

Mia couldn't breathe. She swallowed a lot of water.

Mia choked and sputtered. Mia could feel her chest burning. She began to panic. She flailed her arms as quickly as she could to try to keep her head above water but her arms were too tired.

As she coughed, more water entered her body. Her head was starting to go under.

Mia felt Aunt Colleen grab her again. This time she was thankful for it. Aunt Colleen pulled her up and started pounding on Mia's back. Mia began to cough harder. She coughed so strong, that she ended up vomiting water down Aunt Colleen's back.

Once Mia was breathing again, Aunt Colleen swam them both back to shallower water, neither speaking a word as they went.

When Aunt Colleen could touch bottom, she picked Mia up and carried her out of the water. Mia didn't know what to do, so she kept telling her story.

"They say you can't look at the solar eclipse with your bare eyes or it will do damage. I don't want to have damage to my eyes. We are making boxes with holes so we can look at it through that."

Aunt Colleen placed her down on one of the towels. She picked the other one up and started to gently wipe her back. She did it slowly and by patting.

"I'm painting my box purple. Do you like purple?"

"Not when it's on your back. Now that's enough, Mia." Aunt Colleen was frustrated. "What happened to you?"

Mia wanted so bad to tell Aunt Colleen what had happened, but she was scared. What if Aunt Colleen was so upset that she called Momma right away and told her? What if she called the police? Even worse, what if Aunt Colleen didn't care?

Aunt Colleen finished wiping Mia's back then wrapped her in the towel. She then wrapped herself around Mia.

"I fell out of a tree, remember?"

"I don't believe that anymore. If you just fell and hurt your back, you would have told me right away. It must have been awful, whatever happened."

Mia hadn't thought about that.

"Mia, it's okay to tell me."

Mia opened her mouth but no words came out.

"Mia, talk to me. It's just us here. How did those marks happen?"

"I can't, Auntie," Mia conceded only slightly.

Aunt colleen sighed and leaned her head on the back of Mia's head. She pulled her in a little closer.

"Okay. Can you at least tell me this? Was your mother involved?"

Mia again had no words. Why were her words hiding?

Mia could only nod.

"Was your Dad involved?"

Mia shook her head.

Aunt Colleen said nothing. She kissed the side of Mia's head, then ear, and finally cheek. She rested her face beside Mia's face.

"I'm sorry something happened to you."

No one ever told Mia that they were sorry that she was hurt. What did that mean?

"When did it happen?"

Aunt Colleen's words were soft.

Mia decided to tell her. "The night we ate turkey."

"After I left?"

Mia nodded. Aunt Colleen swore a lot.

Mia was getting uncomfortable. She didn't know the proper way to react to Aunt Colleen's emotions. She wanted this moment to be over. It was getting to be too much.

"Can we go swimming now?"

Aunt Colleen kissed her cheek one more time, then agreed.

"This time, I will beat you to the water."

Aunt Colleen got up as quick as she could and darted toward the lake. Mia smiled as she got up and chased her aunt into the blue of the water.

Mia laughed in a way she hadn't in many years. A full-bellied, large-smiling, skip as she ran, kind of laugh. Mia felt light. Mia felt safe. Mia, in her own way, let go of a secret, and it felt really good.

Chapter Thirty

The moon was in full reflection off the water by the time Aunt Colleen and Mia left the beach. They hadn't been there all day, but most of it, leaving only for lunch, dinner, and a game of tetherball when they found their skin getting too wrinkly from the water. Mia thought the day was perfect. It was just she and her aunt. Her stomach ached from laughing so much.

But now that the sun was gone and the moon glowed brightly, it was time to pack up and go. They folded their towels, put their garbage in the bin, and slipped off the beach together, hand and hand.

"Want some ice cream? I think the tuck shop is still open."

Mia did.

"I don't want this day to end," Mia admitted.

"Maybe it doesn't have to."

Aunt Colleen didn't say more than that. They walked in silence to her cabin, just holding hands and enjoying each other's company. That was the great thing about Aunt Colleen, Mia thought. Her hand could be held and Mia had no fear that it meant that she was going to be forced down. Mia could hold and let go of Aunt Colleen's hand at any time and it would be okay.

As they continued to Aunt Colleen's cabin, Mia could hear the sounds of laughter, singing, and guitars. Aunt Colleen explained that the volunteers were gathering at her cabin that evening to have a little fun. And maybe a few drinks too. Mia loved hearing the sounds that were wafting through the air. It was almost the exact reflection of what she was feeling inside her heart.

As they reached the front steps, Aunt Colleen stopped and bent down to Mia's level.

"Are you comfortable waiting outside the cabin for a moment, while I run in?"

Mia looked around.

"Can I wait on the porch?"

"Of course, silly. There is a nice rocking chair up there. Why don't you have a seat? I will only be a few moments."

Mia agreed and sat down on the rocking chair to wait. She watched her Aunt walk into the sounds of the cabin. She looked behind the chair to the window, and followed Aunt Colleen with her eyes, as she worked her way through the crowd of a dozen people, and over to the sink where a few ladies, Mia recognized as cabin mates, were standing together laughing. Aunt Colleen must have said something real wrong at that point, because as soon as she started talking to them, they all stopped laughing, and became very serious. Mia wondered if Aunt Colleen said something awful about Mia, because at once, they all looked out at her sitting on the porch. Mia immediately turned her head, hoping they didn't see her looking right back at them.

Time seemed to slow down. Mia felt like she had been rocking that chair back and forth for eternity. She thought she might be rocking it until the rapture even. She was wrong. Aunt Colleen came before Jesus did. But it was many minutes later.

"Good news! We can have a sleep over tonight, if you don't mind a little noise as we go to sleep," Aunt Colleen said as they walked to the tuck shop for ice cream. "Once we are done our snack, we will swing by your cabin and get your suitcase. If you like staying with me, we can talk to the registration office on Monday, and if they say it's okay, you can spend the rest of the week at my cabin."

Mia liked this idea very much. She wanted to spend as much time as she could with Aunt Colleen. She knew that once she got home that she wouldn't see her as often. She wanted to get every minute in that she could.

The tuck shop had five flavours of ice cream. Mia couldn't decide between tiger tail and chocolate. Aunt Colleen said that it would be okay if Mia had a small scoop of both. She said decision-making was not always necessary. Sometimes a person could have their cake and eat it too. Mia liked this theory.

They didn't talk much on the walk back to Mia's cabin. Their mouths were too full of ice cream to worry about conversation. The ice cream at writing camp tasted better than any Mia had ever had before.

Cabin 4 was empty when they got there. Aunt Colleen explained that the campers that hung around for the weekend were all at a campfire on the lake. Aunt Colleen asked Mia if she wanted to go to it and Mia said no. She would rather be with her. They left Ellen a note so she wouldn't worry where Mia was, and then left the cabin with her suitcase and Lucy doll.

Aunt Colleen's room was pretty big. Big enough for the two of them, that was for sure. She had a large queen bed, with a thick blue quilt on top. There were four fluffy pillows at the top, two on each side of the bed. A small wooden lamp adorned the side table, casting a glow on the room that was soft and comforting. The only other furniture was a small dresser and an easy chair. Aunt Colleen placed Mia's suitcase on the chair.

"Pajamas and bed? I don't know about you but I'm pretty tired after a day outside."

"Me too!"

Mia grabbed her clothes and toothbrush then excused herself to the bathroom. When she returned, Aunt Colleen was also in her pajamas and under the covers. She patted the empty side of the bed for Mia to join her. Mia hesitated. She didn't like sharing a bed with anyone, even Aunt Colleen.

"What's wrong?"

"Nothing."

Mia took a deep breath, found her brave, and climbed into the side of the bed that was open.

"Want to tell ghost stories?"

Mia shook her head. Ghost stories scared her. She was already nervous enough.

"Want to talk about one of your stories?"

Mia shook her head again.

"Are you okay?"

Mia tried to relax her body. She didn't know what was expected of her.

"Yes," she lied.

"Good. We don't have to go to sleep yet. We can spend some special time together first, talking or whatever.

Special time. Mia was caught in her feelings. She didn't want special time with Aunt Colleen but she didn't want to hurt her feelings either.

Aunt Colleen rolled onto her side to face Mia. "You sure you're okay?"

Mia nodded. She waited for Aunt Colleen to move closer but she didn't. She just stayed still watching Mia. Mia didn't move or speak. Momma always told Mia what she needed to do during special time and Momma wasn't there. Mia was on her own to figure it out. Mia reached down and took her pants off.

"What are you doing? Are you hot?"

Mia stopped. She wasn't doing the right thing. She pulled her pants back up. Aunt Colleen was waiting for an answer.

"No. I'm cold."

"Then keep your clothes on, silly."

Mia was so confused. She didn't want to get this wrong. She moved a little closer and kissed Aunt Colleen on the lips. Aunt Colleen kissed her back, then pulled her in for a hug.

"I don't know what is going on with you kid, but you're scaring me. Let's forget talking for the night and maybe get some sleep. We have another day of fresh air tomorrow."

She kissed Mia on the forehead then moved away.

Mia was really screwing this up. Now Aunt Colleen was mad. She was pushing Mia away. Mia didn't know what to do, so she cried. She was so stupid. How could she not know what she was supposed to do? Stupid, stupid, stupid!

"Why are you crying?" Aunt Colleen rolled back over as she asked.

Mia had lost her words again. She was really tired of them getting up and walking away.

"I'm sorry," was all she could muster up.

Aunt Colleen looked at Mia with such sadness.

"Are you afraid to be in a bed with someone?"

Mia nodded.

"Frank was an…"

"Stop!" Mia said quicker then she wanted to. It wasn't about Frank, or maybe it was. She didn't know anymore. Too many people were telling her too many things. It was best if she didn't talk about it at all.

"Okay. I'll stop."

Mia was glad for that. The truth was, Frank scared her, but Frank didn't make her feel bad at special time, Momma did. Momma changed the rules the night with the peas. Mia no longer knew what adults wanted of her.

"Go to sleep," Aunt Colleen whispered. "Tomorrow is a new day."

"I did wrong didn't I? I'm not very smart sometimes."

"Did wrong? You did nothing wrong, Mia. You're special. You're perfect just the way you are. I promise. And you are so incredibly smart. Now go to sleep."

Aunt Colleen smiled as she said the last sentence. She rolled over and snuggled herself deep under the blankets.

Mia never thought of herself as smart. Aunt Colleen must have been really tired. Mia watched Aunt Colleen's chest move up and down with every breath she took. Mia wondered if maybe Aunt Colleen didn't want the special time that Momma wanted. Did that mean that Aunt Colleen was going to go away? Maybe not want to spend time with Mia anymore. Mia rolled over, facing Aunt Colleen.

She watched her until she fell asleep. Then she reached out her hand and touched Aunt Colleen's back. She wanted to feel her breathe, and more importantly, she wanted to feel the exact moment she left Mia, for not being what she was supposed to be.

Chapter Thirty-One

"It's a frog!"

Aunt Colleen had refused to guess what was in Mia's pocket but by the look on her face, Mia knew that a frog wasn't at all what she was thinking. Aunt Colleen jumped and screamed at the same time. Mia laughed uncontrollably.

"It's a cute frog."

As Mia fought to keep her balance while laughing, the frog made its great escape, slipping through her fingers and landing on the floor. It hopped all around, before ducking under the rocking chair in Aunt Colleen's cabin. Aunt Colleen then did her own impression of the frog by jumping up on the couch and bouncing up and down.

"Mia, find that thing and bring it outside."

Mia caught her breath before getting on her hands and knees to find the slippery creature. She saw it just under the rocker part of the chair. The frog looked back at her. She rubbed the top of his head first, before scooping him back up into her hand.

She lifted him up to show her aunt that she had retrieved him. Aunt Colleen didn't seem happy to see him.

"Outside with him now!" Aunt Colleen was half crying, half laughing.

Mia gave her a big smile, stuffed the frog into her shorts pocket, and walked the frog outside.

When she returned, Aunt Colleen was still standing on the couch.

"Show me your hands."

Mia did.

"Now show me your pockets."

Mia opened up her pockets and pulled them inside out.

"Any other pockets?"

Mia shook her head, laughing again. "No. He's outside, Aunty."

Aunt Colleen shook her head, snort-laughing at the same time. "You're a little rat, you know that? Gave your aunt a heart attack. No more four legged creatures in this cabin, you hear?"

"Sorry!" Mia tried to sound sincere.

Aunt Colleen stepped down from the couch and ordered Mia to wash her hands while she packed them up for another day around camp. They were going to go to the beach again, and walking around taking pictures.

Mia soaped her hands as best as she could and rinsed them off. Her teacher told the class one day that the best way to wash your hands was to soap up while singing Happy Birthday. That way, your hands were being soaped just long enough. Mia sang it in her head though, because she knew she was a terrible singer. She knew her talents were quite limited.

Mia was surprised to see Aunt Colleen still beside her when she woke up. To Mia's surprise, she was still holding on to Aunt Colleen's back. Maybe that was why she was still there, because she couldn't escape Mia's grasp. She decided that morning, that she had to hold onto the people she loved as they were sleeping from then on. To make sure they were there when she woke up.

Aunt Colleen walked Mia all around the campgrounds showing her everything there was to be seen. Mia took 3 rolls of pictures in the 2 hours they were out walking. She took pictures of the trees, the cabins, some volunteers, the classrooms, even a deer that walked across their path. Mia even took almost a whole roll of Tulip the butterfly. Mia couldn't wait to get the film developed and into an album.

They stopped and got their lunch sandwiches to go, then headed to the beach for a picnic. There were people swimming this time, so Mia kept her t-shirt on over her bathing suit.

"Having a good weekend?" Aunt Colleen asked as she bit into her tuna sandwich.

"I'm having so much fun," Mia replied.

"Good. I know you are used to church on Sundays, are you okay missing it? It's routine for you."

The words church and routine made Mia's hair stand up.

"Oh, no!" Mia said, putting down her sandwich. "Oh, no, oh no, oh no!"

"What's wrong, Mia?"

Mia looked down at her fingernails. They were long. Today was nail cutting day. Momma wasn't here to cut them. If she went back next week and they were long, Momma was going to be mad.

Aunt Colleen asked her again what was wrong.

"I need to cut my nails."

"Right now?"

Mid nodded.

"That it? You scared me. I thought something was wrong?"

"Do you have nail clippers?"

Aunt Colleen said that she did.

"Good. I need to cut them today, okay?"

Aunt Colleen agreed. Mia was relieved.

They finished their sandwiches and vegetables then ran off to the water. This day was shaping up to be just as great as the last.

Chapter Thirty-Two

Mia sat in her theatre class looking at all the excited children planning out their costumes for the big play. In the back of the room, Kirk had four tickle trunks of garments for everyone to look at and put together what they needed for the live performance. Each trunk went with one of the play themes that were available at the start of the project. Mia's group had the trunk labeled *Solar Eclipse Group.*

They decided to reenact the solar eclipse while giving the moon and sun a voice. This way it was entertaining and informative. Mia thought it lacked creativity but she was only one voice in a room of many. She didn't push her thoughts too far.

Jennifer, the redheaded girl in her class was playing the sun. A boy, named William, who was slightly bigger than Jennifer, was playing the moon. The rest of the group members were playing children and adults who were experiencing the solar eclipse for the first time. Mia was girl number 3.

She wrote her own line to say in the play. She wanted it as lame as she thought the storyline was so she wrote: 'Hey, where did the sun go?'

The other classes were better. Mia got to work on her short story and poem. She had more control over the topic and the words in these classes.

Mia almost finished her short story that afternoon. She just wanted to add a few touches here and there. She would do that over the next day or two. Her poem was a little harder to write.

Chantal, her poetry teacher had said that they could choose to rhyme their poem or not rhyme it. The choice was theirs to make. The only catch was that they had to pick which way they were going to write it up front. So, on the first day of class for Mia, she chose to rhyme. Mia liked rhyming poems, and Mia was good at it too. Poetry was her strong suit. At least that was what all her teachers had said to her in past years.

The only problem Mia had about the poem for this class was that she didn't have a topic yet and it was almost hand in time. She spent all evening that night trying to think of what to write about but she came up blank.

The next morning, she got up before Aunt Colleen, walked down to the living space, and looked around. She could see sunlight streaming through the window. She went outside on the porch to see if it would inspire a topic.

"The sun always shines, the wind rarely blows, birds sing their song, that's how life goes."

Mia hated it.

She sat down on the outside rocking chair. Tulip fluttered over and joined her. Setting herself down on the arm of the chair.

"Well hello there, Tulip! How are you today?"

Mia knew she wouldn't answer but she looked to her in silence anyway.

"Any thoughts on what I should write about?"

Tulip flew off the arm and landed on Mia's leg. She seemed to like it there.

"I think we're friends now. You keep sitting on my lap." Mia whispered to Tulip. "I should write my poem about you?"

Mia wished she had brought her pencil and paper with her. She would have loved to start writing now. She didn't want to get up and have Tulip move off of her so she started the poem in her head instead.

You're pretty and orange...hmmm.

Aunt Colleen came barreling through the cabin door calling out her name. Mia looked up from the rocking chair.

"Oh, thank God you're here." Aunt Colleen said, slightly out of breath.

"I wanted to start my poem," Mia answered.

"I woke up and you were gone. It scared me."

"Sorry."

"Nothing to be sorry about," she said. "I just worried. I should have known you would be downstairs."

Mia nodded.

"How's your poem going?"

"Terrible. What rhymes with Orange?"

"No, it doesn't."

"Huh?"

"Sorry, it was a joke my dad use to say. Not really funny."

"I don't get it."

"Don't worry about it. Like I said, it isn't really funny. To answer your question, there are no words that rhyme with orange."

"Really?"

"Really."

"Then my poem is worse than terrible."

Mia looked back down at Tulip. "You're going to need to help me little buddy. I got nothing."

Tulip, as if saying she had nothing of help either, jumped up and flew away.

Mia was halfway dressed when she heard a knock on Aunt Colleen's cabin door. She heard a young girls voice asking for Mia, and Aunt Colleen respond to her saying that she would find her. Moments later, Aunt Colleen was at the bedroom door telling her she had a friend waiting downstairs for her.

Mia didn't really have people she would call friends at camp, so she didn't know who it could be. She walked downstairs and peeked outside. She recognized the long blond hair of Kelly. Her old bunk mate from Cabin 4.

"Hi," Mia said.

"Hi. Just wanted to know if you wanted to walk to class with us?" Kelly looked behind her as she said it. Mia looked over her shoulder to see two other girls from the cabin standing at the bottom of the steps.

Mia looked at Aunt Colleen, "That okay?"

Aunt Colleen said it was, so Mia left with the girls.

"So why don't you stay in our cabin anymore? We all want to know," the caramel skinned girl asked. Mia closed her eyes for a moment and thought back to her spy book.

Caramel skinned girl, caramel skinned girl, think Mia. She mumbled inside her head. Mia thought back to the page and remembered writing the word Donna on top of that entry.

"Because my Aunt is here, Donna." Mia added her name, hoping she got it right. "I don't get to see her much so I wanted to stay with her."

"Oh," Donna said. "Do you like it in there? It looks big."

Mia nodded. "It is."

"Is there a TV?" Jennifer, the redhead asked. Mia remembered her name.

"Ya, but it doesn't work."

"That sucks big time."

"Totally!"

"Majorly!"

Mia wanted something cool to add to all the girl's reactions but didn't quite know which words were cool now, so she just repeated one that was already said.

"Ya! Totally."

Mia looked over at them for acceptance. The girls nodded in agreement with her. Mia was proud of herself.

"So, do you like any boys here?" Kelly asked.

Mia shook her head.

"Really?"

"Donna likes William, Jennifer likes Clint, and I like Dominic. So, they are off limits. You'll have to see who you like. We're all planning on kissing them before we leave camp." The girls all giggled when Kelly said the word kissing.

Mia had no interest in kissing any boys at camp. She did not want to have anything to do with anyone touching her lips. Especially a boy she didn't know.

"You need to pick one. It'll be so fun." Kelly dragged out the word *so* for a long time.

Mia conceded, "I'll have to look at the boys. I'll let you know once I pick one."

The girls reached their classroom and took their seats. All morning Kelly kept poking Mia in the back to get her attention. When Mia would look back at her, Kelly would point to a different boy in the classroom and ask Mia if she liked the one in question. Mia said no every time.

Finally, when Kelly got to the last boy and Mia again nodded no, Kelly looked at her disappointed.

"You're one of those lesbians aren't you?"

Mia didn't know what a lesbian was but no one had ever called her that before, so she assumed she wasn't.

"No," Mia answered.

"Okay, whatever!"

Mia looked around at the boys again. She felt she had to pick one, but none of the boys were interesting to Mia. She tried to look at them all again, this time instead of trying to find the cutest though, she looked for the least ugly boy.

"Maybe him." Mia pointed at a taller, chubbier boy. He looked shy but happy. "The one standing with William."

Kelly looked over in the direction Mia was pointing. "Liam?"

"I guess so," Mia answered. "If that's his name."

"The one wearing the Vuarnet shirt?"

Mia nodded.

"Well, not my first choice for you but okay. Get to know him more. Hang out with him a bit."

"When? How?"

"Start now." Kelly got up and pulled Mia from her seat. "We're on personal time. There's only ten minutes left of class. Go up to him and start talking. You should talk to him before you kiss him."

Mia didn't want to kiss him. She didn't even want to go talk to him. She tried to say no to Kelly but Kelly was persistent.

"Go!"

Mia took a deep breath and walked over to where William and Liam were standing. She didn't know what to say so she just stood there. Frozen.

The two boys looked at her after a while but Mia still said nothing. She didn't know how to talk to a boy she was supposed to kiss.

"Ummm…" but that was all she got out.

"Umm, what?" asked Liam.

Mia panicked.

"Nothing. Never mind."

Mia turned around and walked away. As she was leaving, she heard William say, "What a freak."

Mia left class on her own and crying.

She headed to Aunt Colleen's cabin. It was empty. It was nearly lunchtime. All the volunteers were at the lunch hall.

Mia looked for Tulip. She found her sitting on a leaf by the maple tree. Mia put her finger out to see if Tulip would climb on but she wouldn't.

"It's okay to come on my skin. I won't hurt you. I can tame you." Mia tried again. Tulip didn't budge. "The world is pretty scary isn't it, Tulip? So many people trying to tell us what to do. I don't like to do half the things people want me to. Why do they do it?"

Mia slowly pulled the leaf off of the tree. Tulip stayed on. Mia carefully placed herself on the ground. She brought the leaf, and Tulip close to her face. Mia felt water in her eyes.

"Why are people so mean?" Mia's tears were reaching her jawbone. She wiped them away. "And those that aren't mean, I hurt them. I don't mean to but I do. I just can't figure it all out. I can't fix me. Why can't I fix me?"

Mia smacked her hand down in the sand.

"Ahhh!" She screamed to the air. Her scream caused Tulip to fly away.

Mia took a few deep breaths. As she watched Tulip fly out of sight, she came up with an idea for her poem. She pulled her writing book and pencil out of her backpack. She opened it up and started writing. The words flew out of her.

<u>My Dear Butterfly</u>

My Dear Butterfly,
Your beauty is pure gold,
You have a kindness to you
That I like to hold.

You fly around our faces
You show us all your grace
You listen to our cries and cheers
Then you fly to another space.

Mia wrote 9 more paragraphs until she had it complete.

Mia walked into the lunchroom with everyone else to sit down to eat. She made sure she was a few feet away from Kelly and her friends and a lot of feet away from William and Liam.

The meal came and Mia concentrated on her food. Her tray came with a hotdog, a bowl of peas, and a cup of chocolate pudding. A glass of milk and water were already at her seat when she sat down. The camp must have gotten a deal on peas, because they served more today than they had ever had. At least she didn't have to pick them out of her other food this time. They came in their own bowl. She placed them on the table, off of her tray. They were safely out of nose range.

Mia was chewing on her hotdog when she heard laughter coming from where Kelly, Jennifer, and Donna were sitting. Mia looked over. They were whispering and pointing at Mia. Kelly was doing most of the talking.

Mia tried to ignore them.

The laughter got louder. Mia was getting upset.

Kelly leaned over and whispered something to William. William looked at Mia then laughed.

"Freak," he said again. This time though, he said it meaner than before.

"I'm not a freak," Mia said.

"Ya, you are."

William leaned over and whispered something to Liam.

Mia put her head down and ate the rest of her hotdog. She just wanted to finish eating and get out of there.

Mia started eating her pudding. As she went to take her second bite a pea dropped onto her spoon. A loud eruption of laughter followed. She looked up to see William ready to send another pea her way.

"Stop it!"

Mia hated being teased. Moreover, she hated peas. She was afraid one would land on her spoon without her noticing, and end up in her mouth.

"Stop it," Kelly repeated in a mocking tone. Everyone in the group was laughing except Liam.

"Leave her alone," Liam said to his buddies.

"Oooo, Liam has a crush on Mia," said Donna.

"No I don't!" Liam answered defensively. "Just leave her alone. She isn't worth it."

Liam's words hit Mia hard. She knew she wasn't worth much to adults, but kids her age always seemed to feel differently. Until now. Mia was crushed. As tears welled up in her eyes another pea landed on her tray. Mia had enough. She took her tray and flipped it over, sending food remnants everywhere.

"Leave me alone!" Mia screamed. The girls looked terrified. William laughed. Mia got up and started running. She ran straight into the empty kitchen, grabbed the pot of remaining peas still left on the stove, and dumped them all over the floor. She tossed the pot aside and stomped. Stomped on every last pea. Screaming at the top of her lungs as she did. She stomped those peas until they were mush. Adults came running to the kitchen doorway. First the chef, who screamed at Mia's mess, then Aunt Colleen who grabbed Mia up with two arms and held her from behind.

"What the hell Mia?"

"Let me go," Mia cried. She was still stomping the peas.

Aunt Colleen didn't let go.

"Let me go, I said." Mia bit down on Aunt Colleens arm as hard as she could. Aunt Colleen screamed in pain. She loosened her grip. Once free, Mia high-tailed it out of the kitchen, out of the lunchroom, and out of sight.

Mia ran down the path, through the cabins, and into the forest. Mia had fought back. She made something stop. Mia screamed out her pain with a yell so deep she wasn't sure if it was through anger or laughter because as awful as it felt, it also felt so damn good.

Mia kept running until all the pain left her body.

Chapter Thirty-Three

Mia stood in the middle of the forest. It reminded her of the night she spent in the woods at the Bible retreat. The night Momma brought her out there. She was convinced now that she remembered it correctly. She didn't sleepwalk. Momma made her go then left her alone. Mia was starting to hate everyone. Not just Jesus.

She sat on a rock that protruded from the ground a few feet. It was cold but it felt nice to sit on it anyway. Mia took some deep breaths to calm her heartbeat down.

Tulip showed up. Mia shooed her away.

Mia was angry.

Girls her age could be so mean. It frustrated Mia. She never really felt like she fit in with these ones. Most days she could fake it enough to get by but today wasn't that day.

Why did they want her to kiss some gross boy anyway? Why did it matter? And why were they throwing peas at her?

Mia wanted to cry but she couldn't. She was too mad. Knowing she was in the middle of the forest she screamed. She screamed loud and hard.

Every scream felt better and better.

Mia picked up some loose rocks on the ground and threw them against a tree. Each rock thrown harder than the last.

Tulip returned to Mia.

"Go away, stupid butterfly. Or I'll throw this rock at you!"

Mia pretended to throw it. Tulip just fluttered in front of her.

"I mean it. Leave! I don't need anyone."

Mia pretended again. Tulip flew a distance away, landing on a tree trunk.

Why was she so unlovable, she thought? Why did no one want her as she was? Mia kicked some sticks on the ground. She looked down at her ratty shoe. "Pathetic," she said "just like you Mia.

Stupid to think you have friends. People just tolerate you. They don't like you."

Mia looked around. She wasn't quite sure how to get back to the campground. She knew the direction she had come from but couldn't see anything but trees ahead of her. When she was ready, she would just have to start heading that way.

Mia thought about the night of the peas. She thought about Frank and the time with him. Mia thought about the beatings, and the name calling, and the closet. Mia thought about it all. Mia hated who she was.

Mia thought about all the people she tried to tell. All the people that asked if something was wrong. All the people that didn't stay to help her. The people that wanted to help but Mia didn't let them. Maybe, Mia thought, it wasn't all that bad. Maybe?

But she knew it was.

No one else had a life like hers. Not that she knew of anyway. None of her friends showed up with bruises. No one talked about closets. No one had her rules. Mia wasn't special, Mia was different. Unlovable. Unimportant. Mia was garbage.

Mia was mad at Momma for making her garbage. Why did Momma bring her into this world? Mia wanted to destroy Momma. Mia wanted to fight back.

Mia screamed again. Trying to squeeze a tear out of her eye. If she could only cry, she thought, she would feel so much better. But she couldn't. It just hurt so much. Mia grabbed a stick. She smashed it down as hard as she could on the ground. She smashed it over and over again When she had enough of that, she hit the rocks, then the trees, then she hit poor Tulip. Mia instantly regretted it.

"No!" She screamed. "No! Tulip!"

Tulip fell to the ground.

"Mia? Is that you?"

Aunt Colleen's voice rang out through the trees.

"Mia?"

Mia thought about hiding for a moment but she couldn't. The one thing she wanted right now was to be in her Aunt Colleen's arms.

"Over here!" she called out towards where the voice came from.

A few moments later Aunt Colleen came out through the trees. Mia picked up Tulip and ran straight into her aunt's arms.

Aunt Colleen held tight. After a while she stepped back a bit. She pulled out a walkie-talkie and pressed a red button on the side. She told whoever had the matching radio that she had found Mia, and that everything was okay. She also told them they would be back in a bit to clean up the mess in the kitchen.

Aunt Colleen threw the walkie-talkie onto the ground.

"What happened? I hear kids were teasing you?"

Mia nodded.

"They must have been teasing you a lot to get you this upset?"

"It wasn't that bad."

"It wasn't that bad? Mia! You went ballistic."

"I know."

"Well? Is there more to the story? If it wasn't that bad then something else happened. Mia, between the marks on your back, your weird behavior in bed the other night, this, whatever you want to call it, at lunchtime, and your issue with peas. Something really bad is going on. You need to start talking, kid."

Aunt Colleen was right.

Mia put Tulip down on a rock. She paced back and forth. She knew that if she were going to say something, now would be the time.

"Mia? You're scaring me."

"I need a moment."

Aunt Colleen stopped talking. She started pacing back and forth with Mia instead. They paced for 10 minutes.

"Mia, you're killing me here."

"I'm sorry. I don't know what to say first."

"Okay. Would it help if I asked questions? We can start there?"

Mia nodded.

"Can we stop walking in circles?"

Mia shook her head. She needed to keep moving. That's the only thing she knew for certain at that moment.

"Fine. We will keep pacing," Aunt Colleen kept walking beside Mia. She had figured out the pattern now. When Mia would stop and turn in the other direction, so would Aunt Colleen. They were smooth together, in perfect sync.

"Is this more than the teasing?"

Mia nodded.

"Okay, first rule. If I'm asking questions, I need you to verbally answer. Can you do that?"

Mia nodded again.

"Mia!"

"Sorry. Yes!"

"Good. Do you want to start with talking about the teasing?"

"No."

"Nothing at all?"

Mia shook her head.

"Just the peas. They were throwing peas at me, and that made me mad."

"Okay. Peas make you mad. Man, you must really hate peas. I think you flattened about 2000 of them back there."

Mia didn't respond. She didn't think this was a question so a verbal answer wasn't required.

"So, peas bothered you before today?"

"Yes."

"Do they have something to do with the bigger picture?"

"Yes."

"Do you want to talk about the peas?"

"Not now. Later."

"Okay, we will shelve the pea talk. Does this have to do with your back?"

"Yes."

Aunt Colleen took a deep breath in. "I'm going to hate this story aren't I?"

Mia really didn't know how to answer that question. It depended on if Aunt Colleen thought it was wrong or not. Mia felt in her gut that it was wrong. But she wasn't sure. Momma seemed to think it was okay. All of it. Not just what happened that night, but what always happens with Momma.

"I don't know," Mia finally answered.

"Mia, I really need to stop walking. Can we sit down? If you want, we can sit on the ground back to back, so you don't have to look at me when we speak."

Mia thought about it for a moment then agreed. "Okay!" she said.

The two cleared a spot on the ground, sat down, and as promised, Aunt Colleen put her back against Mia's before continuing to ask questions.

"Does this hurt your back?"

"It's okay. Just don't wiggle much."

Aunt Colleen agreed to try not to.

"You said your Momma hurt your back, did she hit you?"

"No."

"Did she push you into something?"

Mia needed to give her more story to go on.

"She pushed me down to the ground."

"That explains the bruises," Aunt Colleen hesitated before finishing her thought. "But that doesn't explain the rug burn marks. Did she? Did she drag you around the house?"

"Yes"

"For fuck sakes."

Mia could hear sadness in Aunt Colleen's voice. She wondered if she should continue. Mia was still on the easy stuff.

"Why did she drag you?"

"Because of Frank."

"Was Frank there too? He was still there when I left but he was leaving. Did he not go? Did they hurt you together?"

"No. He left with Daddy. Momma was drinking lots when you all left. She started acting funny."

Aunt Colleen moved around in her spot a little. Mia winced.

"She was drunk."

"I guess so."

"Tell me what happened."

Mia took a deep breath in. It was now or never. Mia knew she had already told most of the story so she might as well get the rest out.

"Momma asked me to sit on her lap. She started rubbing my hair. She sang to me even. It was nice for a moment. Until Momma…"

Aunt Colleen said nothing. Mia took a breath again. She closed her eyes to remember that night. She hated every part of the memories it brought up, but she needed to get it right. She needed to tell Aunt Colleen everything.

"Until Momma kissed me."

"Kissed you? Like how?"

"I don't know. Like weird."

"Weird how?" Aunt Colleen wanted more details than Mia had at the moment.

"Like how she kisses Daddy."

Aunt Colleen got on her knees and crawled in front of Mia. Mia put her head down. "Like how she kisses Daddy? Like romantically?"

Mia shrugged her shoulders. She didn't know what romantically meant.

"Then what?"

Mia asked Aunt Colleen to sit behind her again. Aunt Colleen was red in the face. Mia couldn't look at her. It made her wonder too much if she was mad at Momma or at Mia. Aunt Colleen slammed a rock hard to the ground before she moved, but then sat back down in the position they were in before.

Once Mia felt her back against her aunts again, Mia continued.

"She asked me why Frank liked me more than he liked her. I think Momma tried to get Frank to kiss her that night too, and he said no. Momma said Daddy didn't want her in the biblical sense, and neither did Frank. She was mad that Frank touched me and not her."

Mia paused for a moment. She could hear her aunt breathing loudly.

"Are you okay?"

"Yes. But your mother won't be soon."

"What do you mean?"

"Nothing. Go on."

Mia closed her eyes and continued to go through the night's events, one step at a time, in her mind. She shared them out loud.

"I backed away from her and she pushed me down to the ground. She dragged me to the front door to lock it, then into the kitchen. She grabbed the bowl of peas. Momma brought me to the living room and climbed on top of me. She said that if I was good enough for Frank, then I was good enough for her."

"Mia, where are you going with this? Tell me your mother didn't..."

Aunt Colleen didn't finish her sentence. Mia could feel her back moving up and down. Aunt Colleen was crying.

"I should stop."

"No. Keep going. What did your mother do?"

"She shoved peas in my mouth. Handfuls and handfuls. I couldn't breathe. Then she...then she."

Mia couldn't say the rest. She was now crying too. Tears were finally coming. She didn't know how to say what Momma did.

Aunt Colleen turned around and hugged her from behind.

"I'm so sorry, Mia."

"It hurt so much, Aunty," Mia cried out. "So so much."

Aunt Colleen kissed Mia's head over and over. She could feel her aunt's tears running down the side of her cheeks and mixing in with her own.

"It was the worst one."

"The worst one?"

Mia nodded.

"This happened before?"

Mia nodded. Breaking the using the voice rule Aunt Colleen put in place. Aunt Colleen didn't call her on it.

"Are you fucking kidding me?"

Mia stiffened right up. "You don't believe me?"

Aunt Colleen grabbed her by the face. "I didn't say that. I believe you. My God Mia, I believe every word you are saying. I can't believe your Momma. That horrible wretch of a woman is going to burn in hell and I would like to put her there myself."

"You can't tell Momma I told you. You just can't."

"We will get to that in a moment. But look at me Mia." Aunt Colleen pulled Mia's face straight towards hers and looked her dead in the eye. "She will never, and I mean NEVER, do that to you again!"

Mia believed Aunt Colleen. Mia just melted on her shoulder and cried. Aunt Colleen sat with her for several minutes then asked Mia if she could ask a few more questions. Mia said she could.

"Does your Dad know?"

"Daddy knows that she doesn't like me. He also knows about the closet. But he doesn't know about this, or Momma's special time with me."

"Special time. Is why you got scared the other night?"

"Yes. I thought you wanted Momma's special time."

"Oh God Mia, I would never hurt you like that."

"I know now."

"Good. And what do you mean about Daddy knowing about the closet. What happened in the closet?"

"Momma locks me in the closet when I do wrong. Which is a lot."

"What? Where is this closet?"

"In my room."

"Is that why there is a lock on it?"

Mia nodded.

"How long does she put you in there?"

"It depends on how mad she is. A few hours usually. One time a whole day."

Aunt Colleen looked like she was about to have a heart attack. Her face was still red, her breathing was fast and hard, and now her body was shaking.

"Are you okay, Aunty?"

"No, I'm not okay. Your mother is pure evil. I hate her. I hate her so much."

"Can I tell you something too, Aunty? Between us? Don't get mad?"

"Of course."

"I hate her too!"

And with that, everything began to go dark.

Chapter Thirty-Four

It was the solar eclipse.

Mia looked at her aunt. Aunt Colleen hadn't said anything to Mia for a long time. Mia could hear her taking deep breaths in and out. She was doing what Mia did when she needed to calm down. But now, she was just sitting there still. Looking nowhere it seemed.

Mia stretched out on the ground looking up at the sky. She didn't have the special box she made for the eclipse but she didn't care. She felt invincible. She felt light. And for the first time in a long time, she felt fearless.

"Look Aunty, the eclipse."

Aunt Colleen lay beside Mia. She reached over and grabbed her hand. They stayed there for the entire eclipse. Mia wasn't sure how much time had passed but she knew that she read that most eclipses lasted about twenty minutes. It had to be at least that long.

When the sun came back Mia sat up. Aunt Colleen was still on the ground crying.

"I'm sorry I hurt you," Mia said.

"You didn't hurt me, Mia. I am angry that I didn't see what was happening to you. I am upset that I didn't stop it. I'm so mad at my brother for allowing this to happen under his roof. I love you so much, kid. Incredible amounts. It hurts my heart that someone you trusted did this to you. I'm sad. You don't deserve this. Any of it."

Mia didn't know what to say. Aunt Colleen was uttering words she had longed to hear her entire life. Aunt Colleen didn't blame this on her, she said nothing about Jesus, and she told Mia that she loved her. Mia hoped it was true. She didn't think Aunt Colleen would lie to her.

"I love you too."

Aunt Colleen sat up and dusted herself off. She had dirt and leaves from head to toe.

"Thank you for telling me. You're so brave."

Mia didn't have a response.

"Okay. Is there more to tell me?"

"Not right now."

Aunt Colleen lifted an eyebrow. "Is there more?"

"Yes."

"Do you want to talk more?"

"No."

"Okay. Let's curb it here. I need to digest this all anyway. We need to make a plan of what to do now. I have to do something, you know that right? To stop this? But we will make the plan together. I will keep you safe, I promise. Can you trust me on that?"

Mia knew she had no choice but to, so she nodded her head.

"Okay. We need to head back to the kitchen. We have a mess of peas to pick up."

Mia felt fear inside of her. Aunt Colleen must have noticed it on the outside.

"What am I thinking? I'll clean up the peas. You stay away from it."

"No. I made the mess, I need to clean it up."

"Most cases, yes, that's the rule. Today is the exception. You're not going near those peas. I won't allow it."

Mia was grateful but felt guilty. It wasn't fair to her aunt that she would clean it all up when she didn't make the mess. But Mia didn't argue. She needed to take her aunt's kindness today.

They got up to leave when Mia remembered about Tulip. She went to the rock where she left her. Mia wanted to bring her back to the cabin. Maybe she could bring her to Mrs. C. and see if she could help her. Mia wondered if Mrs. C. ever fixed a butterfly before. But Tulip wasn't there. Maybe she had the wrong rock? She looked at all the other rocks around. Tulip was nowhere.

"What are you looking for?"

"I hurt Tulip. I was angry. I left her on a rock but she's gone."

"Maybe she flew away."

"I think I killed her though."

Aunt Colleen looked at all the rocks. "You sure you left her on one of these?"

Mia nodded.

"Well then she must not have been dead. Because she flew away."

Mia was happy to hear that she may not have killed Tulip. She knew Tulip would never want to be around her again and that was okay, as long as she wasn't dead.

"Can we leave now?"

Mia said that they could.

Aunt Colleen grabbed Mia by the hand.

"Let's go!"

It was nearly 3 in the afternoon when Aunt Colleen and Mia returned to the cabin. Aunt Colleen set Mia up on the couch with a book, and headed over to the dinner hall. She told Mia she would return as soon as she could.

Mia read for a little while, then fell asleep. She was exhausted. She woke up hours later when Aunt Colleen returned with two plates of food. She brought dinner.

They sat at the table eating. Mia asked Aunt Colleen why she wasn't doing dinner hour volunteering and Aunt Colleen explained that she was given the night off to stay with Mia. Mia was grateful for that. She really felt the need to be with her Aunt.

"So, Mia, I have a few more questions. Light questions. Are you okay with that?"

Mia was.

"Have you told anyone else about this?"

"About which part?"

"What happened that night with Momma, how you hurt your back."

"No. Just you."

"Thanks for trusting me."

Mia nodded.

"Does anyone else know about the closet?"

"A few of my friends. Most of them stop playing with me once they find out. Daddy knows about it."

"Does he ever put you in it?"

"No. Just Momma."

"Does he ever take you out of it?"

Mia took a bite of mashed potatoes and thought about it. "No. He never has."

"My brother is an idiot," Aunt Colleen said barely audible.

"Anyone else?"

"Jesus knows."

"Yes. We already went through that."

Mia shrugged.

"Oh, and Mrs. C. knows about Momma and Frank. She also knows about Momma and the forest."

Aunt Colleen put down her fork.

"Really? I have many follow up questions here."

Mia kept eating. Talking was getting easier and easier.

"Who is Mrs. C.?"

"She was the guest of Daddy's at dinner, remember? Annie?"

"Yes. I like her. I had a feeling she knew something more than she put on. How does she know about Frank?"

Mia explained to her about what happened at the Bible retreat after Mia fell playing tag. She also told Aunt Colleen how Mrs. C. tried to help her clean up without Momma seeing, but when Momma came storming through the door, Mrs. C. told Momma a whole lot of things the Lord Jesus wouldn't want a good Christian woman to be saying. Mia told her that Mrs. C. threatened Momma that if she ever touched Mia again, that Mrs. C. would tell everyone that Momma was more upset over Frank going to jail then what he did to her own daughter.

"I never understood why that upset Momma so much," Mia admitted. "Everyone seemed to know just how much Frank meant to Momma. Of course, she was upset."

"Mia, your Momma should have put you above Frank. You're her very own flesh and blood. Any real Momma would have."

That's what Mia thought too sometimes. But she just figured the feeling was wrong.

"So, what happened with the forest?"

Mia answered that too. Aunt Colleen knew a bit of the story but only what she was told by Daddy. Mia told her about her memory of Momma walking her out there and telling her to stay put. Mia also told Aunt Colleen about how Momma later said that she wanted Mia to die in the forest. Mia shared how Mrs. C. comforted her after and how she and Momma got in a war of words again. When Aunt Colleen repeated how much she liked Mrs. C., Mia then shared how she rescued her from Frank's house that one time.

Mia finished her meal around the same time that she finished her story.

"Do you want more?" Aunt Colleen asked.

"Is that okay?"

"Of course. Let me go get it. I will be right back. Mia, one more question if you don't mind."

Mia looked up.

"Do you want to stay and finish out writing camp? Or do you want to leave and go home?

"I don't want to go home."

"Okay." Aunt Colleen grabbed the empty plate and headed to the door.

"But I don't want to stay here either," Mia said looking down at the ground. "I just want to be with you." Mia couldn't face her aunt. She didn't want to see the rejection alongside hearing it.

"Then that is what we will do. We will leave tomorrow and you will come to my house for a few days. Just us. We won't tell your parents."

"Really?" Mia asked looking up.

"Really. That way we can figure out our next step together."

Mia smiled. Aunt Colleen wanted to be around her too. Aunt Colleen was going to do this with her. She said 'we' will figure it out. Those words meant everything to Mia. She liked it when people said 'we.'

"Now let me go get you some more food. It was real yummy tonight."

Mia agreed as Aunt Colleen left the cabin. The food was yummy. But Mia wouldn't be eating what Aunt Colleen was bringing back. Before Aunt Colleen returned, Mia was fast asleep at her seat at the table, dreaming of a life less complicated. A life without Momma and Daddy.

Chapter Thirty-Five

Mia woke up in darkness. She looked around. She couldn't figure out where she was. She noticed a light behind her. Mia sat up in her small bed to see that the light was coming from the kitchen. Mia waited for her eyes to adjust to the darkness then looked around again. She was on the couch. She had a pillow and a blanket covering her.

She remembered falling asleep at the table but nothing after that. Aunt Colleen must have moved her to the couch. Where was Aunt Colleen? Mia assumed that she was too heavy to be carried upstairs so Aunt Colleen must have left her there.

Mia's throat was dry. She decided to get up and get a drink of water from the kitchen. The minute she stepped out of bed, she found Aunt Colleen. She was asleep on the floor beside her. Mia put her foot back up on the bed but it was too late.

"Mia, you okay?" Aunt Colleen asked in a groggy voice.

"Yes. I just need a drink of water."

Aunt Colleen sat up. "Let me get it for you."

She went over to the sink and ran the water to cool it. She grabbed a glass, filled it up, and brought it over to Mia. Mia took a long drink.

"I fell asleep before you came back, didn't I?"

Aunt Colleen rubbed her eyes and let out a big yawn. "You did."

"I'm sorry. I will eat the food I wasted for breakfast."

"Don't be silly child."

"Food shouldn't be wasted. Many kids go without."

"That is true. Doesn't mean you need to eat it cold the next day. You can waste a meal now and then. Besides, maybe I already ate it."

Mia didn't believe that but she was too tired to argue tonight.

"Okay."

"Do you want to go upstairs to sleep?" Aunt Colleen asked.

Mia was quite comfortable where she was and told her aunt that. She also told her that she could go upstairs if she wanted to. That Mia would be okay if she did.

Aunt Colleen said she would rather stay where Mia was. Mia was thankful. Truth be told, Mia wanted that too.

They decided to go upstairs together so Aunt Colleen could be off the floor to sleep. They crawled into bed and Mia decided that instead of touching Aunt Colleen's back, she would snuggle her whole self up to her. Aunt Colleen said that was okay. Mia felt safe and warm.

Aunt Colleen woke Mia up early. She had to head to the kitchen and talk to the staff about her leaving early. Aunt Colleen said she didn't want Mia to worry if she woke up and she was gone, so she decided to wake her up instead. Mia asked if she could go back to sleep while Aunt Colleen was gone and she said that she could.

Mia slept for another two hours.

By 11 am the car was packed and they were ready to leave.

"Are you sure you want to go? You were quite excited for this camp. You won't be able to finish your stories under guidance, or participate in the final show. That okay?"

Mia nodded. "I think they will survive without Girl Number 3."

"I don't know. I hear she steals the show."

Mia laughed. "Let's go home. Well, to your place."

"That's home. My home is your home, Mia."

Mia liked that thought.

"But I do have to tell you. Your poem was selected to be read at the banquet. Chantal said it was really good."

"It was?"

Aunt Colleen nodded.

"Did you want to stay the last two days so you can read it?"

Mia wanted to stay so bad but she couldn't face those kids anymore. Her mind had images she feared slipping out if she got angry at them again. She couldn't risk it. And she was getting alone time with Aunt Colleen. That meant more to her than her poem.

"I think I want to leave."

Aunt Colleen nodded.

"Will you read me your poem before we go then? Since I won't get to hear it?"

Mia went to the car and grabbed her backpack. She returned to the cabin and pulled out her notebook.

"Sit on the couch. Like you're in the audience."

Aunt Colleen did so. Mia cleared her throat then read her words out load to her aunt:

"My Dear Butterfly,
Your beauty is pure gold
You have a kindness to you
That I like to hold.

You fly around our faces
You show us all your grace
You listen to our cries, and cheers
Then you fly to another space.

My Dear Butterfly,
Thanks for being my friend
I loved having you around
The best gift Jesus could send.

Your wings and your colour
Are the prettiest I have seen
The best thing about you though
Is you're never mean

My Dear Butterfly
It's only a matter of days

You will leave like the others
No friend ever stays

You will leave me sitting still
On this rock waiting for you
Even if I'm a good girl
I know this to be true

My Dear Butterfly
I will say goodbye now
Don't worry it will be quick
I know exactly how

I will forget what you looked like
You will forget my smell
We will never think of each other
Or the stories we did tell

You will flutter away
Pretending that's what's right
I will stay here in the darkness
With no one in sight

If we pass each other again
We will act like perfect strangers
Not talking about the mean ones
Not mentioning of their dangers

This will be our friendship
And we both know why
I just wish it was different
My Dear Butterfly."

Aunt Colleen stood and cheered.

"Bravo! Bravo, Miss Mia."

"You like it?"

"Yes! So much. You're really good, Mia."

Mia smiled. She believed that. Everyone told her that she wrote well. She felt she did well at poetry. She felt great at writing stories. Mia had found what she was good at. Mia had a talent.

"I wish I could see Tulip before we go. I'm so sorry that I hurt her."

"I know, Mia. She's okay. And you will be too."

Mia forced a smile. *Poor Tulip*, she thought. Mia knew what it was like to be struck down by someone you trusted. She hated leaving Tulip behind, this wasn't how she meant to say goodbye. Mia wondered if Tulip was afraid. Wondered if she felt betrayed. Mia wondered if she now mistrusted all humans. Mia was heartbroken. She didn't tame Tulip, she did the opposite. She made her broken. She just wanted Tulip back. Mia wondered if she was now just like her Momma. A hitter.

As they left camp, Mia quietly whispered out her window, "goodbye Tulip."

A few hours later they were pulling up in front of Aunt Colleen's big white house.

The entire ride, Mia kept thinking about the things that Aunt Colleen said in the forest. She thought about how everything that happened wasn't her fault. That Momma was messed up and not a good Momma, and how Daddy should not have allowed it to go on in his home. Mia wanted to believe all of this so bad. She didn't like the thoughts of Momma being sick, or angry, but Mia wanted to believe that maybe she wasn't such a bad person after all.

She again wondered why other kids had a different life from hers. Momma always said that Mia had more than the average kid. What did that mean? Momma said Mia should be happy that she was loved so greatly. That she should be thankful that her parents cared enough to make sure she was growing up with proper values and rules. But Mia never heard any other kid talking about closets with locks. She never even saw another kid with a lock on their closet door. And none of her other friends came to school with cuts and bruises that weren't explained by falls or fights she heard of. Maybe something *was* wrong with Momma. Maybe her life wasn't what it was supposed to be. Maybe she didn't deserve to be hit so much.

The thought seemed so foreign.

She wondered what life would be like the other way. When she was younger, she dreamt about a white castle with a Queen for a Momma and a King for a Daddy. They laughed a lot, fought off evil armies, and threw big parties with lots of food. All you can eat food. Now, Mia found herself dreaming of a bedroom with no door, a Momma who cooked, and a Daddy who adored and protected her. Was that possible? Or was Mia being selfish and not appreciating her life. She was fed, clothed, and had toys and books. Mia was okay.

Mia felt guilty for thinking she should have something better than what she already had. Aunt Colleen said she should want better, but she didn't know. She wondered what Aunt Colleen would have done differently?

As they pulled into the driveway, Mia asked her aunt, "What would you have done differently?"

"What do you mean? In my life?"

"No. In mine?"

"You mean, if I were you, what would I have done to make things not happen? Oh sweetie, as I said, this isn't your fault. You have done nothing to make them do what they have done to you. Changing you isn't what is needed. Changing them is."

"That's not what I mean."

Aunt Colleen took the keys out of the ignition and faced Mia.

"What do you mean then?"

"I mean. Maybe not different, that isn't the word." Mia paused to think about what she was trying to say. When she felt she had it, she continued. "If you came to my house, when Momma was hitting me, or yelling at me, or having special time with me, if you knew what was happening, what would you have done differently?"

Mia felt an instant relief that she could talk about these things freely. She still felt guilty for telling them out loud, but it was nice to have someone know.

"If I had known all these years? Mia, I would have walked straight into your house, knocked your mother unconscious, scooped you up into my arms, and got you the hell out of there. And I would keep you with me, forever."

Mia was shocked. She wasn't expecting that answer.

"Really?"

Aunt Colleen nodded.

Mia bowed her head.

"I wish I would have told you then."

Aunt Colleen reached over and hugged Mia.

"I wish you would have too, but we can't go back. Lord knows I wish we could. But I know now. I will not leave you."

"Do you still want to keep me?"

Aunt Colleen looked at Mia intensely. "I'm not very kid-friendly, and I am probably not the best role model, but you Mia, you deserve to be loved. You belong with me. I love you something fierce kid."

Mia's stomach turned. She wanted to move in with Aunt Colleen. She wanted to not be around Momma and Daddy anymore. But she also loved her parents. And she didn't want to see them hurt.

Mia's insides felt like they were turning in circles inside of her. And with one last thought of her leaving Momma and Daddy's house for good, Mia threw up all over the front seat of Aunt Colleen's car.

Chapter Thirty-Six

Mia sat in a bathtub half full of water and half full of bubbles. The water was still running and Mia loved it, more bubbles were being made.

Mia dipped her head under the water. When she came up, her head resembled Santa Claus. Bubbles were in her hair, on her chin, and over her eyes and ears. Mia kept them on until Aunt Colleen came in. Aunt Colleen thought it was pretty funny too. She wiped some bubbles off of Mia's eyes before reaching over to turn the water off.

"You good in here for a bit?"

Mia said she was.

"I'm going to go throw your clothes in the wash."

Aunt Colleen gathered Mia's clothes and picked up Lucy doll at the same time.

"Where you taking Lucy doll?" Mia asked.

"She got a little puke on her. I'm going to go wash her up."

"I didn't see any."

"It's in her hair."

"No. There's none there."

Aunt Colleen looked at Mia with frustration. "Fine, I will leave her here."

Aunt Colleen put the doll back down on the closed toilet seat. As she placed her down, Lucy doll fell off the seat and onto the floor. A small paper fell out of the pocket.

"What's this?" Aunt Colleen asked.

"That's Mrs. C.'s phone number. Remember I told you she hid it in the pocket? It's still there."

Aunt Colleen opened up the paper and looked at it closely.

"Let me hold onto this for a bit."

"Why?" Mia asked.

"It's paper. You're in the tub. I don't want it to get wet and you lose the number."

Mia agreed that that was a good idea.

Aunt Colleen left with the paper and her dirty clothes leaving Mia alone with her bubbles.

Mia played with the bubbles as long as she could but she got bored quick. She decided to wash herself up. Grabbing the bar of soap from the side of the tub, she slid it under the water and started rubbing it over her skin. She knew she was supposed to use the washcloth that Aunt Colleen had put aside, but she wasn't interested in that. She liked the feel of the soap directly on her skin.

She was only on her second leg when she noticed that most of the bubbles were starting to fade away. By the time she got to her arms, the bubbles were nearly all gone. Mia had no desire to stay in a bath without bubbles so she finished washing then drained the tub.

Getting out, Mia grabbed the towel Aunt Colleen left out, dried off, and put on a pair of pajamas. Mia grabbed Lucy doll and headed downstairs. Aunt Colleen was sitting at her dining room table, head bowed, and on the phone. Mia only heard a part of the conversation.

"I'm glad you agree with me. I don't know what to do now. Maybe the two of us can figure this out?"

Aunt Colleen did a bunch of head nods after that, adding a few aha's and okays in there as well. She ended by telling the person on the other line that she would see her soon.

"Are you going somewhere?" Mia asked as Aunt Colleen hung up.

Aunt Colleen jumped when Mia spoke.

"Mia! What are you doing out of the bath?"

"The bubbles disappeared so I thought it was time to get out."

"Did you wash?"

Mia said that she did. She sat down beside Aunt Colleen.

"Are you going somewhere?" Mia asked again.

Aunt Colleen shook her head. "No. I do have someone coming over later but don't you worry about it. It'll be after you go to bed. Are you hungry?"

Aunt Colleen didn't wait for Mia to answer. Instead, she got up and went to the fridge. She poured a glass of milk and brought it to Mia.

"Toast and peanut butter?"

Mia nodded. She was hungry.

Aunt Colleen popped some bread in the toaster then pulled out a small plate and the peanut butter. Mia thought she looked stressed but didn't say it. It wasn't polite to tell adults that they looked tired or stressed. Once, she told Momma that she looked tired and Momma yelled at Mia for hours. Then Momma spent an obsessive amount of time in front of a mirror. Momma kept repeating that Jesus must have been taking the day off and forgot to tell Momma's looks that they were on their own that day.

Aunt Colleen brought Mia her toast and sat back down.

"You tired?"

Mia was. Her eyes felt as heavy as a garage door. She nodded yes.

"Okay, finish up your toast and let's get you up to bed. I'll read you a story."

Mia did as her aunt suggested. After putting her dishes in the sink, she walked upstairs and got into the bed in the spare room. Aunt Colleen pulled out a copy of the Velveteen Rabbit and started reading. Mia nestled in close to Aunt Colleen and listened to her heartbeat more than the story.

When Aunt Colleen had read the last page, she kissed Mia on the forehead, and said goodnight. Mia was comfortable. She was happy.

Mia watched her aunt turn off one lamp, then another. Once she was at the door she turned back around to face Mia.

"Goodnight mon petit chou."

Mia smiled and tilted her head confused.

"It means goodnight my little cabbage. I don't know. It's silly but my dad used to say it all the time. I'm surprised your Dad hasn't."

"I've never heard that before. It's silly. I like it."

"Good."

Aunt Colleen came back over for one more forehead kiss. Mia gladly accepted it. It was nice.

"Now get some sleep."

"I will," Mia responded.

Mia, as comfortable and tired as she was, was not near ready to fall asleep. Her mind was busy. She kept thinking about her day, and how she shared a lot with Aunt Colleen. She thought about how Aunt Colleen wasn't mad at her for what she said. Mia also thought about how kind Aunt Colleen was.

Mia was in the middle of a memory from years ago, of her and Aunt Colleen at a school event, when she heard someone knock at the front door. Aunt Colleen's guest had arrived.

Mia wanted to run downstairs to see who it was, but she didn't want to risk getting in trouble for being out of bed. She pondered her choices for a while. She wasn't sure if she could go to sleep without knowing who it was. Within minutes, she realized she didn't need to worry about that any longer. With the opening of the front door, and a few quick stomps of shoes being removed, Mia heard the voice of the visitor, and it was someone she knew quite well.

"Hi, Colleen. I'm so glad you called."

"Me too. I'm glad you agree with me," Mia's aunt replied. "Shall we sit at the table, Annie?"

Chapter Thirty-Seven

Mia stayed at the top of the stairs to listen in on what Aunt Colleen and Mrs. C. were saying but she heard very little. Both seemed to be whispering. She took a few steps down to get closer. At her new level, Mia still could not hear many words, but she could now tell that Mrs. C. was doing most of the talking. She said something about Jesus but not in the way her parents said his name. She said it loud and mean, and with his full name, adding the Christ to it. Mia didn't think Jesus would like his name spoken in that tone.

Mia debated going all the way downstairs and surprising them but she knew that if Aunt Colleen wanted her there, she would have invited her. Mia could always tell when her presence wasn't wanted. She tried to slow down her breathing so she could strain her ears more. Mia was getting frustrated. Against her heart, Mia decided to go back upstairs. Just as she turned around to head up, the ankle Mia hurt twisted around the wrong way and caused a pain to shoot right through it, making her miss the step she was headed to. The misstep sent her flying down the remaining three stairs from where she was sitting. Mia landed hard on her back.

"What was that?" Aunt Colleen said running around the corner. Mrs. C. came barreling behind her.

"Mia! Are you okay?" Aunt Colleen reached down and rubbed Mia's face. "How did you fall down the stairs?"

Mia didn't want to answer the latter question.

"I'm okay," she said. Her knee hurt a bit and her ankle burned but otherwise she felt fine. She was embarrassed.

"Sorry, I was just coming for a drink." Mia looked up at Mrs. C., she looked upside down from this angle. "Hi!" Mia said.

"Hi, sweetie."

Mia tried to sit up. Aunt Colleen stopped her.

"How is your neck?"

"Fine."

"Your back?"

"It's okay."

"Are you sure?"

Mia nodded.

"Okay, you can sit up now, then."

Mia sat up with Aunt Colleen's help. Mia said thank you, then headed back up the stairs.

"Where are you going?" Mrs. C. asked.

"Back to bed."

"What about your drink?"

"My what?" Mia asked.

"Your drink. You said you were coming down for a drink."

"Oh, right."

Mia turned toward the kitchen. As she passed Mrs. C., Mia saw her and Aunt Colleen share a look. Mia wondered what the look was for.

Mia grabbed a cup from the cupboard and filled it with tap water. She took the biggest drink she could, but she wasn't that thirsty. She just needed to drink enough to convince them that she had been.

Aunt Colleen and Mrs. C. were standing just feet from her, watching each gulp that she took.

"You haven't asked why Annie is here?"

Mia kept drinking.

"You don't seem surprised."

"I heard her come in," Mia admitted in defeat.

"Do you want to know why she is here?" Aunt Colleen asked.

Mia nodded.

"She is here because we both want to help you."

Mia wasn't sure she wanted to know anymore.

"Mia, sit down?" Aunt Colleen asked, pointing to the table.

Mia topped up her water cup hoping they would change their mind about talking to her while she took the extra time. They didn't.

She walked over to the table and took a seat. The ladies sat on either side of her. Mia wasn't comfortable.

"Mia..." Aunt Colleen started to talk but she had nothing more to say after Mia's name.

"Let me, Colleen," Mrs. C. finished for her. Aunt Colleen moved her hand to say go ahead.

"Mia, we're worried about you. About what happens at home. It isn't safe for you there."

Mia sat silent.

"We know this is a tough situation for you, and it might be a little confusing, but your Aunt Colleen and I love you very much, and we don't want to see you hurt anymore."

Mia looked down at her lap. Her heart was starting to beat faster. She wondered if they could tell.

"Mia, what do you think about us trying to get you out of there? Out of your home?"

"Away from Momma and Daddy?" Mia looked up and asked.

"Yes. Away from Momma and Daddy," Aunt Colleen answered.

"I don't know. I don't want to be away from them."

Aunt Colleen reached over and touched Mia's arm. "I know baby. But they aren't making the best choices for you. You're getting hurt. We can't allow you to get hurt anymore."

"Then talk to them. Can you talk to them?"

"I could. But I'm not sure they will listen. Haven't you asked them to stop before?"

Mia nodded. "But they might listen to you more."

"I don't think they are going to change, Mia. Not without help."

"But they might?" Mia started to cry. She was torn. She didn't want to live in a closet anymore, and she didn't want to be hit, or have special time, and she wanted to be able to eat when she was hungry. But she didn't want to leave Daddy, and she didn't want to see Momma sad.

Mrs. C. reached over and put her arm around Mia's back.

"I know this is hard to understand Mia, but we can't let you go back there. That is a fact. We have to do something. I already tried talking to your mom, and she still hurt you. Right?"

Mia nodded.

"Where will I go? What are you going to do?"

"We haven't decided that yet, but we will make sure you know before anything happens. Is that okay?"

"But where will I go?"

"Well, hopefully here."

Mia still liked the thought of living with her aunt but now that it was more of a possibility, Mia was scared.

"Why would you want me?"

Aunt Colleen pulled Mia's head into her chest.

"You're pretty awesome and I would love to have you with me. Truly. But let's not get ahead of ourselves. Let's take this one step at a time, okay?"

"Okay. You'll tell me first right?"

"Right."

"You promise?"

Both Aunt Colleen and Mrs. C. gave her their pinky finger to shake.

Mia smiled even though she didn't feel like it.

"I want to tell Annie about what you told me the day of the eclipse. Is that okay?"

Mia shook her head.

"She needs to know, Mia. If she's going to help us make this stop."

Mia put her head down. Softly she whispered, "okay."

"Why don't you go back to bed? You can go to my room if you want, sleep with me tonight."

"No thanks."

Aunt Colleen caressed Mia's cheek. "Okay, if you're sure. But if you change your mind, you can always change beds."

Mia agreed. She got up from her seat, gave both ladies a hug, put her cup in the sink, and headed back to the stairs.

"Aunty?"

"Yes, sweetie?"

"Can you please just try talking to them first?"

Aunt Colleen said that she would. Mia left to go back to bed. A little while later, while lying in bed, Mia heard Aunt Colleen and Mrs. C. at the door.

"You know, she may not like what is about to happen?"

"I know," Aunt Colleen answered. "But what can I do? I just hope she'll one day forgive me."

"She will," Mrs. C. replied.

"Thanks for your help."

Depending on what was about to happen, Mia wasn't sure she could forgive anyone. Adults were not kind.

Chapter Thirty-Eight

Mia woke up to sunbeams shining in through the sheer white curtains. She was warm under the covers. She liked the guest room. It had a soft white shaggy carpet, a large bed with a big picture window, and dressers and drawers galore. The right corner of the room held a small writing desk and chair, with a small lamp to light up the creative space. Small highlights in the room were pink. Mia loved the colour pink.

She got up and sat at the desk. It was the perfect height for her. She ran her fingers over the wood. It was smooth. No rough edges or etches like her desk back home. She missed her desk. She missed her house. She missed her parents.

Mia got up and looked into some of the dresser drawers. In the large high dresser, she found extra sheets and blankets. The smaller dresser was empty. Mia walked over to the bedside table. It had only a Bible in the top drawer. Mia was surprised to find one in Aunt Colleen's house. She sat on the bed and opened up the book. Mia wondered what Jesus would think about what was happening. Would he want Mia to stay with Momma and Daddy or would he want her somewhere else?

Mia thumbed through the pages. She looked at her Daddy's favourite verse, Psalm 23. Mia read it out loud.

"The Lord is my shepherd; I shall not want. He maketh me to lie down in green pastures: he leadeth me beside the still waters. He restoreth my soul: he leadeth me in the paths of righteousness for his name's sake. Yea, though I walk through the valley of the shadow of death, I will fear no evil: for thou art with me; thy rod and thy staff they comfort me. Thou preparest a table before me in the presence of mine enemies: thou anointest my head with oil; my cup runneth over. Surely goodness and mercy shall follow me all the days of my life: and I will dwell in the house of the Lord for ever."

Mia ran her fingers over the words she just read out loud. She had heard the verse so often she thought she could say it word for word without reading. Daddy used to say this verse had helped him through many dark times. It reminded him that no matter what was happening, Jesus was with him. It was His will. Even if Daddy didn't like what he was going through. Mia wondered if that applied to this situation too? Would Daddy say that to Mia for this situation?

Mia always thought she knew a lot about Jesus and her Daddy but she wasn't so sure she did anymore. Mia felt lost.

"You awake in here?" Aunt Colleen knocked on the door as she opened it.

"I'm up."

"Pancakes?"

Mia smiled. "Yes please."

"Okay. Be downstairs in ten minutes?"

Aunt Colleen left and Mia pulled out her suitcase. She picked out some black bicycle shorts, and an orange t-shirt for the day. Mia knew that today they were going to visit Momma and Daddy so that Aunt Colleen could talk to them as she promised she would try. A day that Momma would be unhappy was a day Mia had to wear tight clothes. Loose clothes were too easy for Momma to grab and swing her around with. Tight clothes allowed Mia to get away. And sometimes, getting away from Momma was the only thing that lessened the pain. If she could hide long enough, sometimes, Momma calmed down. It didn't stop the closet, but it stopped the hitting. Mia didn't want Momma to hit anyone today, especially Aunt Colleen. Maybe Mia should tell her to wear tight clothes too.

Mia spent the day looking around Aunt Colleen's house. She hadn't really explored it much before. It was a large house. Mia looked all around the main level, checked out Aunt Colleen's room, both spare rooms other than the one she was staying in, and the basement. The basement looked like it could be an entire house on its own. It was large, with a laundry room, a living room with a couch and a recliner, and a television. It also had another bedroom. Why did Aunt Colleen need a house with so many bedrooms? She lived on her own.

It was around 4 p.m. when Aunt Colleen finally finished all of her phone calls. She called Mia to the main level and asked if she was ready to go to her parent's house. Mia was nervous.

"What if Momma gets really mad?"

"Well, she is most likely going to get mad Mia. But I'll be with you. I will not leave you, remember?"

Mia said that she remembered and gave Aunt Colleen her best smile. Those words didn't comfort Mia at all though. Mia was afraid for Aunt Colleen more than she was worried about herself.

"Maybe we shouldn't do this?" Mia suggested.

"We need to do this."

"No, we don't. I can just go back and you could visit lots. Momma doesn't hit me all the time. Sometimes she is nice."

"There is so much wrong with what you just said Mia."

Mia was often wrong with what she said. She just didn't understand what was wrong this time.

"What did I say wrong?" Mia decided to ask.

"Your Momma shouldn't hit you at all, Mia."

"But she is nice to me too."

"I'm sure she is."

The two stood looking at each other for a moment. Aunt Colleen spoke first.

"Mia, your Momma needs help. She shouldn't treat you the way she does. You don't deserve it."

"Will I ever see her again?"

"Of course, you will. But not until she gets some help. And while someone is with you to protect you."

"What about Daddy?"

"To be honest, I don't know what about your Daddy. He isn't acting like the brother I know. I don't know this answer Mia, I'm sorry."

That answer scared Mia. Mia didn't like situations where she didn't know what was going to happen. Aunt Colleen didn't understand that about Momma and Mia. Mia almost always knew what was going to happen. It was comforting. Mia knew the consequence for being late, for talking back, for not cooking a proper meal, for wearing the wrong clothes on the wrong days, for laughing when she wasn't supposed to, and for eating too much when she was hungry. Mia knew it all. She could prepare or decide if it was worth it.

This situation, Mia had no idea what was going to happen and it scared her. Mia could not prepare.

"I just want to go home and stay there."

"You can't Mia."

Mia felt fear and anger setting in.

"I don't want to do this!"

Aunt Colleen crouched down to look Mia in the face.

"I know baby. What's about to happen won't feel good at all. And it may get a little scary. But I will protect you. And I promise, when it's all over, everything is going to feel much better."

Mia wanted to believe her so bad. She wanted to believe that things would feel better. She wanted to believe that Aunt Colleen would protect her. She wanted to believe that she could protect Aunt Colleen in return, but Mia knew better. She knew that the words Aunt Colleen was speaking were only just that. They were words. And words meant nothing to Momma.

Mia's chest felt tight. She was struggling to breathe. She wanted Aunt Colleen to listen to her. She wanted this all to stop.

"No!" Mia yelled out. She reached over and pushed Aunt Colleen to the ground and ran up the stairs as fast as she could. She ran into her room and shut the door. She threw herself on the bed and started to cry. Mia felt broken.

Aunt Colleen opened the door.

"Mia, that's enough! I'm trying hard here." Aunt Colleen paced the floor. "I'm scared too. But we're going to try it your way. Try talking to them. This was your idea. Remember?"

Mia sat up. Aunt Colleen was mad, but so was Mia.

"None of this was my idea. I should never have told you anything. You made me tell you."

"I'm sorry you feel that way."

Mia then uttered the only words she could think of at the moment to express how angry she was. Words that Mia knew hurt. "I hate you!"

Aunt Colleen looked at Mia intently.

"No, you don't."

"Yes, I do!" Then she spoke them again, slowly and as mean as she could. "I hate you, I hate you, I hate you!"

Aunt Colleen sat down on the bed beside her. She rubbed her forehead as she softly spoke.

"Mia, I know you don't hate me. You're mad at me. There's a big difference."

Mia's thoughts were spinning. She didn't know how to respond.

"Now get your suitcase, empty it, and let's go. You can fill it up with stuff from your room for now, until we can get more."

"You know that's kidnapping?"

"What is?"

"Taking me from my house against my will."

"For Christ's sake Mia. You need to be a little bit more on board with me right now. How the hell am I going to fight for you if you are fighting against me too?"

Aunt Colleen got up and grabbed Mia's suitcase. She placed it on the bed. Aunt Colleen opened it and started taking clothes out. She put Mia's dresses to the side, then placed pants and shirts in the large dresser. Mia reached into her suitcase and grabbed her spy book.

"What's that?"

"It doesn't matter. It doesn't work. I can't figure people out."

"What do you mean?"

Mia didn't answer her aunt's question. Instead, she opened up the spy book and started ripping pages out. Sheet after sheet she ripped in half. Throwing the torn pieces all over the bed.

"Mia, stop that!"

Mia continued to rip. She was laughing and crying at the same time. Mia didn't understand what she was feeling. But she kept ripping anyway.

"Mia!" Aunt Colleen reached over and grabbed the book from Mia's hands. She closed it and threw it across the room.

"You're being so mean."

Mia didn't chase after the book.

Aunt Colleen grabbed the dresses and walked to the closet. She opened the door.

Mia froze.

Aunt Colleen reached in and grabbed a few coat hangers and walked back to the bed. Mia knew what the closet meant. That was fine. Mia was talking back. She got up and walked to the closet and sat inside in the corner. Mia wasn't going to let Aunt Colleen have the satisfaction of putting her there. Mia was going to go on her own.

Aunt Colleen looked in at Mia.

"What are you doing?"

Mia looked up.

"Taking my punishment."

Aunt Colleen put the dresses and hangers on the floor.

"Mia, get out of the closet."

Mia didn't know if this was a trick or not.

"Mia! Seriously, we don't have time for this. Get out of the closet."

Mia did as she was told. She walked back over to the bed. Mia stood on the bed just in case she needed to run. It was faster to run from the standing position. Aunt Colleen sat down on the bed.

"I won't ever put you in the closet, Mia. That's not normal. This is why you need a break from your parent's house. I really wish you could see this."

Mia stood in silence. Aunt Colleen got up and faced her.

"Mia, look at me."

Mia looked her Aunt Colleen in the eyes as they stood there face to face.

"You're scared. You're angry. You're confused. That is all okay. We will get through this, I promise. You're going to be okay."

Mia looked deeper into her aunt's eyes.

"I'm so scared."

"I know."

Mia kept eye contact with her aunt for several moments before she finally conceded. Mia sat down on the bed.

"You should wear tight clothing to go see Momma."

Chapter Thirty-Nine

All of the lights were on as Mia and Aunt Colleen pulled up to Mia's house. Even Mia's bedroom light seemed on.

Aunt Colleen said she was going to park on the street instead of in the driveway so it was easier for them to leave when it became time. There were a lot of cars full of people on the street. Mia had never seen the front of her house so busy.

Aunt Colleen stopped the car and took the keys out of the ignition.

"Are you ready?"

Mia said she was, but she wasn't sure that was true.

Aunt Colleen held her hand.

"It's okay if you aren't. I'm pretty scared too!"

Mia looked down at her hand in her aunt's.

"I don't hate you, Aunty."

"I know."

"Thank you for not putting me in the closet."

"Oh, Mia. I will never do that to you."

"Am I really going to live with you?"

"I don't know, Mia. That isn't up to me. But I'm going to fight like hell for you. Is that enough?"

Mia nodded.

"Let's go."

Mia let go of Aunt Colleen's hand and opened up her door. When she got out, she went straight to the back seat door, opened it as well, and grabbed her suitcase and her Lucy doll. She closed both doors at the same time.

Mia headed towards the house. Aunt Colleen looked around at the cars on the street. She waved.

"Who are you waving at?"

"Just to someone who waved at me. Not sure who it is."

Mia continued toward the back door.

"Mia, before we go in, let's discuss something quickly."

Mia gave Aunt Colleen her attention.

"When we go in there, I want you to go up to your room, okay? You don't need to be a part of the talk I'll have with your parents."

"I can't leave you with them."

"Yes, you can. And you will. They won't hurt me."

Mia wasn't convinced. "Momma gets pretty mad when people tell her things that she doesn't want to hear."

"I know. Your Daddy will protect me. He's my big brother."

Mia nodded.

"Also, I want you to listen to me. Only me. I know that's going to be hard but if I say we need to leave, or you need to go somewhere, or come downstairs, I need you to do so. Can you do that?"

"But what if Momma tells me something different?"

"I need you to listen to me. Can you do that? Please?"

Mia agreed to listen to Aunt Colleen. It was going to be hard to go against Momma but she gave her word. Mia always kept her word.

"Okay, let's go in. Remember, they don't know that we came back from camp early. You aren't due home until tomorrow. This will be a surprise."

Mia walked up the front steps. The door was unlocked. She walked in first, making an awful racket with her suitcase as she tried to pull it through the doorway.

"Who's here?"

Momma's voice rang loud through the entrance hallway.

"It's me, Momma, and Aunt Colleen."

Momma came around the corner. She had her apron on and food in her mouth.

"What in heavens are you doing back home, child? You weren't supposed to be here until tomorrow."

Aunt Colleen walked up to Momma.

"We were done early."

"Well, thanks for the call. We weren't expecting to see her for another 24 hours. What if we had plans?"

"Well your plans are about to change anyway." Mia noticed Aunt Colleen's upset tone coming through already.

Aunt Colleen pushed past Momma and headed to the dining room. She motioned for Mia to follow. Mia did.

Daddy was sitting at the table eating. Momma had made one of Mia's lasagnas for dinner. Mia remembered making it before she headed to camp.

"Done early, is that what I hear?"

Mia just nodded her head. She didn't want to answer with words.

"I need to talk to you Richard," Aunt Colleen said to Daddy. She pulled out a chair at the table and sat down.

"Where are your manners, Colleen? You weren't raised in a barn. I know that for a simple fact. Your brother is eating. It's the first time he has eaten all day."

"He can eat while I talk."

"Eat while you talk? Well I never! You can wait until he is done. This isn't good for his diabetes! He's been sick all week."

"What about you Richard? Can you eat and talk? Do you have anything to say? Your wife seems to be doing all the talking for you. When did you become so weak?"

Momma didn't like that. "Get out! Get out of my house right now!"

"No," Aunt Colleen replied to Momma. "I will not leave until we talk. Mia, go upstairs to your bedroom for a while, please. I will come get you in a bit."

Mia didn't want to leave but she remembered her deal with Aunt Colleen. She picked up her doll and her suitcase, and left the room. She didn't go all the way up though. She couldn't. Aunt Colleen just wanted her out of the room - she didn't say that she couldn't stay close enough to listen to what they were saying. Mia put her stuff in the corner then placed herself on the first step. They couldn't see her, but she could hear them.

"What is this all about Colleen?" her Daddy asked. She could hear his fork clinging and clanging against his plate. Daddy was still eating.

"We need to talk about what happens in your home Richard."

"What are you talking about Colleen? There is nothing happening in my home. And even if there was, it's none of your business."

"She's my niece, Richard. It is my business."

"You're talking about Mia? Oh, I wouldn't listen to a lot that child has to say, she likes to tell stories."

"I didn't need to listen to her Richard. Her back says it all. Bruises and scratches everywhere. A damaged ankle. Scars from God knows what that may have happened before."

"She is a clumsy child," Momma finally added to the conversation. "What can we say?"

"Clumsy? Or Abused?"

Mia heard Daddy's chair scrape against the floor, then his fist slamming down on the table. "What are you saying exactly, Colleen? Do you think I abuse my child?"

"Not you, Richard, but your wife, yes. Although standing by like you do, letting her hurt Mia, that's pretty fucking pathetic in itself. Neglect."

"Neglect? You brought Mia back and you have interrupted our dinner. You have also upset my husband when he is sick. I think you have done enough here. Time for you to leave Colleen." Momma's voice was calmer than Mia expected.

"I told you, I'm not leaving."

"You are leaving."

"Fine, then I'm taking Mia with me. She isn't staying here anymore."

"Try to take Mia and I will call the cops." Momma's voice was getting shaky.

"Go ahead. Call the cops. I have a few things to say to them too." Aunt Colleens voice seemed calm. "And a child's back to show them."

"Richard, do something."

Mia heard Daddy's footsteps.

"You heard Lee-Ann. Get out."

"Really Richard. I come in here and tell you that your wife is abusing your child, and you want me to leave? What would God think? You have the devil right here in your own home and you don't even see it."

"Mia is a tough child to raise. You don't understand that. You spend a few hours with her and now you think you know how to parent her?"

"I've been with her the entire two weeks at camp, Richard. I know everything."

"Well, I know everything too. Sometimes Mia needs a strong hand to keep her in line."

"Huh! You know everything Richard. Did you know that your wife rapes her?"

Aunt Colleen said the last part of her sentence slow. Mia was shocked by the word. She knew what raped meant. But Momma never called it that.

Mia then heard what she had feared she would the entire time. A loud flwap! The sound of someone being hit hard. Mia couldn't wait on the stairs any longer. She ran into the dining room. Aunt Colleen was on her knees.

"Don't come into my house and say these lies, Colleen."

Mia went running to Aunt Colleen. She wrapped her arms around her.

"Aunt Colleen, are you okay?"

"I'm fine. Go back upstairs."

"No."

"Mia, what lies are you telling?" Daddy asked.

"Mia, go upstairs?" Aunt Colleen seemed to be begging Mia but she still couldn't leave.

"No. I won't leave you either."

Aunt Colleen stood up. Mia wrapped herself around Aunt Colleen's waist.

"Mia!" Daddy grabbed Mia by the arm and whipped her around. "Tell your aunt the truth, Mia. Tell her that you're lying." Daddy was shaking Mia as he spoke.

It took Mia a bit to get up the courage but finally she looked at her father as bravely as she could and spoke clear. "It's not a lie, Daddy."

"It is a lie, Richard. Why would I do something so awful?" Momma looked at Aunt Colleen. "I just don't know why you are trying to break up my family."

"*I'm* trying to break up your family? I think you're doing a good job of that on your own."

Aunt Colleen turned Mia around so her back faced Daddy. She lifted up Mia's shirt, exposing the pale brown markings where dark purple bruising was just the week before.

"Do you see this, Richard?"

Daddy stood up straight. He wiped his chin and walked over to the table. He sat back down in his seat and took a few more bites. Daddy closed his eyes as he chewed. His forehead wrinkled. He wasn't thinking happy thoughts. Everyone in the room just watched him.

Momma walked over to him. "Richard, you know these are lies, right? I didn't do that."

"Of course, I do, Lee-Ann. I just need a moment to think."

"Are you kidding me?" Aunt Colleen shouted. She pulled Mia's shirt down and held onto her tight.

Momma turned around with a smile on her face.

"Well, I think your little charade is over. If you don't mind leaving now, Mia and I need to talk, and Richard needs to finish his meal."

Mia didn't want to talk with Momma. Mia squeezed as hard as she could to hold onto Aunt Colleen's waist. Aunt Colleen matched Mia's strength in the hold.

"I'll leave. But like I said, Mia is coming with me."

"Like I said. You aren't taking her. You try to take her, and I will make sure it's the last thing you do."

"Your threats don't bother me. I'm not leaving without her."

Momma reached out and grabbed Mia by the shoulder and pulled her towards her. Mia didn't get far because of how strong she was holding onto Aunt Colleen. Momma's hands slipped right off of Mia. It hurt, but Mia was thankful in this moment for her choice of tight clothes.

Momma reached out again, this time tighter. Aunt Colleen slapped her hand away. "Don't touch her."

"She's my child. I'll touch her if I want to." Momma grabbed onto Mia with two hands and pulled hard. Mia screamed in pain. She let go of Aunt Colleen because it hurt too much not to. Aunt Colleen didn't let go. Mia was being pulled in two different directions. The burning in her arms was almost unbearable.

"This hurts," Mia cried. "Someone let go, please!"

Aunt Colleen let go, sending Mia flying hard into Momma. Momma grabbed her by the hair and started walking her toward the staircase. Aunt Colleen tried to follow but Daddy got up and stopped her.

"Mia was wrong to get you involved Colleen. You're going to be quite disappointed in yourself when you realize you let a 10-year old girl manipulate you. You'll really need Jesus on your side then."

"Oh, get your head out of your ass, Richard."

Momma pulled Mia up the stairs. She heard Aunt Colleen shout, "Get out of my way, Richard."

Daddy said he wouldn't move.

Mia was half way up the stairs when she heard the house door slam shut. Aunt Colleen left. Mia was devastated. Aunt Colleen did what she promised she wouldn't do. She left Mia alone with her angrier than usual parents. Mia had no one now.

Chapter Forty

Momma threw Mia into her bedroom and slammed the door behind them. Mia knew that the door being shut was a bad sign. Mia was going to feel pain. Mia crawled as far away from Momma as she could.

"You stupid little bitch," Momma started. "How could you say those things? I'm your Momma. You don't do that to me. I brought you into this world child, Lord knows why, but I did. And this is how you thank me?"

Momma picked up Mia's dictionary and threw it at her. It hit Mia in the cheekbone. Mia felt instant blood rush down her face.

"Momma, I'm sorry."

"Sorry? Well, you're sorry. I guess it's all good now."

"Momma."

"Don't *Momma* me. You don't respect me as a Momma. You only think of yourself."

Momma walked over to Mia and kicked her in the stomach.

"Momma stop!"

"You know I did all of those things because I love you. And this is how you thank me? I'm just trying to make sure you turn out okay. You need help Mia. You're not a good girl at all."

"I'll be better Momma, you will see."

"No. This is as good as you get my child. No one will love you now. Not even Jesus can love you after what you have done. You disgust me."

Momma spit on Mia.

Mia wanted to cry but she didn't. She couldn't. That would make Momma laugh and the last thing Mia wanted right now was to see that look on Momma's face. She wanted to fight Momma. She wanted to scream and shout and punch and kick but if she did that, Momma would just make this last longer. Mia didn't think she could last through a long fight today.

"I know you can't help it Mia. This is who you are. I tolerate it and you because I know where it is coming from. You're misguided. Jesus sent you to me so I can fix you. Show you. But you don't see what I do for you. You don't care. You're a selfish little bitch. You don't deserve me. You don't deserve anything I give you. I wish you were never born."

Mia sometimes wished that too.

Mia heard the downstairs door open again. This time Mia heard voices, a lot of voices. Momma looked at the bedroom door.

"What the hell is going on now?" Momma started toward the bedroom door but turned toward Mia instead. She grabbed Mia by the hair and dragged her to the closet door. "Get in there. I don't need you running downstairs again."

Mia happily went inside. She wanted away from Momma. The door shut and Mia heard the sound of the lock click. Mia was alone in the darkness. Her face full of blood, her lip swollen, her head feeling hot and sore, and her stomach in pain. Mia could only guess what was going on downstairs. But even her best guess was probably wrong. All she could hear was a lot of shouting. And not one word was clear.

Mia pressed her ear against the door of the closet. She had to go on the right side because the left side of her face was too sore. She pressed as hard as she could but nothing was getting any clearer. Mia gave up. She sat back in the dark, tried to wipe the blood that was dripping.

There was a knock at the closet door. "Mia, are you in there?"

"Aunt Colleen?"

"Yes, sweetie. I'm going to get you out okay?"

"Where's Momma?"

"She's downstairs. Mia where is the key?"

"Momma has it. It's around her neck."

Mia wondered how Aunt Colleen got by Momma. She also wondered why she came back. Did Aunt Colleen change her mind and decide not to leave?

"Mia, it's Mrs. C. darling. I'm just outside the door too. Are you okay?"

Mia struggled to answer. She placed her hand against the door. Quietly she whispered, "I am now."

Why was Mrs. C. there? She really wanted to be with Aunt Colleen and Mrs. C. right now. She wanted out and to be with them.

Mia leaned forward and slid her fingers under the door. She felt Mrs. C. touch her hand.

"I got you," she said. Mia was happy to feel Mrs. C. really there.

"When did you come?" Mia asked.

"I was always here. I was just waiting outside."

She was always there? Mia wanted to ask more questions but she didn't know what to ask so she just sat there a few moments with her fingers touching Mrs. C.'s.

"What is taking so long?"

"I don't know. I think I hear someone coming upstairs now."

Mia heard Aunt Colleen's voice enter the room.

"Bitch doesn't have the key. This is all I could find. It was in the basement."

"What are you going to do with that?"

Mia wondered what they were talking about.

"Cut her free. Any other thoughts?"

Mrs. C. must not have had any because she stayed silent.

"Mia, I need you to get as far back in the closet as you can okay? As far back."

"Okay." Mia did so.

"Okay, are you there?"

Mia said that she was.

"You're going to hear a loud noise. I don't have the key so I'm going to saw a hole in the door. One big enough for you to crawl out of. It's going to be loud. Stay back until I'm done okay?"

"I will."

"Okay, here we go."

The saw was loud in Mia's ear. As the blade went down the door, Mia could see light coming through. The saw was noticeable now as well. It looked and sounded scary. Mia closed her eyes.

Soon she heard the saw stop and an arm reach in and touch her.

"Come on out."

Mia uncovered her face to see her Aunt looking in at her. Aunt Colleen raised her hand to her mouth and gasped.

"What did she do to you?"

"I'll go get a cloth," Mrs. C. said as she got up.

Mia crawled out through the hole and straight into her aunt's arms.

"Is it over?" Mia whispered.

"Almost," Aunt Colleen replied.

Mrs. C. returned with a warm wet cloth and ran it down Mia's face.

"That's a big cut. It might need stitches. We should bring her to the hospital."

Aunt Colleen took over the washing of Mia's face. Mia liked the way Aunt Colleen looked at her. It was always so gentle.

Sirens began to blare from outside. Mia got up from her aunt's arms and looked out the window.

"There's an ambulance here?"

"Yes Mia, it's for your Daddy."

"Daddy, what's wrong with Daddy? Did you hit him?"

"He collapsed downstairs. Mia. Your Daddy needs a doctor too."

"I want to see him." Mia headed to her bedroom door. Aunt Colleen stopped her.

"No Mia. Let's let the paramedics take care of him first. I'll bring you to the hospital and you can get your cheek checked out then see your father.

"I want to see him. Please!"

Aunt Colleen stood up. She rubbed her forehead. "Okay."

Mia walked to the door but could barely move. She fell to the ground.

"Mia! What's wrong?" Aunt Colleen asked.

"It hurts when I walk. Everything hurts so much. Especially my heart."

"Let me help."

Aunt Colleen reached down and picked Mia up. "Better?"

Mia nodded.

When they reached the first floor of the house Mia saw Daddy on a stretcher. His eyes were closed. He had a tube in his nostrils and wires attached to his chest and arms. Two paramedics were fussing over him. Momma was in the corner crying, being comforted by a neighbour. There were many neighbours there, and some people Mia didn't know.

The one paramedic looked up and at Mia.

"What happened to her?"

"She needs stitches I think."

The paramedic came over and looked at Mia's cheek.

"I think so too. Are you hurt anywhere else?"

Mia told him about her other pains. He pushed on her stomach and looked at her back and foot.

"What happened?"

Mia didn't answer.

"We have to call someone about this," the paramedic said to Aunt Colleen.

"Oh, don't worry. I plan on it. I'm going to take her to the hospital now."

"I can't let you leave with her, ma'am."

"She's a doctor." Mia said, pointing to Mrs. C. It worked at the Bible retreat, Mia thought.

Mrs. C. just smiled.

"I'm a doctor of veterinary medicine." Mrs. C. showed the paramedic her badge. "Not quite the same. But you can trust that we will get her straight to the hospital."

The paramedic looked at Aunt Colleen and Mrs. C. for a second then said okay. He went back to attend to Daddy.

Moments later, Mia watched as the paramedics rolled Daddy out of the house and outside. Momma came into the dining room.

"They will take good care of him, Mia." Aunt Colleen assured her.

"He's probably going to die, Mia."

Mia looked over at Momma who was visibly upset.

"He's going to die. And you know why? Because of you, that's why. Between your nonsense here tonight, and that lasagna you cooked that he was eating. You killed your Daddy. I hope you're proud of yourself."

Momma left the house with the neighbour who said she would drive her to the hospital. Mia stood and looked at the floor. There were garbage papers from bandages scattered about. Mia looked at the leftover food on the table.

"Come on, Mia. Let's go to the hospital."

Mia took one more look around. She couldn't leave yet. She had one thing she needed to do.

Mia walked into the kitchen and grabbed a container. She went back to the table and scooped up some of the lasagna. The doctor was going to need to see what hurt Daddy, Mia thought. And Mia was going to be brave enough to show him what she had done.

Chapter Forty-One

Mia sat on a stretcher. Her cheek was still numb from getting stitches. She watched as Aunt Colleen and Mrs. C. stood outside the curtain talking to a female police officer. Mia wanted to know what they were saying. Aunt Colleen looked over at Mia every few moments and smiled.

When the police and Aunt Colleen came in, the policewoman asked Mia a whole bunch of questions about what happened at her house, and about the things that happened before. Mia was honest through it all. Aunt Colleen said it was probably best that she was. Aunt Colleen stayed beside her the whole time. Mia had to show the officer her back, just like she had showed the doctor. Mia offered to show the policewoman the lasagna a few times as well, but she didn't want to see it. Mia didn't blame her. It must have been pretty awful.

The policewoman was upset with Aunt Colleen. The officer said Aunt Colleen should have called them before going over, and before bringing Mia there as well. Aunt Colleen said she understood that now. She said she thought it was best, at the time, for Mia, but now she knows that was wrong. The officer seemed to be okay with that answer, at least with her words. The officer's expression said a little different.

When the questions were over, Aunt Colleen said that Mia could go check in on Daddy. She asked the policewoman if it was okay, and if she could escort them and the officer said she could and would. Mia jumped down from the stretcher, took her aunt's hand, and went with them down the hall. It wasn't a far walk to where Daddy was. Mia could hear Momma's voice in the distance, but couldn't see her.

Daddy was in his own room with glass windows, lying on a stretcher, his eyes still closed. He had tubes everywhere. Mia could hear a monitor beeping. Another monitor showed Daddy's heartbeat. Her Daddy looked like he was sleeping.

"Is he okay?"

"He's in a coma right now, Mia. They call it a diabetic coma."

"My lasagna did that to him?"

"No, baby. Your Dad's diet and exercise did it."

"But I cook for him."

"Well, it's more than just his dinners. It's also because he refused to take the medicine that he needed to help him. Your Daddy did this, not you."

Mia saw him eating her lasagna that night. He was fine until he did. Mia knew, that even though Aunt Colleen said differently, that she was the one that did this to Daddy. Mia felt bad.

She walked up to her Daddy and rubbed his arm. She looked at him and whispered that she was sorry. She didn't know if Daddy could hear her, but if he couldn't, she was pretty sure that Jesus could. She hoped Jesus knew that she was sorry.

"Mia, we need to leave now. People can only stay for 10 minutes at a time."

"Can we stay at the hospital?"

"Yes. We need to stay. Want to go get a snack? You must be hungry."

Mia was hungry.

She said goodbye to her Daddy then left with Aunt Colleen.

Aunt Colleen took her to a gift shop and let her pick out anything she wanted. Mia picked out ketchup chips and an orange pop. Aunt Colleen grabbed a bag of chips as well.

Aunt Colleen was just finished paying when alarm bells went off in the hospital. A woman's voice came on the speaker.

"CODE BLUE. Emergency code blue, ER, room 6, section red. I repeat, CODE BLUE, ER, room 6, section red.

Mia looked up at Aunt Colleen.

Aunt Colleen hung her head.

"Is that Daddy's room?"

"Yes, sweetheart, it is."

The walk back to Daddy's room seemed longer than the one that took them to the gift shop. Everything seemed to move in slow motion. Sounds were different, the hallways were darker, and Mia's thoughts were blank.

When they reached Daddy's room they saw two police officers standing outside. Momma was there now, lying across Daddy's chest, screaming at the top of her lungs. Two nurses were moving around Momma, taking the wires off of Daddy's body. The monitor no longer made a sound.

"What happened?" Mia asked. She knew the answer but she just needed someone to say it out loud.

When Aunt Colleen didn't, Mia looked at her. Aunt Colleen's mouth was covered by her own hand and she was crying. Aunt Colleen dropped to her knees on the floor. Mia didn't know what to say, so she just sat down beside her. Mrs. C. came from around the corner and sat down on the ground beside Aunt Colleen as well. She wrapped her arm around Aunt Colleen's shoulder.

Mia looked back and forth between Momma and Aunt Colleen. Was Mia supposed to be crying too? She didn't feel like crying. She didn't know why. Her Daddy was dead.

Mrs. C. wasn't crying either.

Aunt Colleen wiped her eyes and stood up. She helped Mia up too. She walked her over to some chairs and sat her down. She asked Mrs. C. to keep an eye on Mia. Mrs. C. sat beside her. Aunt Colleen walked off and spoke to a nurse nearby. Mia sat, looking into her Daddy's room, listening to her Momma's cries, and waited.

When Aunt Colleen returned, she sat with Mia and Mrs. C. They all watched as the officer Mia spoke to earlier got off the phone at the nursing station and met up with her partner. They walked in to speak to Momma. Momma yelled at them both. The officers stayed calm while Momma screamed.

Aunt Colleen tried to cover Mia's face but Mia wouldn't let her. She needed to see what was happening to her Momma.

A lady in a red pantsuit walked up to them. She had the longest, curliest, and puffiest brown hair Mia had ever seen. The lady's bangs were teased high above her forehead. Mia instinctively reached up to her own hair to see how high it would go. She was no match. The red pantsuit lady joined them at the chairs.

"You must be Mia?"

Mia looked at her and nodded. She put her attention back on her Daddy's room.

"Hi Mia, my name is Katherine. I'm with social services."

Katherine held her hand out to Mia. Mia shook her hand without looking at her.

"Can we talk for a bit?"

Mia nodded but still didn't turn to look at Katherine. She couldn't stop looking into her Daddy's hospital room. Momma had stopped screaming by now. She looked tired. Tired and sad.

The officers walked Momma out of the room in handcuffs, passing Mia as they went. Momma looked at Mia and with a hard voice said, "I will never forgive you for this. I hope you rot in hell, kid. You deserve to die for what you did."

"That's enough," the officer told Momma. "Stay here and keep your mouth shut while I get your papers."

Momma stopped at the counter with the officer tight beside her. She kept her mouth shut, but glared at Mia the entire time.

But Momma didn't need to say more. Mia heard the message. Momma was right.

Mia looked down at her feet, into Aunt Colleen's bag. There was the container of lasagna Mia had brought with her. Mia reached down and grabbed it.

Mia opened up the container and scooped as much of the lasagna up as she could. Mia shoved it into her mouth.

"What are you doing?" Mrs. C. asked, getting Aunt Colleen and Katherine's attention too.

Mia had too much food in her mouth to answer. She cried as she tried to swallow it all.

Aunt Colleen reached into her mouth and removed some lasagna. Mia pulled her head back to stop her.

"You're going to choke."

Mia didn't care. She just wanted to die like her Daddy.

Mia chewed and chewed what was left. She tried to go for more but Mrs. C. stopped her.

"Mia!"

Mia swooshed the food around in her mouth. Something was wrong. What was wrong?

Mia looked down at the container of lasagna. She pulled apart layer after layer looking inside.

"What is going on, kid?"

Mia now had two hands digging in. Where was the cottage cheese? There was no cottage cheese. Mia always added that to her lasagna. It wasn't there.

Momma didn't though. Momma never put it in. This wasn't Mia's lasagna.

Mia looked up at Momma who was still glaring.

"This isn't mine."

Momma turned away.

"Momma, this isn't my lasagna." Mia was talking out of turn but didn't care.

Momma didn't look back.

"Momma. I didn't make this. I didn't do it. I didn't kill Daddy. Momma? I'm not bad. Momma, please! Look!"

But Momma never turned around to face Mia again. She was taken away by the police officers moments later. Mia, Aunt Colleen, Mrs. C., and Katherine just sat there together. First looking at Momma walk away, then to the room that held Mia's dead daddy.

Mia put down the container of lasagna and slowly stood up.

"Mia?" Mrs. C. asked. "What's going on now?"

Mia walked towards her Daddy. Aunt Colleen reached out to stop her but Katherine told her not to stop her.

Mia walked to the doorway.

Her Daddy was still.

"I'm leaving soon Daddy," Mia called to him. She knew he wouldn't answer back. "I'm going to go with Aunt Colleen. Is that okay?"

Mia had to ask even if her Daddy was dead.

She walked closer to him. She touched his hands. They were swollen.

Mia looked at Daddy's face. She tilted her head from side to side and looked at him in many different directions. He looked different dead. It might have been the tape on his eyes that made that so.

Mia pulled over a chair and stood on it. She got as close to her Daddy's face as she could. She kissed his cheek. She backed up and looked at him again.

She reached over to his cheeks and slowly pulled off the tape that covered his eyes. First the right, then the left. She took her fingers and spread his eyelids apart. Daddy's big brown eyes stared straight up to the ceiling.

"There," Mia whispered. "Now you can see Jesus when he comes to take you to heaven."

Chapter Forty-Two

Mia didn't need to talk to Katherine for long. She met with both Aunt Colleen and Mia separately. Then she let them leave together. Katherine said she would talk to Mia more on another day.

Mia asked to go back to her house to get some things, but Aunt Colleen said that they weren't allowed to go there for a few days. Mia would have to wait to get her stuff.

Aunt Colleen set up the spare room just for Mia. They even went shopping to get a few things for the room that she would like. Aunt Colleen bought her a pink Care Bear, a ghetto blaster with some cassette tapes of her own, and a poster of New Kids On The Block for her wall. Mia even got some new clothes including a new dress for Daddy's funeral.

Mia found Daddy's funeral to be hard. She felt bad for him. Not because he was dead, or for how he died, but because neither his best friend nor his wife were there to see him off to heaven. Momma could have attended but Mia overheard Aunt Colleen say on the phone one night, that Momma wasn't going to come because she didn't want anyone to see her with a police escort. Momma needed to have an escort at the funeral because Mia was going to be there. Momma and Mia couldn't be in a room alone together without the proper authority on hand.

The funeral was long and sad. Many of Daddy's church friends were crying and praying loudly in their church language. Mia felt like everyone was watching her. Secretly blaming her for his death. It was okay that they were, she still kind of blamed herself too.

They played Amazing Grace, and read some of Daddy's favourite Bible verses. The Psalms verse was the first. Mia never thought this would be the place she heard that scripture next.

When it was all over, everyone met at the cemetery and the minister lowered Daddy's body to the ground. They all took turns throwing a bit of dirt over his coffin then said their goodbyes. Mia followed suit, not knowing if it was right. It seemed weird to throw dirt on a dead person.

When the funeral was over, Mia was handed a brown envelope from someone she didn't know that said it was a package of all the stuff from Daddy's pockets the night he was brought into the hospital. Mia looked inside and pulled out the contents. It held her Daddy's wallet, his car keys, two sticks of gum, and a single key Mia recognized as the key to the closet door. Why did Daddy have this? She felt hurt. She put the closet key in her pocket and placed the rest of the stuff back inside the envelope. She handed the envelope to Aunt Colleen. She needed nothing else.

When Mia got home, she found a string and placed the key on it. She was never going to let that key out of her sight again. She would always carry it to keep safe.

The days after that were quiet. Mia spent most of them watching movies with her aunt. Mia was still trying to comprehend everything that had happened. Momma was spending some time in a mental hospital but was charged with child abuse. She was awaiting a trial and sentencing. Mia wondered if she would end up in the same place as Frank if she went to jail. Mia kind of hoped she would, so that she and Frank could be together again.

Katherine had worked out everything so that Mia could stay with her Aunt Colleen until everything was settled with Momma. If Momma were found guilty, then Mia would stay with Aunt Colleen permanently.

Mia didn't want to live at home anymore. Daddy was gone, Momma was mad, and Aunt Colleen was kind.

Aunt Colleen told Mia she would drive her back and forth to her therapy appointments and school. She liked that Aunt Colleen was driving her to school. That way she could stay at her old school with all of her friends. She missed Abby so much, and if she couldn't be living by her anymore, at least she would see her at school.

Mia had received a new spy journal from Mrs. C. with a card that told her to keep writing. Mia was grateful to be able to document things again.

Mia finally felt what Aunt Colleen had said, that when it was all over, she was going to be okay. Mia felt okay.

The best thing of all for Mia was what happened on the second week of being at her aunt's house. Mia went up to her new bedroom to find a picture on the wall that wasn't there before. It was the picture of Mia and Tulip that Aunt Colleen took at writing camp. Aunt Colleen put it in a frame and hung it up for her.

"You like the picture?"

"Yes."

"Then you're going to like what's behind you too."

Mia turned around. The closet door was completely removed. There was just a curtain strung up to keep the stuff on the inside hidden. Mia looked around her room and twirled.

"Does that help?"

Mia nodded. She reached into her backpack where she kept the closet key from her old house. She held it tightly in her hand. After a few moments, she walked over to her dresser and opened the top drawer. She placed it inside. Shutting the drawer, she whispered to herself, "yes, it helps a lot."

Acknowledgements

It takes an entire community to write a book. This one is no exception. To my readers that hit the ground running with me on the first draft…thank you for meeting me in the basement of this project.

For the readers who came at a later draft, your participation is equally appreciated..

To the fabulous copy-editor Marnie Woodrow. You teach me something every time we talk. I am grateful for you and your skills.

Thank you to the Ontario Arts Council for the funding to get the bulk of this story written. You made time for this possible.

To Lize, for helping me get into the space to be able to share a story like this.

Thank you to the Aunt Colleens, and the Mrs. C's in the world. You are brave, you are bold, you are desperately needed. You make a difference simply by showing up. Because really, that's where healing starts…when someone shows up.

About the Author

Sarah began her writing career when she won a National broadcasting scholarship from Global Television in 1999. Starting out in Journalism, Sarah furthered her education with a post-grad course in Writing, Directing, and Producing, for Television, specializing in Creative Writing. Years later, she published her first fiction novel *Where the Stream and Creek Collide*, that is currently being made into a feature film. She has written works in the media both print and to-air, as well as magazines, novels and short stories, film, and television. Two of her feature screenplays were accepted into the Female Eye Film Festival Good To Go Program, as well as one winning the award for Best Fresh Voice in 2014. Sarah just completed her first short film, *Dearly Not So Departed*, as both writer and director. After a four-year battle with Cancer, Sarah is happy to be healthy again, and able to write more stories for people to enjoy. Evanesce is Sarah's second novel.